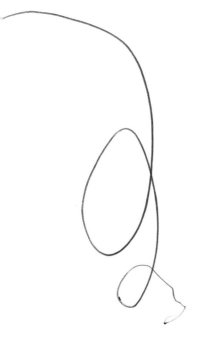

Mara's Choice

By Anna Jacobs

THE PENNY LAKE SERIES

Changing Lara • Finding Cassie
Marrying Simone

THE PEPPERCORN SERIES

Peppercorn Street • Cinnamon Gardens
Saffron Lane • Bay Tree Cottage
Christmas in Peppercorn Street

THE HONEYFIELD SERIES

The Honeyfield Bequest • A Stranger in Honeyfield
Peace Comes to Honeyfield

THE HOPE TRILOGY

A Place of Hope • In Search of Hope
A Time for Hope

THE GREYLADIES SERIES

Heir to Greyladies • Mistress of Greyladies
Legacy of Greyladies

THE WILTSHIRE GIRLS SERIES

Cherry Tree Lane • Elm Tree Road
Yew Tree Gardens

THE WATERFRONT SERIES

Mara's Choice

❧

Winds of Change • Moving On
The Cotton Lass and Other Stories
Change of Season • Tomorrow's Path • Chestnut Lane
In Focus

Mara's Choice

ANNA JACOBS

Allison & Busby Limited
11 Wardour Mews
London W1F 8AN
allisonandbusby.com

First published in Great Britain by Allison & Busby in 2021.

Copyright © 2021 by Anna Jacobs

A CIP catalogue record for this book is available from
the British Library.

First Edition

ISBN 978-0-7490-2616-5

Typeset in 11.5/16.5 pt Sabon LT Pro by
Allison & Busby Ltd

FSC
www.fsc.org
MIX
Paper from
responsible sources
FSC® C020471

The paper used for this Allison & Busby publication
has been produced from trees that have been legally sourced
from well-managed and credibly certified forests.

Printed and bound by
CPI Group (UK) Ltd, Croydon, CR0 4YY

This book is for my friend, Deborah Smith, with thanks for all the help she has given me and my books. Thank you so much, Debs! You're a star and a pleasure to know.

Chapter One

When Mara Gregory went into the kitchen to make a cup of tea, her mother looked up with a guilty expression, crumpled the letter she was reading and stuffed it into her apron pocket. The envelope missed and wafted to the floor to land at Mara's feet.

After picking it up, she glanced at it automatically and froze when she saw her own name, not her mother's, in the address. 'This letter was for me. Why did you open it?'

'I knew who it was from.'

She turned the envelope over to read the sender's address but the name A. Buchanan meant nothing to her. 'Who is he? Or is it a she?'

'Nobody who matters.'

Mara waited because her mother seemed to be fumbling for words, stuttering slightly, as she'd done a few times lately.

'You don't need any more trouble. You've just lost your fancy London job. Concentrate on finding a new one nearer your family and leave any other problems to me. That's what mothers are for.'

'I'm thirty and perfectly capable of dealing with my own letters and troubles, thank you very much.' She held out her hand.

Kath took a step backwards, shaking her head.

'Mum! Stop this!' Mara tried to snatch the letter out of her mother's apron pocket and failed, but she managed to block the doorway and didn't intend to move till she'd got her missive. '*Give it to me!*'

'You two don't usually quarrel before breakfast.' Phil moved his stepdaughter gently to one side and joined them in the kitchen. 'What's the matter?'

Kath shot a warning look at her daughter. 'Nothing.'

Mara wasn't backing off. 'I just caught Mum opening a letter addressed to me and she won't let me have it.'

He looked sharply at his wife.

'She doesn't need this,' Kath said. 'You know we agreed—' She broke off. 'I'll get your breakfast. Let it drop, Phil.'

'After you've given her the letter.' His voice was unusually firm. 'It's about time, don't you think?'

'Phil, no! You *agreed*.'

'Years ago and only because you made such a fuss. I never approved of what you were doing about Buchanan and it's been on my conscience, so I'm glad it's coming out into the open.'

Kath crossed both hands protectively across her

apron pocket but he was strong enough to move them away, doing it as gently as he did everything. He passed the crumpled letter to his adopted daughter. 'Here, love. But don't pass judgement on your mother till you know the whole story.'

He turned back to his wife, who was sobbing and rubbing her forehead as if it ached. 'Ah now, don't. Don't cry on me, Kath. I can't think straight when you cry.' He tried to put his arms round her but she pushed him away.

Mara scanned the letter and after a few minutes she looked up, frowning. 'I don't understand. This man says – he says he's my father.'

'Never stops causing trouble, that one,' Kath said bitterly. 'Even after all this time.'

Shock made Mara's voice come out as a hushed whisper. 'He really is my father?'

'Only biologically and that was by sheer accident.'

'But you told me he was dead! You told me that when I was little and started asking, before you two even got married.'

'As far as I was concerned, that man was dead!'

Mara reread the letter, which was just a page long. There seemed to be a warmth in the way he wrote. Or did she just want there to be?

Dear Mara,

This letter is so hard to write. I've sent two previous letters, the first one to what sounded like a flat in London, the second to this address. I've not *received an acknowledgement that either of them arrived, though surely at least one must have done.*

I only found out a few months ago that I had conceived a daughter with my then partner before I emigrated to Australia.

It was sheer coincidence that I recently met someone who knew your mother. Since Kath and I both came from the same village in Wiltshire, she wondered whether we might have known one another.

I was gobsmacked to hear that Kath had a daughter who was 'just turned thirty' and couldn't help wondering if you might be mine. The mere thought of that delighted me, you can't know how much.

I did some research online and discovered the date of your birth, which told me I was highly likely to have been the father. Kath simply wasn't the sort to play away from home.

I hired a private detective to trace you, and when he found you, he said you and I resemble one another greatly.

I'd very much like to meet you. Is that possible? You can contact me at either of the above addresses.

Very best wishes,
Aaron Buchanan

Mara couldn't think straight with her mother watching her with anger in every line of her body. She went into the hall, grabbed her coat and shoulder bag and headed towards the front door.

She turned as the sound of a sharp argument followed her and saw her mother shove Phil roughly aside and step into the hall.

'Where do you think you're going, Mara Gregory?'

'Out. I need to think.'

'Don't get in touch with him. He's not worth it, will only hurt you, as he hurt me. *Please*.'

There was such desperation in that last word, Mara actually thought of giving in, but only for a few seconds. She'd wondered about her father all her life and couldn't bear to miss this opportunity to meet him, just couldn't. If she didn't write back to him now, there might never be another chance. She shook her head and opened the front door.

'*Mara, no!*' It was a shriek.

She turned to say bitterly, 'How do I know whether he's worth it or not, Mum? All you've ever told me was that he was dead. You've refused to talk about him, and heaven knows I've begged you for information a few times. You wouldn't even tell me the colour of his hair, for heaven's sake!'

'You were better off without him.'

'It was up to me to decide that, especially once I became an adult. And how *dare* you intercept my mail?'

'It was better that way,' she repeated with her usual stubbornness.

'Well, just to set the record straight, Mum, it wasn't

better for me because it's always hurt not even to know what my father was like.' It still did. A lot.

'Well, it's never been proved that he was your father. I was quite in demand in those days. It could be – someone else.'

She didn't believe that for a second. And her birth father hadn't done, either. Her mother was straight-laced and set in her ways, would never have cheated on a steady partner, or cheated about anything, come to that. Kath was blunt to a fault.

Mara left the house, not letting herself slam the front door behind her. But she wanted to. Oh, she definitely did.

If she weren't unemployed, she'd move out again because her mother was treating her as a child in other ways too. Only, she couldn't afford to leave and set up in a new flat till she got a job, so thank goodness Phil was there to keep the peace. Her adopted father was a wonderful man, putting up with her mother's moods – and with her own lately, Mara had to admit.

It did that to you, losing your job. Made you grumpy. Especially when the choice of who should be made redundant hadn't been fair and you could do nothing about it.

And she knew who to blame for that: Darren, her former partner. Bad mistake, getting together with him. After they split up, he'd told damaging lies about her to her manager.

'What's wrong, Aaron love? You're looking a bit down.'

He turned round, smiling involuntarily, as he always

did at the sight of Emma in the morning, her auburn curls in a wild tangle, coffee mug in her hand, eyes bright with hope for what the day might bring. She was a delight to wake up to.

Then her words sank in and he couldn't hold on to the smile. 'I was thinking about Mara.'

Emma closed her eyes for a moment and when she opened them the happiness wasn't quite as bright. 'You've sent her another letter, haven't you?'

He nodded.

'Oh, Aaron, you said you'd not do that to yourself any more. She's had two chances to reply and there's not been a word from her.'

'Well, it seems she moved house in the middle of it all. So I just – well, had to try one last time.'

'You should hire that detective again if you can't accept the situation. He'll make sure your letters are actually getting through to her.'

'I will contact him if nothing comes of this one.'

Emma came to put her arms round him. 'It still hurts, doesn't it, that your ex didn't even tell you that you had a daughter. Let's face it, Aaron love, if anyone is intercepting your letters, it's likely to be your ex and the new letter won't get through either now Mara is living at home again. This Kath knew who you were working for in Australia right from the start. What harm would it have done to tell you about the child?'

'She was very stubborn about me not taking a job so far away, said it was her or the job and she'd never leave Wiltshire, let alone England. I realised after a while that she couldn't have coped with such a major life change. Life isn't easy for people as rigid as her, even when things go well.'

'She could still have told you later on and allowed you the chance to meet your child. You'd think after all these years the stupid woman would have got past how you two broke up.'

'Ultimatums and quarrels don't make for good decision-making on either side. I've grown wiser since then, I hope.'

'I must admit that from what you've let drop, it's always seemed to me that you were both at fault. You were both young and stubborn. And you at least have well and truly paid for that.'

He nodded against that silky mass of hair, seeing the silver threads in it now, but not caring. 'I love your hair.'

'Don't try to change the subject.' Emma pushed herself back a little, studying his face anxiously and briefly caressing his cheek. 'Let's set a time limit before we bring in the detective again, eh? How about two weeks?'

'I suppose.' He nodded but couldn't raise even a slight smile. 'If she doesn't reply by then, we'll definitely call George in again. He's good at his job. He was the one who found her for me in the first place.'

'What if he finds out for certain she doesn't want to meet you? Will you accept that?' She waited a moment or two, then prompted, 'Aaron?'

'Yes, love. Well, I'll try anyway.'

But he wondered if he could ever accept a total rejection when she hadn't even met him. It had blindsided him to find out he had a daughter. He'd missed the first thirty years of her life – that was probably a third of it and he was now fifty-three, so how many years would be left for him to interact with her now? Why, she might even have children, who'd be his grandchildren and he'd have missed part of their lives too.

It had been cruel to keep Mara's existence from him. He'd never forgive Kath for that.

If Emma had been able to have other children after her first marriage ended, maybe this recent discovery wouldn't have touched such a raw nerve. Well, she'd made him a stepfather at least and he'd thoroughly enjoyed helping raise her son and daughter by her first husband. But the longing for his own child had always been there and he knew Emma was well aware of it.

If Mara didn't want to meet him, he might go to England and at least take a look at her from a distance, maybe even manage a sneaky photo or two.

What a sad sack he was!

He had a good life, was just in the middle of selling a thriving business and moving into early retirement. And yet . . . the longing for a child of his own blood had always been there.

Mara waited till her mother went out to the shops, which Kath always did at the same time each Tuesday and Saturday, then sneaked back into the house to change her clothes for the job interview she hadn't told her mother about, because Kath would fuss and worry.

When she went home again mid-afternoon, the

sound of sobbing began to echo down the stairwell. She hadn't heard that note of strangled anguish for years. Had she interrupted this sob-session or had her mother been watching for her return and started it when she came into the house? It wouldn't have surprised her either way lately. Her mother was once again behaving unpredictably, as she had in two past incidents.

She went into the kitchen, amazed to see that it hadn't been cleared up and that her mother's shopping had simply been dumped on a surface. These were serious omissions from the queen of neat and tidy.

Well, the situation was serious for Mara, too, far more important than the other tussles she'd been facing ever since she moved temporarily back home and her mother started trying to reorganise her life.

As the sobbing continued unabated, she looked up and frowned. She wasn't going to give in to emotional blackmail. She'd decide what to do about her birth father herself.

Trying to ignore the sounds, she put the kettle on and started stacking the breakfast crockery into the dishwasher, banging and rattling things on purpose. But the noise wasn't enough to bring her mother downstairs or even drown out the sobs, so she turned on the radio loudly.

That blocked the noise from upstairs but it didn't drive away the worries. Her mother had had a nervous breakdown when Mara was eighteen and been hospitalised for a few weeks. There had been another episode when Mara was twenty-five, but by then there was a new type of medication that was more effective for her problems and Kath hadn't had to go into hospital. Instead Phil had taken time off work to be with her until the pills took effect and she settled into her routines again.

Had the letter from this stranger been enough to undo all that? Apparently so. Well, not just the letter itself but the thought of Mara getting in touch with him.

But oh, she wanted so much to meet her birth father!

When she turned the radio down a little and peeped into the hall, there was no sound of sobbing, thank goodness.

She made herself a slice of cheese on toast because she'd missed lunch. She ate it slowly, wondering what to do for the best. It was a relief when she heard the front door open and close. Phil must have come home early. Thank goodness. He'd retired recently but still went out regularly to play golf. It was the one thing he wouldn't let Kath control.

As soon as the door opened the sobbing immediately started up again.

He came into the kitchen, glancing upstairs, then rolling his eyes and giving her a quick hug. 'Don't back down, love. You have every right to meet your birth father.'

'Do I? Even though the mere thought of it upsets my mother this much?'

'Yes. She isn't the only person in the world, you know. You have needs too. She's utterly selfish, has been getting worse over the years.'

His tone was sharper than she'd expected.

'Is it worth upsetting everyone, Phil? I shan't be able to *meet* the man, after all. He lives in Australia.'

'Why not? People travel to and from there all the time.'

'It'd cost far too much to go, that's why. I daren't dip into my savings without a job to come back to and who knows how long I'll be out of work?'

Unfortunately she felt sure a certain person in her old company was blackening her name in other places too and making it difficult for her to get another half-decent job. She wasn't ambitious to climb up the management ladders, but she did want a job that interested her.

'You could write back to the poor man. He deserves that, at least, after the way he's been treated.'

'You believe he really is my father?'

'Yes, I do. She wouldn't make such a fuss otherwise.'

She nodded agreement and passed Phil a mug of coffee. He never said no to it.

He raised it in a thank-you salute. 'How did the interview go this afternoon?'

'Not well. I reckon they've already got someone lined up for the job. It was pretty obvious from their lack of real interest in what I was saying and the way one man kept glancing at his watch.'

'Sorry to hear that.'

'So am I. No offence, but I do miss having my own flat, Phil.'

'I don't blame you.' He sighed.

She shot a quick glance at him and saw how strained he was looking. Well, who wouldn't get tired of being a permanent support figure to a rigid woman who never gave an inch when she wanted something? No wonder he refused to budge on his golf. It was his only escape.

He laid his hand on hers. 'Write to Aaron Buchanan straight away, Mara. I'll post it for you when I go out to pick up a takeaway for tea.'

'Thanks but there's an email address. It'll be easier for me to contact him that way. Save me a week or more of angst about what his reply may be. Only, well, I feel I need a little longer to think through the implications of making contact.' She couldn't help glancing up above their heads again as she said that.

'Then take as much time as you need, but be certain you do what *you* want. It's *your* decision, not your mother's.'

'But it'll upset her big time if I get in touch with him. And you'll bear the brunt of that.'

He shrugged. 'Her choice to hold a grudge all these years. My choice to stay with her . . . or not. And your choice what you do about your birth father.'

She went across to hug him. '*You* will still be my father, whatever happens with this man.'

He gave her an even longer hug in return. 'Good. I feel like your father. But there's no law that says you can't have two fathers, is there?'

'Oh, Dad, you're so generous. You're the kindest person I've ever met.'

He shrugged, but she could see that her compliment

had pleased him. When he glanced upstairs again and frowned, she wondered if the way her mother had grown worse in the past couple of years meant she was going to need serious medical help again.

Mara had felt for a while as if a thunderstorm was gathering over their lives. There was nothing definite, just a growing discomfort within their small family. She hadn't realised how bad it was getting till she came back to live at home. Maybe she shouldn't contact this Aaron, should be content with the people who'd raised her?

Would that make her mother feel better? No. She shook her head grimly and the decision was made. She'd always longed to know what her real father was like. Always. She needed to do this.

Mara tried writing an email to say she was interested in taking things further, but it was harder than she'd expected to deal with a complete stranger about such an intimate subject, blood relative or not. She read and reread Aaron's letter, then read her own reply even more times, deleting her first effort.

Did she have the right to set her mother and Phil at odds with one another when she couldn't afford to go and meet this man anyway? Why, she didn't even have a flat of her own in which to talk to him if he came to England, really talk and start getting to know him, not make polite and meaningless conversation as you usually did with strangers.

When her mother and Phil had another loud quarrel the following day, the cruel things her mother said carried round the small house and showed that she not only wasn't going to change her mind about her former partner; she was making threats about what she would do if Mara dared go and see him.

Only, why shouldn't she get to know her biological father? Why should Kath's desires always take precedence over other people's feelings?

Chapter Two

When Peggy Buchanan went back to the flat in Perth, she found that Mike had come home early. She was about to fling herself into his arms when something about the way he was standing with one hand behind his back made her stop and stare at him. 'What's wrong?'

He held up a soggy package. 'This. I found it in the rubbish before I went to work. The bin liner bag had split and there it was.'

'Oh.'

'How long have you been eating on the sly?'

She shrugged. 'Just now and then, when I get too hungry to bear it. If we were married—'

He cut her off sharply. 'I made it plain before you moved in that I don't like fat women and also that I'm never getting married. You said you were OK with that.'

She moved to put her arms round him but he sidestepped and gestured to the table. 'Sit down, please.

We need to talk about our whole relationship, Peggy. Let's do this in a civilised way.'

She took the chair he'd indicated, her heart thumping. She'd never heard that tone in his voice before, cold, as if he were speaking to a stranger. 'Do what?'

'Split up. You clearly can't live by my rules and I shan't be able to trust you again. That's spoilt the relationship for me.'

'No! Mike, no! I'll never eat anything unhealthy again.'

'I'm sorry, Peggy, but I simply won't be able to trust you. I think it's best to end our relationship. I was coming to that conclusion anyway. You've been talking about friends getting married and buying houses. I don't intend to do that, not ever. This flat suits me just fine. I know where this is leading. You'll be asking me to father a child for you next and that's something that utterly repulses me.'

He began to tick things off on his fingers. '*I do not want – children, a mortgage or marriage.* Not ever. I'm perfectly happy with my life here.'

'But what would be so different, apart from the child?'

'Permanency. Staleness. Toys, chaos and noise.' He shuddered.

She wept, pleaded, but he was adamant. This was a side to him that she'd never seen before, though she'd heard people he worked with say he could be tough to deal with.

In the end he stood up. 'Enough. Get it through your head that I will never, ever change my mind.'

'But—'

'I'll spend the night in a hotel. When I come back after work tomorrow, I want you and all your possessions gone. If you're still here, I'll evict you legally and have your things packed and sent to your parents' house in Mandurah.'

He walked towards the door and though she jumped to her feet, the look he gave her across the room was so chill, so implacable, that the plea died in her throat.

He was gone before she could say another word.

She wept for a while, then fumbled for her phone and called her brother, sobbing out her story.

There was silence for a few moments then Rufus said, 'I doubt he'll change his mind.'

'But Rufus, I love him so much.'

'That's not love. That's – I don't know, obsession. It takes two to make a marriage, Pegs. To be frank, Mike Cruikshank isn't the sort of fellow I'd want you to marry. He's been bossing you around ever since you got together. I hate to see that. And you've got thinner and thinner, eating as he dictates. You're starting to look ill. Where's your pride, anyway, letting someone boss you around and decide what sort of body shape you'll have?'

'I don't have any pride. I *love* him.'

'Well, I'm sure he meant exactly what he said, so he can't love you. You'd better move out. No, don't cry.'

'But where am I going to go?'

'To Mum and Dad's. They'll take you in, just as they took me in when I was transferred to Perth for three months.'

She could only sob.

'Good thing I was working late tonight. I'll phone Mum to let her know, then I'll come round and help you pack. You'll have to put some of your furniture into storage till you decide what to do.'

'A lot of my stuff is already in storage because Mike doesn't like clutter. I'd been thinking we could find a proper house to live in then I'd get it out of storage again.' She dabbed away another tear.

'Well, leave it there for the time being. Mum and Dad won't want all of it dumped on them. They've got their house just as they like it.'

'I suppose.'

'Chin up. You'll get through this. You won't be on your own.'

No, she'd known her family would help her. But that didn't make this whole thing hurt any less.

Sobbing intermittently, she began to gather her clothes and personal possessions, going through the flat methodically, for all her unhappiness. Mike had called her a pack rat when they first started living together. She was in one sense: she knew exactly what she owned.

When the doorbell went, she checked who it was then flung it open. Rufus came in and gave her a big hug. 'I've ordered some boxes delivered. They're sending them express.' He glanced at his watch. 'Come on. Let's get to work.'

'Did you phone Mum?'

'Yes. She says of course you can go there. They're going out tonight but I have my key. You're to take your old bedroom.'

'Do you think they'd let me use the guest suite? I might want to – you know, be alone.'

'No. Mum said specifically that you can't use that as they're expecting a special new friend to visit soon.'

'Who?'

'She wouldn't say.'

He helped his sister pack, chivvied her along and told her to follow him down the freeway to Mandurah. 'And for heaven's sake, drive carefully.'

'OK. OK. I'm not suicidal.'

He gave her another hug. 'Chin up! You don't want people laughing at you.'

'I don't know what I want now.'

Chapter Three

Two days later, a lively interview for a job in Gloucester raised Mara's hopes briefly, and cut them abruptly off forty-eight hours after that as she was told she hadn't got the job, but they'd like to keep her on their reserve list, if that was all right.

As if anything would come of that!

Phil cornered her while Kath was out at the hairdresser's. 'Have you heard about the job?'

She nodded. 'I didn't get it.'

'It's been over a week now since you heard from your birth father, love. Don't let your mother stop you contacting him.'

'She'll go mad – and take it out on you.'

'I'm used to it.' He stared into the distance for a few seconds then went on, 'I can't abandon her, because I promised our marriage would be for better or worse and I always try to keep my promises. Besides, she'd never

cope with the practicalities of life on her own now. She's
getting worse.'

'Frankly I don't know how you can live with her rigid
rules for what to do or not do.'

'Golf.'

'What?'

'I play golf a lot more often. Or I tell her I'm off to
play golf. Being retired has its advantages. I find it very
soothing to be out in the open air with cheerful people,
or even just to sit in the club room chatting to my friends
or making new ones. The game and my golfing buddies
are my lifeline. It's still your choice what you do, but I
wanted to sum up the situation: your decision not to
meet this Aaron guy has left three people unhappy and
the fourth is never really happy, only determined to get
her own way. Think about those statistics: three to one.
And then do what *you* really want.'

He was right but her mother hadn't always been this
bad and that was holding her back. Mara had some
good memories of their relationship from her childhood
as well as bad ones.

The day after Phil's frank talk, he went out early to
play golf. Mara abandoned the idea of a late breakfast
because she knew her mother was waiting to pounce on
her in the kitchen. Kath was well aware that something
was going on and wouldn't rest till she found out what
it was.

It might be cowardly but Mara crept downstairs,
grabbed her jacket from the hallstand and called, 'Just

going out for a walk.' She slipped out of the front door before her mother could protest or try to come after her. There was a large park nearby and she'd started going there on fine days for the same reason Phil played golf so often: to find some peace and quiet.

She was still smiling when she got there but the smile gradually faded when she saw a man of about her stepfather's age watching her. She'd noticed him twice before and there he was again today, strolling along behind her, stopping when she did. Was she being stalked now? She wasn't putting up with that.

Feeling safe in an open area with several other people walking nearby, she strode across to confront him. 'Don't tell me you're not watching me because I've spotted you hovering nearby twice before. What do you do with yourself on rainy days? Stalk the family cat round the house?'

To her surprise he looked at her with a rueful smile. 'I must be losing my touch. But it's such a pretty park you can't help relaxing here.'

'Well, find somewhere else to relax because I have enough problems on my plate without you hassling me.'

When she started to turn away, he said quickly, 'Wait! Please, Ms Gregory!'

She paused, surprised by him knowing her name.

'Have you got a minute? I'm not stalking you in the way you think, I promise. I've been hired to find you and give you a message. Today I've been waiting till you got somewhere quieter in the park to do it.'

'Well, that's a new excuse for pestering a stranger!'

His smile crinkled his eyes at the corners and made his whole face light up. He didn't look at all threatening now, so she waited, curious to see what he'd say next.

He spread his hands in a helpless gesture. 'It does sound a bit corny, doesn't it. And it's going to sound even cornier when I tell you that I'm a private investigator sent by your father to ask you something important.'

'I talk to Phil every day and if he needs anything he asks me straight out.'

'I meant your birth father. Here's my ID.' He pulled out a laminated card with his photo on and held it out to her.

She gasped and looked at the card, then studied him carefully. Actually, he was quite pleasant looking, with the sort of face you'd buy a used car from. 'What's this alleged birth father's name?'

'Aaron Buchanan and he lives in Australia or he'd be speaking to you himself. You two haven't met yet, but he's hoping you will.'

It was so unexpected she turned all wobbly at that and had to sit down on a nearby bench.

He came to stand nearby. 'Mind if I join you?'

She waved one hand permissively and he sat down at the other end of the bench.

'My name's George, by the way, George Walters. But you probably saw that on my ID. These are my personal contact details, which I don't give to everyone.' He fumbled in his pocket and took out a business card, offering it to her.

She glanced at it only briefly before shoving it into the

side pocket of her shoulder bag. When she felt she could control her voice, she asked, 'What's the message?'

'First, Aaron wanted to be sure his recent letter got through to you.'

'Yes, it did.'

'You didn't reply. He'd really like to meet you.'

'I'd like to meet him too, but I'm out of work and I haven't the money to go gallivanting off to Australia.'

'Would you agree to meet him if he paid your fare?'

'Seriously?'

'Yes. He was a bit worried because he's written three times now and you haven't replied.'

'My mother has been intercepting the letters. I caught her red-handed a week ago, so his third letter did get through to me. It's a lot to take in. She'd destroyed the others so I don't know what was in them.'

'Ah. I see. Do you know much about him?'

'Nothing whatsoever. It came as a big shock that he was even alive because all my life I'd been told he was dead.'

It was George's turn to look shocked.

'I've never even seen a photo of him,' she added wistfully.

'That's easy to remedy.' He got out his mobile phone, fiddled around with it and held it out to her.

The man on it looked like an older, masculine version of herself. There was no mistaking that determined chin or the way his dark hair grew. And his eyes were very similar to the ones that looked back at her from the mirror every morning.

'You're so like him physically, Mara, that I have no doubt you're his daughter. But he'll take a DNA test should you wish. If you'll give me your email address I'll send this photo to you now. And may I take one of you to send to him? He's desperate to see you now that he's found out about your existence. I'd have taken a photo before but he said it seemed unfair to do that without asking you.'

'He's being very scrupulous about all this.'

'He's a decent, honest chap. I've known him for years.'

And suddenly her decision was made, because, as Phil had said so sadly, the numbers were three to one in favour of her doing it.

She couldn't raise a smile but looked steadily towards the mobile phone until George had clicked it a couple of times and lowered it.

'Um, what happens next?'

'You really do want to go and see him?'

'Yes. Give me another day to tell my mother. It — won't be easy.' She'd have to get Phil's advice on how best to do that.

'All right. He'll pay your return fare to Australia and help you through the formalities. I'm assuming you have a passport?'

'Yes, of course.'

'Good. Oh, in case you're worried about the cost, he's not short of money. He's been very successful in business.'

'I can't believe it.'

George gave her another charming smile. 'He'll be

over the moon. I'll see how he wants to arrange it all. I'm assuming you don't want me to come to the house, given your mother's attitude, so maybe we could meet here again tomorrow? If it's raining there's a café at the other end of the park.'

'I know the place.'

'I should have had an answer from Aaron by then. He doesn't hang about when he wants something. Ten o'clock suit you?'

'Yeah.' Words still seemed to be in short supply in her brain.

'If anything happens to prevent our meeting or to prevent you going, could you please let me know, Mara? It'd be beyond cruel to raise Aaron's hopes then dash them.'

'I won't do that. My mother will try to prevent me. She's desperate to stop me meeting him, but now that I've decided, I won't go back on my word.'

'Is there any way she might be able to prevent you coming to Australia?'

A huff of cynical amusement escaped her. 'No. And as I lost my job recently, I'm free to do what I want.'

She glanced down at her watch. 'I'd better get back now. If I'm away too long she'll make an even worse fuss. I'd rather she didn't suspect anything yet, so definitely don't come to the house. I'll tell her later, when Phil's back from golf.'

George inclined his head. 'All right. I'll get back to my office, then. Nice meeting you properly.'

When she got home her mother was out and there

was what looked like a business letter waiting for her, propped up against the kettle so that Mara couldn't miss it. It hadn't been opened; at least she didn't think it had. It had been posted in London but she didn't recognise the company whose name and logo were on the envelope. She definitely hadn't applied for a job with them.

The contents made her suck in her breath in amazement. It was a legal demand on behalf of her former employer for return of the children's software program that someone alleged she'd developed while working for Perisson Toys.

She had developed a program, but it wasn't the one they used and anyway, she'd developed it totally in her own time, mostly at weekends.

'Do they want the blood from my veins as well?' she muttered.

Phil had come into the kitchen to make a cup of coffee. 'Problem?'

'Yes. See.'

He scanned it quickly, then read it again more slowly. 'And do you have this program?'

'Of course I do. But I developed it in my own time and it wasn't connected with anything I worked on at Perisson; it was preparatory work for marketing the toys I make in my spare time. So the intellectual rights belong to me.'

'Why are they asking for it, then? How do they even know about it?'

She'd already worked that out. 'Must be Darren's

idea to claim it. He's the only one who knew what I was doing because he saw me working on it at home when we were living together.'

'Did anyone else see your work?'

She frowned. 'Not exactly, but I shared some information with a friend of mine a few times. Pete. I asked him about a few things. All the programming was done at home on my own computer. There's nothing whatsoever on the system at Perisson because I knew better than to do any personal work there.' She flicked the letter. 'You have to be really careful, if you want to avoid this sort of thing.'

'What are you going to do about it?'

Tears filled her eyes and she dashed them away angrily because she hated showing a weakness. 'I don't know. The last thing I can afford now is to get involved in an expensive court case and Darren knows it, the cheating scumbag.'

'Then let's find someone who'd be able to check what you've been doing. You didn't even switch on your computer this morning.'

'I wasn't in a creative mood and didn't want to pick up any messages. I went out for a walk round the park. And something strange happened there.' She told him about meeting the PI and her birth father offering to pay for her flight to Australia.

Phil gave her a quick hug. 'Well, that's good news, surely?'

'I suppose so. But if I'm embroiled in a court case, it'll be a bad time to go to Australia, won't it?'

'Well, we'd better sort out the court case first, then, eh? You're quite sure you never did any personal stuff on your work computer?'

'Definitely not.'

'Could Darren have got into your computer when you were living together and made a copy of your work?'

She let out a scornful puff of laughter. 'No way. He's more into marketing than computer programming, so he wouldn't have the necessary skills. I have all my private stuff very well protected, believe me.'

'Right then. I know a guy who's very knowledgeable about legal matters. He may be able to help us or at least find us someone who can prove your work has only been done on your own computer. Then if we challenge these people to produce any part of the program as evidence you did it at work, I think they'll shut up and leave you alone.'

'Trouble is, if word gets out about their claim, even if I'm proved innocent, it'll throw a shadow on my honesty that'll be hard to get rid of.'

'Well, first things first, I'll just give my friend a call and see if he's free. I think if we clear your name, it'll make Darren look a fool, so anything he says won't be given as much credibility.'

The friend was free and she felt as if she'd been caught up by a whirlwind as Phil drove her round to this man's office, which was in an old-fashioned block of four suites.

When Phil rang the bell next to his friend's name in the foyer, a man answered and his voice sounded familiar to Mara. It wasn't . . . It couldn't be . . .

'Come up the stairs and turn left, Phil. My office is the only one there. My secretary has nipped out for a few minutes and my partner's out on a job, so I'm on my own here.'

The man who opened the door was her stalker. He grinned at her. 'Small world, eh?' He shook hands with Phil and the two clearly knew one another.

Phil was also smiling. 'Are you really a private investigator? You always say you have a boring old backroom job in computer stuff when anyone asks and that you're semi-retired now.'

George shrugged. 'I don't advertise what I do, for obvious reasons. And I really am semi-retired. I only take on cases that interest me and leave the rest to my junior partner.'

He locked the door again behind them. 'Can't be too careful these days and I'm not always here to protect my secretary if some nasty type gets angry at me. Mind you, she does have a black belt in some martial art or other, so she's fairly confident she can look after herself, if necessary. I'd rather she didn't have to prove that, though.'

Phil put the laptop on the desk and said, 'Well, I already know and trust you so you being a PI is going to be really helpful, George. I'll let Mara explain the details.'

She did that, then Phil took over again. 'So, we need to find someone to check out her work on this computer and show it hasn't been imported from elsewhere. Is that possible?'

George looked at him and then at the laptop. 'It may be. I'm good with computers, but not expert enough for your purpose, nor am I an impartial witness, being a friend of yours. However, I have an acquaintance I can ask to deal with it. He owes me a few favours. Sounds like a simple job for someone like him.'

Mara didn't like the thought of letting her precious laptop out of her sight, though of course she'd got everything on it backed up. She looked from one man to the other. 'I'm still not sure this is the right thing to do.'

'It absolutely is,' Phil insisted. 'You're not giving in to that Darren creep.'

George was watching them, his head moving to and fro from one speaker to the other like someone watching a tennis match. He asked a couple of questions and she explained about Darren, then found herself going on to talk about how she'd left the company.

When she saw Phil and George exchange glances, she realised she'd given away her suspicions about dirty tricks being played by Darren to make sure he got the promotion. This pretence that she'd stolen a program she'd produced in office hours might even have been part of why she'd been made redundant, so she definitely had to prove herself innocent.

George seemed to understand her worries. 'It'll be all right, Mara. My friend really is one of the best. I won't tell you his name unless we have to take it to court, but if you like I can deal with your old company. In fact, I'm sure your birth father would want me to do that for you.'

He put the laptop on a set of low cupboards behind the desk and bent down to pull an older one in a well-worn case from the end cupboard. 'You can borrow this for the time being if you'd like.'

'Thank you, but if it's only for a day or so I'll make do with my tablet. I'm sorry to be a nuisance. If there's any charge for this—'

'None at all.' He gestured towards a seating area to one side. 'Let's sit down more comfortably. I was going to get in touch with you today about going to Australia.'

He glanced at Phil, hesitated, then turned to her. 'Aaron responded to my email straight away. Mara, he'd be delighted to pay your fare to and from Australia if you'll go out to visit him and his wife for a few weeks. He can't come over to the UK at the moment because he's in the middle of some important negotiations for selling his business and has to be available in that part of the world. But he's very eager indeed to meet you.'

It was all becoming very real suddenly.

Phil nudged her. 'It's generous of him. You should do it, love. There would be so many advantages to going just now. You'd get away from your mother and give her time to grow used to the situation, as well as finding out how you get on with your birth father. George and I can sort out this spurious claim. I never did like Darren, by the way, but I didn't expect him to do something like this.'

'He fooled me for a time. He can be very charming when he wants to.'

'He's a smarmy rat. When you brought him down to

meet us that day, I took an instant dislike to him.'

'I could tell you didn't warm to him. I didn't think you felt that strong a dislike, though. Um, you're sure you wouldn't mind if I left you to look after Mum? She'll be angry big time.'

'I'm well used to her little ways. You need to go.'

She reached out to squeeze his arm. 'I won't let this Aaron come between you and me, Dad. You know that.'

George had been watching them and now said firmly, 'He won't even try. I've worked with him before. He's a thoroughly decent chap.'

She looked at Phil. 'I'll be coming between you and Mum, though, won't I?'

'Well, I'll deal with her and you deal with your new situation.' He smiled at her. 'There you are, then, your immediate future is settled and you're heading off to the sun.'

'You'll keep in touch while I'm away, won't you, whatever she says or does?'

'Try to stop me.'

She turned to George, who was smiling benignly at them. 'So – what do I have to do?'

'Say yes, give me a date you can travel and leave it to Aaron to make the arrangements. I don't think it'll take him more than a few days, though, if that.'

'Really? Wow. Any time will do me for travelling, the sooner the better, actually.'

'I can deal with all that for you.'

'Really?'

'Or rather, Aaron can. He has some excellent

connections, has done jobs for the Australian government. You'd better let me have your passport details after you get back home.'

She chuckled and waved her phone at him. 'Got them here. I'll send you a copy.'

'That's great.'

Once that was done, he said, 'Now, if you take my advice you'll get ready to leave at a few hours' notice. Aaron doesn't let grass grow beneath his feet when he wants something done. Oh, and don't forget when you're packing that Australia is in the opposite season to us. It'll be coming up to summer there, which can get very hot in Western Australia.'

'I could do with some sunshine.'

'Don't forget your swimming things. Aaron and his wife – her name's Emma by the way – live in a waterfront home situated on some man-made canals in a seaside town called Mandurah. It's about an hour south of Perth, the capital of Western Australia.'

'Wow, sounds like a Hollywood dream home.'

'It's a nice place to live, that's for sure. I'll get your laptop back to you by tomorrow afternoon at the latest and I'll contact you to confirm that we've proved you were working at home.'

Phil put an arm round her shoulders. 'There you are, then, Mara love. Fate has stepped in to help you. I think you need a break, so make the most of this holiday in the sun.'

Nothing had actually been done yet, but she felt as if a huge burden had already been lifted from her shoulders.

Chapter Four

When his phone played a tune that signalled an email from George, Aaron read it, reread it and rushed out of his home office into the kitchen. He grabbed Emma by the waist and danced her outside and round the back patio, moving in and out of the patches of sunlight, chanting, 'She's coming to visit us, she really, really is.'

Emma laughed but slowed him down until they were standing next to one another looking at the canal that bordered their garden. 'I presume you mean Mara. When is she coming?'

'Within days, as soon as I can book her a flight. And I know just who to tell about my sudden discovery. She'll push things along for me.'

'You always know somebody. I suppose you mean Nancy.'

'Yes. She's big on family reunions. Well, you would be in a country with so many migrants, wouldn't you?

You see how the separations hurt people. If you have any compassion, that is.'

'Yes. Migrants like you who make a success of their new lives. I'm sure you'll play that card well.'

He heaved a happy sigh. 'Mara needs to get away from her mother as well as wanting to meet me, it seems. I doubt Kath will have got easier to live with as she's aged. Well, George told me she's very difficult to deal with.'

'No one is perfect.'

He raised her hand to his lips in one of the sudden romantic gestures she loved. 'You are.' Then he sighed. 'I'd have done things differently if I'd known she was carrying my child, though.'

'Families can be – difficult.'

He knew she was thinking about Peggy. Their daughter was so thin she looked ill, thanks to that damned Mike she was shacked up with, and they were both seriously worried about her.

'It sounds as though the mother is going to make things difficult for Mara.'

Emma shook her head. 'What's with the woman? Hasn't she got a life of her own that she has to take over her daughter's?'

'George has met her. Phil is worrying that she's got a lot worse lately. Turns out George knows Mara's stepfather quite well because they're golfing buddies. Coincidences do happen in this funny old world of ours, don't they? It's not just in fiction that you meet them.'

'Poor woman. Mental illness or a different slant on

the world can be very difficult for the person as well as everyone else. Your daughter will have had to cope with it for years. It's bound to have marked her.'

'Another reason she needs a holiday down under.'

Emma looked at his beaming face, hating to spoil his happiness in any way after the frustrating months of setbacks in his search for his daughter, but there were other people to think of. 'Um, there's something else to think of. When are you going to tell Rufus and Peggy about it? She's still rather fragile after breaking up with Mike but you can't leave it much longer.'

Aaron looked at her in surprise. 'I hadn't thought about that. This all came together so quickly in the end. Our two will cope all right, won't they? Make her welcome and all that, even though she's not related to them?'

'Maybe. Who knows? You didn't tell them you had a daughter, wouldn't do that till you'd found her, you said, in case Mara refused to see you. They're not going to like having been left out of the loop because they regard you as their father in every way. What's more, if you show them that glowing face, well, to be frank, they're going to feel you regard them as second best.'

'Oh, hell. They're not second best, definitely not. I love them to pieces. I even loved them when they were teenagers.'

They both chuckled at the memories of teenage rebellions, then he said thoughtfully, 'This is a different type of love, I think. If you can pass your genes down the generations, it's the nearest you can get to immortality.

And I'm weak enough to care about that, which doesn't stop me loving our two.'

'You did pass on your genes. You became a sperm donor when you found out I couldn't have any more children.'

'That's not the same. I haven't a clue what, if anything, came of that, and I never shall have. They made that clear to me when I donated.'

'You might. You never know. The rules for such things keep changing.'

'Nah. Any resulting children probably won't have been told they're not the result of their parents getting together biologically. I was warned not to expect any contact whatsoever.'

'Well, I'm giving you another warning: be prepared for tangled emotions and maybe even storms from Peggy when you introduce this complete stranger into the family. She's more fragile than she lets on. I found her crying her eyes out last night. She confessed that she'd been feeling really broody for a while. Who'd have thought that of our Pegs?'

'Not me. Mike must have fancied her initially, though.'

'Well, she's gorgeous looking. Or she was when she was a normal size. Anyway, I'm glad she came back to us. We can keep an eye on her, get her help if she needs it. I'm more than a bit worried about how little she's eating.'

He gave her a wry smile. 'And we thought we'd have this place to ourselves when we built it. They deserve the title of Boomerang Generation, the way they come and go. Rufus has moved out of here twice and come back again. Peggy's only come back once since she graduated.'

'Give her time. She's younger than he is. And if we continue to live in such a desirable spot, what can you expect?' Emma gestured to the water slapping gently against their jetty and wall.

Aaron was back to frowning at the water. 'I thought Mike really cared about her, you know, the forever kind of caring. My old aunty from Lancashire used to say: "There's nowt so queer as fowk," and she was right.'

'Translate that into Australian English, please, Aaron.'

'It means: there's nothing as strange as people.'

'Your aunty was right about that.' Emma went across to pat him on the cheek. 'No more ifs or buts – tell them about Mara tonight.'

It was an order. She didn't often use that tone of voice and when she did, everyone in the family usually jumped to attention. He supposed she was right and he really ought to have told them sooner, but he'd wanted to hug the news to himself, sharing it only with his wife, who was very much his forever love. He'd known that from the first day they met, even though she was widowed and had two young children from her first marriage.

The more he thought about it, the more Aaron agreed with Emma. He'd better not delay bringing his stepchildren up to date on the news. He'd hate Rufus and Peggy to feel that he considered them second best. How could he? He'd been their father for most of their lives, and had loved every minute of it. He couldn't understand anyone not wanting children.

But he didn't want Mara to feel she was second best, either. It was going to be a delicate balance. And it had happened at a bad time, with the sale of his business not yet resolved.

When they'd finished the family meal that evening, Rufus started to push his chair back. 'We'll clear up quickly then we're going out to our favourite bar to drown Peggy's sorrows.'

Aaron grabbed his sleeve. 'Could you wait a few minutes please? I have something rather important to tell you both.'

'You can clear the table then we'll stay in here,' Emma said. 'It's better to hold this sort of discussion across a table, I always think. And keep your phones switched off, please, you two.'

They exchanged puzzled glances and Aaron could almost see the cogs going round in their brains. This switching off phones was one of her rules for mealtimes, and she was unyielding about it. So if the rule was to continue to be applied, it'd be clear to them that whatever this was must indeed be important.

When the table was clear and the dishwasher loaded, they came back to sit down. Aaron hesitated, wondering how to start.

Peggy looked at him anxiously. 'You're not ill, are you, Dad?'

'No, honey. And before you ask, neither is your mother. No, it's some good news that I received a few weeks ago. It was so unexpected that I had to catch my breath, so to speak, and come to terms with it before I shared it with anyone else – except your mother, of course.'

They waited, still frowning slightly.

'I found out I'd fathered a child before I left England all those years ago. The woman I was with at the time refused point-blank to emigrate, which was no surprise to me after weeks of quarrelling about it. But she kept the information that she was pregnant from me – out of sheer spite I have to presume. It's been – a huge surprise.'

'What sort of child did you have?' Rufus asked.

'A girl. Only she's thirty now, so it'd be stupid to refer to her as a girl.'

'What's she called?' Peggy asked.

'Mara.'

Rufus nodded. 'Cool name, Mara. How did you find out about her? Did *she* get in touch looking for her father?'

'No. She'd been told I died years ago. I had my first clue about her existence at the Lucases' barbecue for their cousin from England.'

'Several months ago, then, not weeks,' Peggy remarked rather sharply.

'Turned out their cousin came from the same village as me. They didn't tell me till I got there, wanted it to be a surprise because the cousin had recognised my name. It's a very small village, so Di and I knew one another vaguely back in the day, though we weren't friends, or even in the same year at school. She knew I'd been close to Kath, so assumed we'd kept in touch.'

The pause went on for so long, Peggy tapped his arm. 'Hello? Anyone still there?'

He jumped. 'Sorry. When Di was bringing me up to date on people, she mentioned that Kath had settled down in the village with a stranger from London, who was, she said, a really nice man. They hadn't had any children but Kath already had one. When I did the sums, that child could only have been mine, so I went online and started checking the census information. The birth date fits and the researcher I hired said she even looked like me.'

There was dead silence, then Peggy asked, 'Are you going over to the UK to meet your daughter?'

'No, Mara is coming over here for a few weeks.'

'Have you done DNA tests?'

'No need to. I don't see how anyone else could have fathered her. Her mother is very much against us making contact, so things would be a bit awkward if I went there. But as Mara has just been made redundant, it's a good time for her to take a break and come out here.'

Rufus shrugged. 'She's a few years older than us, then.'

'Three years older than you, five years older than your sister.'

Peggy was frowning. 'That's a bit risky, isn't it? There's no guarantee that you'll like her or that we will, yet you've invited her here to our home for several weeks. We've all seen relatives from overseas come here for long visits and nearly drive people mad after a couple of weeks. We've even seen people quarrel and go back earlier than planned.'

'I'm sure Mara won't be like that.'

'There's no guarantee. And don't assume you can shove her off on us to entertain if you have to go away. You know what you're like when work calls. I know you've got the business up for sale, but it hasn't attracted a genuine buyer yet.'

Aaron didn't like the continuing sharpness of Peggy's tone. He shot a quick glance at Emma and she shook her head slightly, warning him not to take issue with that.

Rufus pushed his chair back and stood up. 'Well, if that's news time finished, we'll be off. Coming, Peggy?'

'Yep. My first foray as a single woman.'

'Don't rush into anything,' her mother warned.

Peggy smiled brightly but unconvincingly. 'Of course not.'

The two of them were gone so quickly Aaron didn't have the chance to tell them anything else about Mara. Not that they'd asked for it.

He went across and put his arms round Emma. 'How did I go?'

'Six out of ten.'

'Huh? What did I do wrong?'

'Gave them the bald facts, didn't say much about how you're feeling, didn't ask their help, just assumed it'd be forthcoming. Add to that, Peggy's still in hyper-sensitive mode, still shocked that her relationship could have ended so abruptly, so I doubt she'll feel positive about anything for a while.'

'And you? How do you feel about Mara? I didn't even ask you how long I could invite her here for. Sorry.'

Her smile crinkled her face into the adorable wrinkles she was developing at the corners of her eyes to match the faint frosting of silver in her hair, so he kissed them.

She kissed him back, then pushed him away to continue their discussion. 'I won't know how I really feel till I meet her, will I? But she'll be a guest so I'll treat her nicely, even if she turns out to be, um, a challenge.'

'Why should she be?'

'No saying what she'll be like, is there? Her mother didn't sound to be easy to deal with. Her difficult attitude to life might be inherited.'

'George says he likes Mara.'

'Well, that's a start. You've known him long enough to trust his opinion. Let's hope we'll all like her too.'

Aaron was starting to worry, but he didn't get a chance to ask Emma anything else about how she felt because she changed the subject very firmly.

She tugged his arm. 'Come on. You can make us our Friday night cocktails and then we'll watch that movie and not worry about anything else tonight.'

Which meant she didn't intend to go on talking about it. Not worrying was easier said than done for him, though.

And was no one happy for him to have found a daughter? Didn't they have any idea of how much it mattered to him?

What sort of welcome would the others offer Mara if even tolerant Emma was guarded about her feelings? He did so want his daughter to feel welcome in his life, and for himself to have a chance to make up for all the years they'd missed, wanted it desperately.

When Phil and Mara got home from their meeting with George, having visited a coffee shop to delay their return, they entered the house through the garage as usual. They'd seen all the downstairs lights blazing as they turned off the street.

'Uh-oh! She's ready for a confrontation,' he said with a sigh. 'I know the signs.'

Mara glanced quickly sideways. 'Then she'll have one with me. You stand back, Dad.'

'But I was going to—'

'Do what? Protect me from her? Not possible, because all that will satisfy her is my abject submission to her will and that's not going to happen. So as I'll be leaving and you'll be staying, I might as well do what I can to protect you.'

'I can usually manage her moods. Not so well lately, though.'

She didn't say it but she didn't think he should have to. She doubted she'd ever marry. Most of her friends had found partners by now and two had divorced again. Perhaps she didn't have the happy marriage gene anyway. There must be some subtle factor that predisposed you to it. Look at how Darren had taken her for a ride.

Kath was waiting for them in the living room. The television wasn't switched on but the three table lamps were blazing as well as the overhead light, and she was sitting bolt upright at one end of the sofa, strategically facing the door.

'You're late,' she threw at them. 'I had my tea at the usual time and I'm not messing up the kitchen again just because you two can't keep an eye on the clock.'

'That's all right. I'll go out and get us a curry takeaway after I've told you my news.' Mara dropped her bag on the floor near the armchair where she usually sat.

'Pick that up this minute. You know I don't like anything messing up my nice tidy room in the evenings.' Kath's voice was at its sharpest. 'And I'm not having a curry stinking up the house, either.'

'I'll pick my bag up when I go out for our takeaway. Until then it's doing no harm. And we'll keep the curry in the kitchen, but we're hungry, so we're having one. Now, do you want to hear my news or not?'

Kath tossed more words at her. 'I know what your news is: you've been in touch with *him*. I can tell from the expression on your face. When I read his letters, I knew he'd come between us if he ever found you.'

'You were wrong to read my letters and he hasn't come between us because I've not even spoken to him yet.'

'But he's got through to you. I can tell. Who's his messenger?'

Phil's voice was calm. 'A friend of mine, actually: George Walters.'

'I suppose Aaron's promising you the earth if you'll toady up to him.'

Mara had had enough. 'For heaven's sake, Mum,

what's got into you lately? Few people have the nasty
motives you ascribe to them. Why should this man want
to come between us?'

'I know him and you don't. Well, just you wait and
you'll find out how worthless what *he* says is. He'll
promise you anything to get you away from me, then
he'll play nice for a while but drop you once he's tired
of you.' Her voice grew more shrill. 'The same way he
dropped me when I wouldn't let him boss me around
and drag me to the other side of the world.'

Mara managed to continue speaking quietly and
evenly. 'Thanks for your confidence in me, Mum, but I
usually make my own decisions. You're right about one
thing though: he's offered to pay for me to visit him in
Australia. And I'm going.'

She waited for the usual explosion of anger and it
erupted almost immediately.

'Then you can get out of this house tonight. I'm not
having anything from him contaminating my life.'

Phil intervened. 'Stop making a drama out of nothing.
Mara's not going anywhere tonight except to fetch us a
takeaway. I really fancy a curry.'

'Go on! Side with her.' Kath's voice rose shrilly. 'She's
not staying here if she's going to see him! I won't let her!'

Phil sighed quite audibly. 'I'm not siding with anyone,
though I would like a calmer life, by hell I would. And
I'm definitely *not* kicking my daughter out of my house.
You do remember that we put it in my name, don't you,
Kath? Mara, love, you know you'll always be welcome
under my roof, don't you?'

Kath stared at him in shock at this unexpected counter-attack. 'Whose side are you on? You can't mean that! She's not even your birth daughter.'

'Why can't I mean it? She's become my daughter and I love her dearly. I've been too weak before, letting you have your own way in just about everything because I despise quarrelling as a way of communicating. That was because your silly little rules didn't matter to me. But this does matter, Kath, it matters very much. Mara is staying here till she leaves for Australia, and she'll be welcome back here when she returns.'

'*You traitor!*'

'Don't do this, Mum,' Mara pleaded. 'There's no need. Meeting my birth father will make no difference to how I feel about you and Phil.'

'But it'll make a huge difference to how I feel about you, you ungrateful creature. You're *my* daughter, not his. He went away and left me to have a child on my own.'

'Are you changing your story now?' Phil asked. 'You've always said you didn't tell him you were having his child. And he told George he'd only just found out about Mara, so I reckon that was the true story on both sides. You always told Mara he was dead, and that was an outright lie.'

'She was better off without him.'

'You can't know that. Stop making simple things difficult. That lass is going to Australia to meet her biological father, then she's coming back to carry on with her life here. She may get on well with him or she may not. Whichever it is, I'll back her up on what she does about it. What's so hard for you to accept about that?'

'She won't want to come back. He'll poison her mind. And I won't want her back if she's on his side. She must make her choice now: him or me.'

He sat down on the sofa beside his wife and tried to take her hand. 'Look, love—'

But she shoved him so hard she took him by surprise and knocked him off it.

There was dead silence in the room as he got to his feet. 'I'll move my bedding and clothes into the dining room till Mara leaves, then I'll sleep in the second bedroom permanently. Be very careful what you say and do from now on, Kathleen Gregory, because I'm just so far from leaving you.' He held up his right forefinger and thumb, with the tips nearly touching, to illustrate this.

Kath let out a whining sound and began to rock to and fro, tears running down her cheeks, but this time he ignored her play for pity.

He turned to Mara. 'Get me a chicken korma please, love. With all the trimmings. I'll stay here with your mother and I'll have the table set in the kitchen for when you get back.'

She nodded, wondering what he'd say and do while she was out. Perhaps he wouldn't say anything new. He rarely ever argued with his wife.

She phoned the restaurant and set off immediately. She'd be a little early but that didn't matter. She needed some thinking time.

This wasn't just about Aaron contacting her, though

that was a major issue at the moment; it was as if her mother was increasingly desperate to control every single detail of what they did.

After her last breakdown Kath had refused any kind of further medical assistance, insisting she was fine and only needed a peaceful life to be happy.

Mara wanted a more peaceful life too, of course she did, but on her own terms not someone else's. If making her own choices led to mistakes, well, she'd learn from them and try to do better next time. She was going to go to Australia and meet her father, see what he was like, and was hoping they'd get on well.

She admitted to herself that she liked the idea of a holiday in the sun and time to think about her future without her mother hovering and nagging. It was strange how sunny weather seemed to lift your spirits in so many ways.

George had spoken well of her father. She hoped he was right because she would be very much at Aaron Buchanan's mercy once she got to Australia. But she believed George's opinion of him rather than her mother's tangled skeins of hostility.

When she got home with the food, the light was on in her parents' bedroom and Phil was sitting in the kitchen, so lost in thought he didn't immediately look up. Then he did and said brightly, 'You know, I really am hungry. Perhaps standing up for yourself gives you an appetite.'

'I hope so. I got us all the trimmings.'

They talked of other things, politics, a book Phil had just read and enjoyed, which he offered to lend her to read on the plane, a television series they'd been watching together.

And for once, her mother stayed out of the way.

But Phil's bedding was sitting in a corner of the living room and when they said goodnight, he started making up the couch for himself, avoiding looking at her.

Mara didn't comment. It was his choice where to sleep and whether to stay with her mother. Whatever he decided to do wouldn't affect how much she loved him.

Chapter Five

Hal Kendrell had been lost in thought and jumped in shock when the taxi driver said loudly, 'We're nearly there now, sir.'

As they turned off the main road, he saw the street sign and was pulled fully back into the present. In a few moments he would have to start dealing with what had happened, something he'd been dreading during the whole flight from the UK to Western Australia. His loss seemed more real here, where his mother had lived her last years – and died alone.

The taxi driver said, 'Here you are, sir, Waterfront Gardens. It certainly lives up to its name, eh? If I ever win Lotto, I'll buy a house here or somewhere like it, that's for sure.'

It was an effort to answer him. 'It looks pretty.'

'Yes, very. Not been to this part of Mandurah before, sir?'

'No. I've never visited Western Australia. My mother moved here a couple of years ago and I've been working flat out, travelling between the UK and North America.'

She hadn't told him she was terminally ill, or Hal would have come to see her regularly. But knowing her, when she found out that her cancer was terminal, he'd guess she'd preferred to spend her last months in peaceful solitude. That didn't stop him wishing he'd managed to say a proper farewell and at least told her how much he loved her.

As far as he was aware, she'd not confided in anyone how short a time she had left; well, unless you counted the lawyer he'd just been talking to in Perth. Mr Coates had drawn up her will and she'd briefed him about what to tell her son after she died, which he'd done gently and carefully today, making sure Hal understood all the basics.

A reclusive woman, his mother, communicating even with her own family mainly by email in recent years. She'd sent one to Hal every Friday, regular as clockwork, and the messages had followed him from country to country. In each she'd replied to his previous email – at least he'd just about always replied to her – then she'd given a summary of what she'd been doing. Even her briefest descriptions had been beautifully expressed. She'd always been good with the written word, even before she gained fame as a poet.

The taxi stopped at the end of a street where large, luxurious houses lined one side, which ran along the edge of the water. Smaller but still quite large houses lined the other side without a water frontage. The main visual feature of the street seemed to be garages, triple or quadruple, with broad paved areas in front of them. Well, of course! These would be the rear of the waterside houses and the sides facing the water would be the front.

Hal got out of the taxi and tried the front door keys the lawyer had given him on the ornate door to the left of the garage. To his relief it opened easily. When he stepped inside, a harsh beeping sound reminded him to enter the code he'd been given. That stopped the ghastly noise, thank goodness.

After paying the driver, who had got his suitcases out of the boot by now, Hal refused further help and carried the luggage inside himself. He didn't want any more meaningless chat, however kindly meant. By the time he'd moved all three cases and his backpack inside the hall, the taxi had driven off.

Once he closed the door, he found that the late afternoon light filtering down into the hall from a window above the door wasn't good enough for a stranger to find his way round easily. The stairs leading up to a dimness suggested closed curtains upstairs. He found a light switch then locked the front door behind him.

He usually travelled with only minimal luggage but this time he'd brought three loaded suitcases with him, paying for the extra weight because he'd intended to spend some time here even before her lawyer had told him that his mother hoped he would enjoy her house for a few months before he sold it, or even settle there.

Maybe he would stay on if he liked living here. He was tired of the rat race and wanted to chill out for a while. His only certainty at the moment was that he was making a much-needed major mid-life change, the sort people called a sea change.

He'd meant to look round as they drove through the town but had got lost in his memories of his mother and his sadness at losing her so young. Well, sixty-two seemed to him far too young to die, only thirty years older than him.

He'd been extremely surprised when the lawyer told him how much money she'd left him. She must have been more business savvy than he'd realised.

He tried saying, 'Good on yer, Ma!' with an Aussie accent at that thought, but his voice broke and he had to stop and take a few deep breaths before continuing to explore. But his thoughts wandered on.

Like her, Hal had come here to Mandurah on his own. He'd never married, though he still had a vague hope that it might happen 'one day'. So far, however, he'd not cared enough about any woman to feel like spending the rest of his life with her. He'd enjoyed a couple of longer relationships, one lasting nine months and another just over a year.

He'd made it plain at the start of each move into shared accommodation that he didn't want to marry yet and had chosen partners who felt the same. Both had been intelligent women, successful in their careers, and the partings had been amicable, caused more by their jobs than by disagreements. He still kept in touch with them both.

And why was he standing here like a fool thinking about his past? It was the future he should focus on from here onwards.

He looked round again. To his immediate right was a door which he found opened into the garage, a big, dark space. Another fumble found the light switches on the wall. As the lawyer had said, there was a medium-sized Toyota parked there, looking rather lonely in a three-car garage. The car belonged to him now, already insured for him, thanks to his mother's thoughtful preparations.

It'd be good to have a vehicle to get around in, but Hal didn't care much what a car was like as long as it was comfortable and reliable, so he didn't go to check it out more carefully.

He moved back into the hall, closing the garage door, leaving the suitcases near the front door until he'd done a tour of the place and chosen a bedroom for himself. The hall stretched right through to the canal side of the house, its length showing that behind the fortress-like outer wall was a much larger dwelling than he'd expected his mother to own.

The first door on the right led into a splendid modern kitchen, which occupied the rear of a huge room. He smiled. She hadn't been much of a cook, so he'd bet it was almost unused. Between it and the canal was a generous dining area and seating area.

He walked slowly towards the other end, thinking how sad it was that the maroon leather suite near the window took up less than half the living space and that only one of the two recliner armchairs seemed to show any signs of having been used. The sofa and the other chair looked pristine, as if they'd never been sat on.

Surely his mother would have made one or two friends here to come and visit her?

This part of the ground floor ended at a wonderful wall of windows looking out onto a covered patio and, beyond that, water. These were artificial canals, his mother had told him when she moved here, and her house sat at the very end of the watery cul-de-sac, looking down towards the main canals. The canal ended in what would have been a turning circle in a street and he supposed served the same function here for boats. Not that he knew much about boats.

She'd told him she'd bought the house because it faced some of the most beautiful sunsets she'd ever seen in her whole life and she loved watching them.

He fiddled with the key ring until he managed to find one which unlocked the huge sliding glass door. As he stepped outside, he breathed in the fresh, salty air with pleasure and felt the tension in his shoulders start to ebb.

The outdoor furniture consisted of a small table and four chairs, stacked now to one side of a patio which could have fitted several large tables on it without looking crowded. He could imagine her sitting here sipping a glass of wine in the evenings and enjoying the sunsets. He'd be doing the same.

'Thank you, Ma,' he said aloud. 'You bought a beautiful home and I'm going to enjoy living here.'

He went back inside, hesitated then locked the outer door again. Better safe than sorry, because people could approach the house from both sides.

The other half of the ground floor contained three large rooms. The one near the street had French windows at the side of the house leading out to a Japanese-style garden. The room was unfurnished but contained several large cardboard boxes.

He couldn't gather together the energy or the courage to find out what was inside them and made a fending-off gesture with one hand. 'Not yet.'

The second room was totally empty and his footsteps echoed as he walked across to stare out again at the stark garden of strategically placed rocks and gravel.

The final room might have been intended as a second living area. It offered more of those breath-taking watery views. His mother had used it as her office and it was set up with a desktop computer and other necessary equipment. He could use this room too, only to do that he'd have to deal with his mother's computer. He wasn't sure he could face her private thoughts yet, but the idea of wiping the whole system clean of her imprint seemed worse.

No, he needed to check it for the last of her delicately beautiful poetry. He was immensely proud of the way she'd made a name for herself over the past twenty years, still remembered her joy when her first collection of poems was accepted for publication. After that, every year or two the same respected publisher had brought out a slender volume of her exquisite poems.

It suddenly occurred to him that she might have written enough for a posthumous collection to be published. He would definitely have to check the computer for that – but later, when he could summon up the courage, see past this wall of grief.

He went back into the central hall and walked slowly up the broad staircase to explore the bedrooms, opening curtains and blinds to let in the light. Two huge bedrooms at the canal side each possessed an en-suite bathroom, walk-in wardrobe and dressing room. 'Sumptuous' was the word that came to mind.

One of them still had his mother's clothes in it, as well as some medical equipment. He moved quickly out again, closing the door, because it was another area he found it hard to face.

He peered cautiously into the other front bedroom, relieved to find the walk-in wardrobe and drawers completely empty. The en-suite bathroom was dusty but not dirty, looking as if it had never been used. Good. He'd take this bedroom for himself.

Four other bedrooms were arranged in pairs, sharing a bathroom each. They too were completely unfurnished.

'Were you happy to be completely alone here, Ma?' he asked softly as he closed the door of the last bedroom. It was increasingly feeling that she'd been like a wounded animal, coming here to die on her own terms, without having to pretend to others how she felt.

He went back to explore the kitchen, hoping there would be some food left in the cupboards or freezer so that he wouldn't need to go out until tomorrow to buy fresh fruit and vegetables.

He glanced at his watch, set now to Perth time. It was

only five o'clock but he was exhausted after the long flight from the UK, followed by the painful visit to the lawyer. He felt like lying down and giving in to the urge to sleep, but if he allowed himself to do that he'd wake up in the middle of the night.

He'd found when he first started travelling to different time zones that it was best to try to fit in with the local time of day as quickly as possible. If there was something to eat and maybe a bottle of wine, he should be able to push himself on for another hour or two, but not much more because he hadn't slept on the plane, for all the extra comforts of business class, only dozed occasionally. Aircraft beds weren't adequate to fit a body over six foot tall.

The fridge was empty and switched off, but there was plenty of food in the freezer, as well as dry goods and tins in the cupboards. He opted for soup and a roll from the freezer, and left half of it because exhaustion won over reason before he could open the bottle of white wine. 'Tomorrow,' he told it and put it in the fridge in solitary splendour, added a carton of long-life milk for his breakfast cereal and a packet of frozen berries that could defrost slowly overnight.

It was all he could do to tidy the food away then trudge up the stairs with his main suitcase, but his mother had taught him that if you didn't let things get untidy, you never had to do major clear-ups. He couldn't bear to go against her lifelong habits in her beautiful home.

The bedroom felt strange, as soulless as a hotel room. He unpacked some pyjamas and his toiletries, briefly debated fetching up the other suitcases, but couldn't be bothered.

He was half asleep by the time he approached the bed, newly showered and ready to let go of the world. But when he pulled back the fancy bedcover there were no sheets underneath it. Groaning softly, he trudged round the upstairs floor looking for a linen cupboard. There was a huge one at the rear of the landing, but it had only a couple of piles of bedding and towels in it, sitting forlornly on the middle shelf, presumably all she'd needed.

A few minutes later he gave a long sigh of relief as he crawled into the newly made-up bed and let himself slip into oblivion.

As Emma was fiddling with the TV she looked outside, stopped what she was doing and went over to the window. 'There are lights on next door. Come and look, Aaron. Do you think someone's broken in?'

He went to stand beside her. 'I doubt it. The security system makes that place seem like Fort Knox. Claudia told me on one of our rare encounters that she always slept soundly, because if she needed any sort of help it was only a press of a button away.'

'Perhaps her son's arrived, then. She said he was living in London and mentioned once that he would inherit everything. I was always amazed at how calmly she spoke of dying.'

'I don't think you get much choice once you've been handed a death-sentence diagnosis. You can either leave your family with memories of you ranting and railing, or grit your teeth and depart with dignity.'

Aaron moved further along to get a better view of the neighbouring house. 'I wonder if he's as reclusive as she was. Look, the lights have gone off upstairs but a couple are still on downstairs. He was probably jetlagged and went straight to bed.'

'We'll no doubt find out tomorrow. Come on. Let's watch that film we chose.'

But Aaron couldn't settle to it, or to anything. He was still too excited about George actually contacting his daughter. In the end he stopped pretending and went to sit outside on his own near the water, enjoying the path of shivering light the moon was painting along the calm surface of their canal. He was glad the other residents were having a quiet night. Parties could be a bit noisy sometimes, echoing across the water, especially those thrown by the weekend-only occupants.

What would his daughter be like? He'd seen a photo now, but her solemn expression gave no clue to her personality.

He hoped she didn't take after her mother, hoped she'd get on with his two stepchildren, hoped most of all that he'd be able to form a good relationship with her from now on.

Emma appeared beside him, took his hand and pulled him to his feet. 'Come to bed, sleepy-head. You were starting to nod off, literally.'

He fought back a yawn. 'Sorry I spoilt your film.'

'We can watch it another time. I couldn't settle to it,

either, after you gave up.'

'I'm being selfish.'

'No, you're being a normal human being. It's a momentous time for you. And remember, if you need me to do anything else to help you through it, you have only to say.'

'I know.' He smiled and they went upstairs hand in hand and fell asleep holding hands, as they often did.

Chapter Six

As George had foretold, three days later Aaron phoned him to say that he'd snapped up a very convenient cancellation and booked Mara on a non-stop flight from Heathrow to Perth for late that same evening. A messenger would be waiting for her at Heathrow near the business class check-in with the necessary paperwork and would be able to identify her from the photograph.

Would George please arrange everything that end? Aaron had an important meeting coming up which he wanted to get over and done with before she arrived. There might be a possibility of the sale of his business.

When George phoned her with the news, Mara closed her eyes briefly and muttered, 'Thank goodness!' because she was finding the atmosphere at home even more uncomfortable than usual. The air felt literally heavy with her mother's simmering anger.

'You can make it, then, Mara?'

'I most certainly can.'

Wishing Phil had come home from his golf game, Mara went downstairs to tell her mother and get the initial unpleasantness over with.

'I forbid you to go!' Kath said at once.

'What? You can't do that. I'm thirty years old, not thirteen.'

Her mother burst into tears, so Mara went straight back upstairs to finish packing her clothes. She was feeling both excited and nervous. The shoes and various personal oddments she was taking were already in the suitcase, but she could now add more things than expected, given the extra luggage allowance. She'd never travelled business class before. It would be a much more comfortable way of travelling.

When she'd finished packing, she would book a taxi to get her to Heathrow this evening and— She suddenly felt the presence of someone and guessed before she turned that it would be her mother. Her busy excitement vanished like a burst balloon.

Kath must have come upstairs quietly. How long had she been standing in the doorway? She wasn't sobbing now but scowling at the suitcase and backpack. 'So you're definitely going there, however much it upsets me?'

'Of course I am. Apart from meeting my biological father, it's a great opportunity to see something of Australia.'

Her mother's tone grew harsher. 'You pretend to care about me but you don't. I'm the one who bore you and raised you. I've given my life to you, but you don't *care* how I feel.'

'I don't like upsetting you, but this isn't about you.'

'Well, you're wasting your time hoping it'll turn out well. Aaron Buchanan is a liar. Don't believe a word he says.'

The venom in her voice upset Mara. 'How do you know what he's like now? You haven't seen him for thirty years.'

'I don't need to. Leopards don't change their spots. He's a manipulator and he always has to be in charge. He'll try to turn you against me.'

'Why would he do that, Mum? Tell me why you keep saying it?'

'Because it's his nature to be king of the castle. I found that out the hard way. His wife won't want you, either. Why should she welcome a stranger who might get between him and her children's inheritance?'

'Mum, really—'

Kath suddenly raised her voice to a screech. 'You'll have broken up our family out of sheer selfishness.'

She turned round, slamming the door of Mara's bedroom before going downstairs again.

As Mara's bedroom door showed its resentment of being slammed so hard by bouncing open again, she heard her mother turn the kitchen radio up to maximum volume and a horrible thumping beat filled the air. Her mother was doing that on purpose, aware of how Mara hated that sort of din.

It nearly drove her mad as she tried to concentrate

on packing her things and she knew it would do little good to close the door. This was a small house, a two-up, two-down in a terrace in which bathrooms had been added over the stairwell during a modernisation phase decades ago, before she was born.

The radio was turned off abruptly and there was the sound of voices down in the kitchen, then her stepfather's footsteps came up the stairs. She could always recognise them because he moved quickly and lightly, while her mother trudged slowly.

Thank goodness Phil had come home.

He tapped on her half-open door and peered inside. 'You all right?'

'Yes.'

'How long has she been acting up like this?'

'A couple of hours, give or take.'

'Oh, dear. Can I come in a minute?'

She nodded and watched him close the door carefully.

'Your mother says this Aaron has found you a flight.'

'Yes. I leave tonight.'

'Well, I just wanted to let you know that I've put a bit of extra money in your bank account today in case you run short while you're over there or want to come back before your time is up. Good timing, eh?'

She was surprised. 'Has Mum persuaded you that everything will go wrong?'

'No. It's just in case. I'm hoping things will go well for you, actually. I see no problem in you having two fathers.'

So Mara had to give him a big hug, rocking to and fro.

He was such a dear, kind man, he brought out the best in people. Even her mother had acted almost normally with him for the first few years.

'I'll drive you to the airport.'

'Are you sure, Dad? Is it worth the rows and sulking you'll have to face afterwards?'

'My choice, not your mother's. And for the record, I think you've made the right choice, too.'

'Thank you. Driving to Heathrow with you will be lovely. We haven't had much time alone together recently, have we? Mum can be very, well, intrusive.' It was so typical of him to offer both practical and emotional help.

Later that afternoon her mother locked herself in her bedroom and refused to answer when Mara knocked on the door in an attempt to say a proper goodbye.

Phil beckoned from the foot of the stairs. 'You might as well leave her be. You'll get no sense from her in this mood.'

'Why does she do it, Dad?'

'I've never understood what starts her off. Sometimes she copes just fine and she can be pleasant to live with for a few days, then off she starts again. I've always thought there's something that misfires in her brain from time to time. I'm worried that she's getting really bad again, has been going downhill for the past couple of years, but I can't persuade her to see the doctor.'

Mara didn't answer. What could you say? They had both lived with her mother's problem on and off for years, but her behaviour had never been this strange. Mara had escaped to work in London; Phil never had. How did he cope with such stress? Golf was no substitute for human affection and companionship.

The approach roads to Heathrow were all bustle and looked like a human ant heap. When they got near their terminal, Mara said, 'If you stop in the drop-off area, I'll get my own things out of the boot and you won't need to pay for parking.'

'You sure? All right then. I hope your flight goes well, love.'

'Yes. It's a long time to be on a plane. Thanks for bringing me.'

'You must try to get some sleep or you'll feel like an old dishrag when you arrive. Leave your worries behind, Mara. She'll be easier to manage when you're not there. She always is.'

She leant across when he stopped, kissed his cheek and got her things out of the boot quickly.

Then he'd gone and she was standing alone on the brink of a new stage of life. She felt more than a little nervous, if truth be told.

I can do it, she told herself, and moved steadily forward, wheeling her suitcase, following the signs, envying people who were travelling with their families or friends.

Contrary to what she'd expected, Mara found some aspects of the flight pleasant and she actually began to relax. She'd only ever travelled cattle class before, so enjoyed the comfort and excellent service of business class. She took one free glass of wine with her meal, but declined a refill, then ate the two delicious chocolates out of the fancy little box they gave her afterwards. She finished off with a glass of her favourite liqueur, Grand Marnier, which she only normally splurged on at Christmas.

She sighed happily, feeling nicely pampered.

When the flight attendant had made up the bed, she lay down on it, just to try it out, but felt so tired she closed her eyes.

She woke up later to a dim cabin with all the lights turned low and it was a few seconds before she remembered where she was. She squinted at her wristwatch and to her amazement found she'd slept for several hours. How marvellous was that?

As it was a non-stop flight, she didn't have to gather her things then get off and on a second plane in the Middle East, so as the plane droned along above the clouds, she watched a movie she'd been wanting to see for ages. After that she ate another meal and read her book till they arrived in Perth.

Business passengers were first off the plane and she got through customs quickly. She paused in front of the exit to gather her courage, took a deep breath and walked out into the terminal. Her father had said he'd meet her himself.

Here we go! she thought.

Aaron recognised his daughter the minute she came through the doorway of the arrivals area. George hadn't said how tall she was, but that was another physical characteristic of his family. He moved forward quickly, waving one hand and trying to catch her eye. 'Mara?'

'Yes. And you're Aaron.'

'You look just like your photo.'

'So do you.'

They stared at one another, then he gave her a wry smile. 'It's difficult to know what to say, isn't it? It must be even harder when you're jetlagged. Did you get any sleep?'

'Several hours. Thank you for booking me business class.'

'My pleasure.'

People hurried past them, various happy and tearful reunions were taking place nearby and all they could do was stand staring at one another. This wasn't what he'd expected because he could usually cope gracefully with any sort of social situation. But this first meeting with his grown-up daughter was a once-in-a-lifetime event, and there was nothing to prepare you for the rush of emotion that made your voice wobble.

'Let's go and find the car. Here, let me push the trolley.'

As she walked beside him, it felt strange that he was taller than her when she was five foot ten old style, slightly taller than her stepfather. Aaron also looked much younger than Phil, though she guessed he must be about the same age. Perhaps he'd had an easier life – or an easier wife.

When they reached his car, she had a further surprise because it was a large new Mercedes, which must have cost a lot, so he was obviously far more affluent than her parents, more than merely comfortably off.

'Do get in. I'll see to this.' He heaved her suitcase and backpack into his boot as if they weighed nothing and took the trolley to the nearest parking point, by which time she'd fastened her seatbelt.

He got in and pulled smoothly away. 'Mandurah is an hour or so's drive south of Perth, depending on the traffic. We're seven or eight hours ahead of the UK depending on the time of year.'

'Yes, they told us on the plane.' She looked round as they drove, feeling a little disappointed because mostly there was only busy traffic and the road passed through unattractive industrial areas. It wasn't at all what you imagined when you thought of Australia.

She stole the occasional glance at him. His hands on the steering wheel were large and strong-looking.

'Is the traffic always this busy?'

'Well, it's the main freeway south from the city. The traffic usually thins out by about halfway towards Mandurah, but as you can see, the scenery in this area isn't all that pretty, especially when the summer heat bleaches the grass beige as it'll have done by the end of this month. It's the sea itself that's beautiful round Mandurah, very blue compared to the sea in the UK, I always think, with white sandy beaches, not pebbles.'

'You go back there sometimes, then?'

'I used to do a lot of travelling when I was setting up my company, not so much now. I leave that to the younger and more energetic folk I employ. I like to spend as much time as I can with my wife. I've been married to Emma for almost twenty-five happy years. We were empty nesters till recently but her two grown-up children are living with us again now: Rufus and Peggy, twenty-seven and twenty-five respectively. They keep moving out of home then coming back. I've enjoyed being their stepfather, so I hope you'll get on with them.'

She didn't think it tactful to ask what his stepchildren thought of a previously unknown daughter suddenly turning up, so compromised with, 'I'm not usually the argumentative sort.'

'Neither am I.'

'I hope you don't mind me asking, but did Emma get a divorce or did her husband die? I don't want to put my foot in it.'

'She's widowed.'

After a few moments he said, 'George tells me you're living at home.'

'I had to move back recently because I lost my job. It was too expensive to stay in London without one.'

'What happened? Company go bust?'

'No, just a minor downturn and I was the one made redundant. Only it wasn't my turn, because it's usually last in, first out in those circumstances. I suspect someone stabbed me in the back.' She didn't elaborate, hadn't meant to tell him that much, actually.

'It happens. Hard luck, eh?'

They drove mostly in silence except for the faint purring of the motor and the road noises around them, then he signalled and began to slow down. 'We turn off the freeway here and drive almost into the heart of Mandurah. Our house is on the water, part of a man-made canal development.'

'That sounds gorgeous.'

'It is. We love living there. I'm trying to sell my business and I've reduced my involvement with it so that I can enjoy more time with Emma.'

She liked the way his voice grew warm when he spoke of his wife.

In Mandurah he deliberately drove by the water, which the locals called the foreshore. As he'd said, the sea looked beautiful, such a vivid blue in the afternoon sun.

When they turned into what was clearly a new development, she was amazed at how big the houses were. The small terraced house where she'd grown up and been living in again until yesterday was tiny compared to these.

She began to worry that she'd be out of her depth with Aaron and his friends. Working with toys wasn't most people's idea of an exciting job, even when you worked on the IT side of the company. And added to that, she knew losing her job had shaken her confidence more than a little.

'We're here.' Aaron slowed down and turned into a street that seemed to consist mainly of garage doors, most of them triple or even quadruple ones.

Definitely rich people's houses, she thought.

He sent her a quick smile. 'The street itself isn't very

attractive because the fronts of the houses face the water.'

'Yes, I suppose they would.' And what sort of feeble response was that?

He clicked on a small gadget and the garage door of one house at the far end of the street began to rise smoothly. As they got closer to it she could see that the street wasn't a dead end as she'd first thought, but carried on into a fairly sharp U-turn round this house and the next one. After he'd driven into the garage, the door rolled down just as smoothly behind them, but the area was well illuminated. Another new car stood there with the third space fitted out as a workshop.

He opened his car door. 'Emma's at home. The other two are at work. Come and meet her before we do anything else.' He opened a door at the rear of the garage, got her suitcase out of the car and dumped it in the hall, then carried on past it, calling, 'We're back, darling!'

Mara followed him into the house, dumping her backpack next to the suitcase. She felt suddenly shy, remembering all the dire forecasts her mother had hurled at her about how her father's wife would behave towards her.

Only, Aaron didn't seem like a manipulative person. He had a lovely smile, a bit like her stepfather's in some ways, with twinkling eyes and a subtle warmth that was hard to fake. Smiles could tell you a lot about a person, she always felt, and this man's said to her that he really liked people.

He seemed to be finding it difficult to know what to

say to a stranger, even if she was his daughter, which made Mara feel better because she was having the same problem speaking to him.

A woman was waiting for them in a kitchen area that was bigger than the whole of the ground floor in her home. Emma's red hair was genuine, not coloured, and slightly frosted with silver. Her smile seemed a little guarded.

'Welcome to Australia.' Emma held out her hand then jerked it back. 'Oops. I've been baking and I haven't wiped my hands properly yet. You don't want covering in flour.'

'It's good to meet you. Thank you for inviting me to visit.'

'How could I not welcome you when it means so much to Aaron?'

The look she gave her husband was deeply loving, and if his smile had been warm and friendly before, it was positively glowing now it was focused on his wife.

It had been a long time since Mara had seen her parents look even moderately affectionate, and she had never seen them look at one another like this. She couldn't help feeling a twinge of envy towards these two people. They seemed to have everything: money, a beautiful home and most important of all, mutual love.

She couldn't help staring at the view out over the water but forced herself to turn away when Emma spoke.

'Would you like some refreshments or would you rather take a shower first? I always feel I have to wash off the smell of an aeroplane once I arrive, so do what you really want. I shan't take offence.'

'My beloved is a typical Aussie, very relaxed about life,' Aaron put in. 'You won't need to tiptoe around us, just be yourself.'

'I'd love to shower and change my clothes if it's not too much trouble. I do feel rather grubby after so long on a plane.'

'No trouble at all. We've put you in the guest suite and you have your own shower room there, small but perfectly formed. Rufus and Peggy's bedrooms are both en-suite too so you won't be disturbing any of us. Show her up to her room, Aaron love, then leave her in peace. Just come down when you're ready, Mara.'

Her father picked up her suitcase in the hall and led the way upstairs to a large bedroom with twin beds and a small sofa. It was at the side of the house, but had a tall, narrow window that looked along to the gap towards the water.

Aaron put her suitcase on the bed and patted her arm tentatively. 'I'm glad you've come, Mara, and I hope you'll be happy with us. We'll probably be outside on the patio when you come down. We sit there a lot; it's so lovely to watch the water. We get dolphins swimming right past the house.'

'Wow! I hope I see some.'

He chuckled. 'You'll see plenty of them. They're one of Mandurah's attractions.'

He moved towards the door, then stopped and snapped his fingers. 'Nearly forgot. I'm supposed to tell you that the chest of drawers is empty and there's plenty of hanging space in the wardrobe. As if you'd not have found that out for yourself.' He gave her another of his lovely smiles and left her alone.

When the door had closed behind him she let out her breath in a long slow stream, then looked round the bedroom. What a lovely home! The kitchen had been magnificent and this was charming. The bedrooms near the canal must be stunning.

Emma looked like a person with money, somehow. Her hair was beautifully cut and even her casual clothes were elegant. How much did her easy confidence stem from the normality and love that had been lacking in Mara's mother and how much came from having money behind her? Probably both had an effect on a person.

She stared in the mirror, grimacing at how rumpled she looked. Her long hair was simply tied back and her clothes were cheap and dark for practicality. She couldn't help wondering what Aaron and Emma had thought of her appearance.

Then she told herself to stop being silly. As if that mattered. She should get on with unpacking some clean clothes and taking a long, hot shower. Bliss.

Chapter Seven

Hal was awake for an hour or so during the night, but sheer exhaustion helped him get back to sleep again.

When he woke, he looked at his watch in surprise. It was morning and he'd slept for over twelve hours in all.

He made a rapid trip to the bathroom then padded to the window to look out. The sunlight was bright and clear, the sky utterly cloudless. And what a view! He lingered, taking in the sparkling water and a small boat bobbing up and down at a jetty further down towards the main canal.

Wow!

Then his stomach rumbled, reminding him that he'd hardly eaten the previous day.

He had a rapid shower, loving the warmth of the day and putting on shorts and a top. No more suits and ties if he could help it! A thought slid into his mind: never again! Was that possible?

When he picked up his watch, he found that it was now nearly nine o'clock. No wonder the sun was so bright. Goodness! He rarely slept that long. But he'd been exhausted when he got on the plane, after sorting out the final details of what he'd hoped would be his last job in the company his partner had bought him out of. He'd only dozed intermittently during the long flight.

He'd been going to take his time and semi-retire, but thanks to his mother's unexpectedly large legacy, he could fully retire if he wanted. Thank you, Ma!

In the freezer he found some ready meals and odds and ends like packets of frozen peas and beans. Ah! A packet of waffles. He pulled it out and decided to have them toasted with jam after his cereal and fruit.

But even though he ate the whole packet of waffles, he still felt hungry for protein and something that crunched like a big juicy apple or carrot. Time to buy some food, which meant he had to find a big shopping centre.

But first, he was tempted to go outside and stand at the edge of the garden looking down at the water and a crowd of tiny fish swimming by. And surely those were mussels on the wall? Were they safe to eat? If so, he'd be having *moules marinière* regularly.

Hearing a sound, he turned to see a red-haired woman wiping the top of a huge outdoor table next door.

She looked across at him, her head on one side, as if asking whether he wanted to speak. So he took the initiative.

'Hi, there. I'm Hal Kendrell.'

'Ah yes. Claudia's son. She said you'd be coming here.

I'm so sorry for your loss.'

He nodded in acknowledgement of the condolences. He never knew what to say in response. It was a relief when the neighbour took that as a signal to carry on a conversation.

'We miss having your mother as a neighbour. She and I had some pleasant chats across the garden wall. I'm Emma Buchanan, by the way. My husband's Aaron and he's around somewhere. We'll look forward to getting to know you, but I promise we're not pushy, intrusive neighbours.'

'That'll be nice. I wonder if you can direct me to a shopping centre? I need to buy some fresh food.'

'That's easy. There's a big one where you can get just about anything.' She gave him its name and told him which street to put in the satnav.

'If there is a satnav,' he said ruefully. 'I haven't even looked at the car.'

'Oh, there is one. Your mother didn't go out a lot but once I'd shown her how to use it, she found the satnav very helpful, especially when she first came here.'

'I'm glad.'

She looked a little puzzled. 'About the satnav?'

'No. That she found neighbours she could chat to. She's always been something of a loner, the sort who stands at the edge of a group at a party, watching and listening. Not antisocial, just . . . quiet and reserved.'

'Well, she seems to have understood people. Her poems are beautiful and sometimes so simple you could be forgiven for thinking them just a few easy words – till the ideas and images sink in and make you think about the world a little differently.'

'That's a brilliant summary of how her poetry can affect people. Her words will be a memorial to her, I'm sure.'

'Yes. She wrote what I call real poetry, not meaningless jumbles of clever, show-off words.'

He nodded and stepped back from the low wall separating their properties. 'I'd better get going. I have a desperate hunger for some protein.'

She chuckled. 'Good luck with your shopping, then.'

The car started easily and Hal found the satnav simple to use. It led him straight to the big shopping centre his neighbour had told him about. He did a rapid walk through to get a feel for the place, then headed back to a huge supermarket at one side of the food area, where he proceeded to fill his trolley with food: lots of cheese, fresh fruit and vegetables, a cooked chicken, some steaks, and a couple of sourdough loaves.

Then he set about looking for pantry staples like flour, his favourite coffee and tinned food. He'd been fending for himself for long enough to know what he would need. His mother had left a few bottles of wine, but he was tempted into buying a few more bottles as well as his favourite whisky and some inexpensive Prosecco.

Another thing he wanted was something to read – not electronic, though. He didn't enjoy reading on his phone, or whatever device the boffins thought up next. He much preferred paper books.

He'd looked up the history of books once out of sheer curiosity. The technology of using movable type on paper had been in operation from the fifteenth century right through until the later twentieth century. And even with electronic advances in formatting for printing in the twenty-first century, they were still producing paper books as the end product.

Another reason he preferred paper was that they wouldn't keep needing 'updates'. Technology changed formats and devices too often for bookaholics like him. He wanted permanent copies of his 'keepers', copies that would still be perfectly usable in a few years' time.

He gave a wry smile at his reflection in a shop window. It looked as ephemeral as he felt. At least his mother had left her poetry behind and a son to carry on her name. What would he be leaving when his time came? Figures in a bank account for a distant relative to gloat over? There was nothing like losing someone you loved for making you contemplate your own offerings to the world and your place in it.

When he went back to the car, the sun was still shining and he raised his face to the warmth, so welcome after the misty chills of late autumn in England. He'd noticed a petrol station as he came into the shopping centre, so he drove across to it and filled the little car he'd inherited, as well as checking what he thought of as its 'life support systems'. Oil, water and so on were all present and correct.

This vehicle would do him for a while. If he decided

to stay for longer than a few weeks, he might buy himself something bigger and more comfortable that he could use for trips into the country. Or he might not. Who knew?

He felt suspended between yesterday and tomorrow, marvelling at the freedom his inheritance plus his own earnings and careful attitude towards money had given him. He now had a large, mortgage-free home and time to seek a rewarding new path in life, possibly even time to return to his youthful passion for art.

He was very lucky.

When he got back he found a car parked on the paved area outside his garage. Presumably someone was waiting to see him, so he got out wondering who could know he'd arrived. It was a large, showy vehicle with a sign that meant nothing to him on the driver's door.

A sharp-featured woman dressed in rather tarty clothes got out of it as soon as he stopped and came across to join him. 'Mr Kendrell?'

'Yes.'

'I'm Diana Vincenzo. Have you a few moments to talk business?'

He didn't know why, but he felt like a dog whose hackles had risen at the sight of an enemy. 'What sort of business?'

'Could we go inside, perhaps?'

'Not till you tell me what you want to talk about. I'm busy at the moment.'

Her lips tightened in annoyance for a moment then

she forced a false smile. 'I was sorry to hear about your mother passing, but life goes on, does it not?'

Hal didn't like this way of referring to a person dying. Passing, indeed! Where had that come from? Modern society's desire to avoid facing up to death, he supposed.

'I have a client who would like to buy this house. We presume you'll be selling it when you've sorted your mother's possessions out? He'd like to be given the first chance to buy, which could save you a lot of trouble.'

Hal was a bit taken aback by this. 'Why the urgency? I only got here yesterday.'

'Well, you see, my client likes the situation of this particular house, but unfortunately your mother snapped it up before he could buy it, so he wants to make sure of it this time. I'm sure you'll appreciate being saved the hassle of putting it up for sale.'

She was standing too close to him, so he took a step backwards. 'I don't know what I'll be doing about the house yet, Ms Vincenzo.'

'My client is prepared to pay a very good price.'

She named it, but what did he know about property values here? Or want to know at the moment? Hal held up one hand to stop her going on. 'Selling the house is not something I wish to discuss right now.'

'But surely you—'

He turned to get back into his car, intending to drive it into the garage and was annoyed when she moved swiftly to thrust a business card at him before he could close the door.

He came very close to letting the card drop on the ground, but couldn't bring himself to be so rude.

'I'm sorry for intruding on your grief. I'm sure when you're ready to let go, you'll find my client's offer very generous, Mr Kendrell.' Her voice was soft now, not matching her earlier tone or her sharp features. It seemed as false as everything else about her, an attitude worn briefly like a change of clothing.

'I have your card so I'll call you if I'm interested. But it won't be for a while, if at all. Now please let me move my car into the garage.'

She stepped back, frowning, and he drove into the huge empty garage, clicking the gadget to close the door on her before he even switched off his engine.

That woman had timed her offer badly and she hadn't been good at reading his body language. He'd not have given her a job in his company – his ex-company, he corrected mentally.

Oh, to hell with her and her offer! He didn't want to think about that sort of thing today. And if he did decide to sell, he doubted he'd choose such a sharp-featured female to deal with. Something about her set his teeth on edge.

He was about to throw away the business card, but on second thoughts, he decided to keep it, if only to remind him of whom to avoid and which company she worked for. *R.E. Real Estate* it had said on the car door, which meant nothing to a stranger to town. If she'd been hired to come after this house, presumably she dealt with the higher end of the market.

He forgot her as he set to work to unpack his shopping and put it away. Afterwards he went into the office and stared at his mother's computer.

And still couldn't bring himself to touch it.

Chapter Eight

When Aaron came downstairs after showing Mara to her bedroom, he looked at his wife a little anxiously. 'I tried to set her at ease, but she still seems on edge.'

'Who wouldn't in such a situation? She not only has a newly-found father and his long-time family to face, but also a new country. It's a lot for anyone to deal with.' Emma hesitated then added, 'She doesn't look very, um, affluent, does she?'

'No. Her clothes are definitely at the cheaper end of mass produced, even a mere male like myself can tell that, especially after years of living with you. You always look great without being a slave to fashion. But she's got that beautiful, rosy English complexion. Shall we count her teeth to confirm how old she is? Don't you do something like that with horses? I wonder if it works with humans.'

She gave him a mock slap. 'Don't be silly. She looks

so like your family there's absolutely no doubt she's yours, even without a DNA test. I've seen photos of your mother at that age and they could have been siblings. I'm just trying to understand Mara's accent. I can't work it out. What is it exactly?'

'Well, she was born and bred in Wiltshire, but there's an overlay of London in the way she speaks now, I think. She's been working there for the past few years, George found out. She's had a couple of promotions but hasn't exactly rocketed up the managerial ladder.'

'No man in her life?'

'There was a recent relationship that fizzled out.'

'Does she have a passion in life?'

'If so, George hasn't discovered it yet.'

'Did she say anything to you about her mother?'

'Not a word. George found out that Kath has personality problems. That doesn't surprise me. When I knew her, she was a bit of a control freak and rigid in her views. She did it quite nicely, and could be fun when she relaxed, but once she'd decided on something she considered important, that was it. Her way or the highway.'

'Don't push Mara to talk about her mother, Aaron love. Let her settle in with us at her own pace. She can give us further information about her family if and when she wants to. We could take her out and about tomorrow, show her the town, go for a short stroll along the foreshore. We'll have to be careful she doesn't get sunburnt. Or should we take her for a tourist boat ride round the canals? Visitors usually love that and you're not out in the sun on those bigger boats.'

'We'll ask her what she'd like to do. Not everyone is into boating.' He wandered to the foot of the stairs but could hear nothing so came back. 'I wonder how she'll get on with your two.'

'I've warned them to behave till she settles in. And why are they suddenly mine? They've been "ours" since we married.'

'Yes, sorry.' He couldn't help wondering how they'd react to the newcomer and he was quite sure they considered themselves well past the age of being told what to do. In fact, Peggy seemed to him to have become rather stroppy lately. That was not only bad-mannered but foolish, considering she was living rent-free in this house. He was on the verge of reminding her of that.

It was mainly Peggy's poorly hidden pain at the break-up with Mike that stopped him saying anything, and the fact that Rufus, always more tactful than his sister, seemed to be handling her very gently and watching her anxiously. Rufus was only in Western Australia for a few months anyway, would be moving back to Sydney next but he seemed to be increasingly interested in Jenn, who was a nice lass, so he wasn't always around.

As Emma went to the kitchen to continue preparations for the evening meal, Aaron wandered outside to look out at the water. He hadn't realised how awkward he'd feel with Mara, how unsure of what to say or do, how terrified he'd be of upsetting her. You'd think, given all the people he'd had to deal with successfully through his business, he'd be making a better job of getting to know her.

After pacing up and down for a few minutes, unable to think how to act differently, he went back into the house to join Emma. 'Champagne tonight, do you think?'

'Good idea. Better open a Prosecco, though. Don't waste your good champagne on my two.'

'They probably won't hang around. Do you think Mara will like bubbly? Most people do, don't they? It usually relaxes them.'

Emma dropped a stray kiss on his cheek as she passed him on her way to get out the champagne flutes. 'Stop overthinking things, my darling. Just go with the flow and it'll be all right. After all, there's goodwill on both sides, isn't there?'

But he couldn't help worrying. Getting on well with his only biological child seemed so important. And there was no flow to go with yet. That was one of the problems.

Mara walked out of the en-suite bathroom wearing only a towel and stood gazing out of the narrow window that gave her a view down the side of the house towards the water glinting in the late afternoon sun. She put on clean clothes, leaving her hair to dry naturally, just fluffing it up a little with her fingers.

She could never see the point in blowing it dry and shaping it in one of the sleek styles. Her hair wouldn't hold one for long anyway, because although it wasn't curly, it had built-in waviness and its own view of what it wanted to do. She'd saved money lately by letting it grow longer and tying it back, as she'd done when she was a teenager.

She studied her reflection in the mirror. She'd never cared desperately about her looks or keeping up with fashion, but for once she was worrying about what to wear and how she'd look to these strangers, worrying about the whole situation now she was here, because Aaron clearly had plenty of money. She hadn't expected that.

He seemed a nice, caring person, but so had Darren and look how that relationship had turned out. She didn't trust herself to make snap judgements about people now.

Once she was ready, joining the family couldn't be delayed any longer, so she grabbed her shoulder bag, more for emotional comfort than because she needed the things in it, and walked steadily down the stairs.

Following the faint sound of voices, she went into the huge kitchen-dining-living area, from where she could see through the glass door that Aaron and Emma were sitting at a table outside on the patio. She paused for a moment, struck once again by how together they looked, as if they genuinely enjoyed one another's company. It was nice to see.

As she set out to join them, the front door slammed open and two people burst into the house behind her, causing her to stop moving.

Before she could turn round a young woman's voice carried clearly. 'Let's go and inspect the cuckoo that's joining us in our cosy little nest before we do anything else.'

'Keep your voice down, you fool,' a man's voice said.

'It's my home more than hers so I'll say what I like when I like.'

'It's our parents' home, actually, Peggy, and if you reckon Mum will put up with you being rude to a guest, you've lost the plot, my girl.'

'Well, I don't trust this woman. She's probably here to rip Aaron off. I hope he's going to get her DNA tested.'

Stiffening indignantly at this assumption, Mara moved quickly out onto the patio before the newcomers came into the kitchen. Cuckoo in the nest, indeed! Had they decided to think the worst of her before they'd even met her?

She kept her back to them, trying to act as if she hadn't overheard the jeering words. It must be Peggy acting like a spoilt brat who resented a newcomer's arrival on 'her' scene. Mara had never ripped anyone off in her entire life, thank you very much.

Well, forewarned was forearmed. She'd be on her guard against them from now on.

She realised her father had spoken to her and turned towards him. 'Sorry. I was miles away looking at that beautiful water. What did you say?'

'I just asked if you'd like a glass of bubbly.'

'I'd love one.'

He looked beyond her and raised his voice slightly. 'You two must have come straight home from work today. Come and meet Mara.'

They moved outside and she got her first look at them. The young woman was quite a bit shorter than her, with bright blue eyes and hair that was almost pink in shade. She was pretty or might have been if she hadn't been so painfully thin. The man was far better looking, seeming fit and healthy. His hair was a rich auburn in colour rather than red like his mother's and he was a little taller than his sister, though still not quite as tall as Mara and her father.

Peggy gave her a mere nod on being introduced, so she did the same in return.

Rufus, however, came forward and shook her hand, then did one of those meaningless kissy-kissy gestures above each cheek in turn. 'Welcome to Australia.'

His voice and expression weren't exactly warm but he was at least being polite, so she replied in a similar vein. 'It's nice to be here.'

Aaron beckoned to her. 'Come and sit next to me, Mara. Here's your glass.'

Peggy had been moving towards him but threw another scowl at the newcomer and changed course to plonk down next to her mother.

Rufus stayed where he was, letting the others sit down before taking the seat next to Mara on her other side, so that the group was arranged in a semi-circle facing the water.

Aaron was filling two more champagne flutes but Peggy said sharply, 'Not for me, Dad. You know I don't drink much nowadays.'

'I thought that was when you were living with Mike.'

'No, it's my own healthy lifestyle choice.'

'Grab some fizzy water, then.' He handed his son the

glass, staying on his feet and waiting till Peggy re-joined them. He lifted his glass, inclining his head towards the newcomer. 'Welcome to Australia and to our family, Mara.'

Everyone except Peggy clinked glasses with her and murmured a welcome. Peggy merely waved her bottle of water around without touching its contents to her lips.

Mara took a sip and said, 'Mmm,' then leant back in the comfortable outdoor chair and tried to look relaxed. She doubted she'd succeeded. This felt like a fantasy world full of rich people and she felt uncomfortably out of place.

'How was the flight?' Rufus asked.

'Wonderful. I slept for nearly half of it. I've never flown business class before.'

'I mostly have to go cattle class now that I'm an independent adult,' he said. 'When I've made my first couple of million, I'll switch to business class like our lord and master here.' He gave his stepfather a cheeky grin.

Peggy was staring blankly at the water, not attempting to join in. She looked unhappy underneath her sharpness and Mara remembered Aaron saying she'd split up from her boyfriend.

'Do you good to live within your income like the rest of the world, Rufus my lad,' Aaron said. 'How did the meeting go today?'

'It was interesting. I think the deal will go through OK. Though you can never be sure, of course, and I'm only one cog in the machinery.'

'Rufus is working for a big international company, still gaining experience in various areas,' Aaron explained to Mara. 'I'm semi-retired, in the process of selling my company.'

'I'm not sure what you do.'

'We offer an international front for various smaller businesses, among other things, and help them sell their goods in Europe and North America.'

'I see.' She didn't really but didn't know what else to ask so kept quiet.

Emma filled the awkward silence. 'What do you do, Mara?'

'I've been doing the software for a toy company, only I got made redundant a few weeks ago.'

'Last in, first out, eh?' the older woman asked in a sympathetic tone of voice.

'Something like that.' She wasn't going to sound like a complaining sort by giving them any details.

'What's for tea, Ma?' Rufus asked. 'I've got a hot date tonight and don't want to be late.' He twirled an imaginary moustache.

Peggy rolled her eyes. 'Idiot. It's only Jenn.'

'Why do you say "only"?' Emma asked. 'He's been out with her a few times now since he's been back. I like her.'

'Because he can do better than her. She's way overweight, so she'll be even fatter when she gets older. Must pig out a lot when she's on her own.'

Her brother glared at her. 'Jenn does not pig out! She has an underactive thyroid and that can make it hard to keep her weight down. I've told you before to stop making judgements about other people's bodies. Just because you've decided to get scrawny doesn't mean everyone else has to walk around looking like a stick insect.'

'I don't think we want to spoil this occasion by bickering,' Aaron said quietly.

The two of them subsided but continued to scowl at one another.

What was all that about? Mara wondered. She agreed with Rufus, though. Peggy was far too thin.

Emma got up and went into the kitchen, coming back with a big platter, which she offered to Mara first. 'Grab one of those small plates and try some of my crispy bites. If you'll just fetch the vegetable kebabs, that'll be a help, Peggy.'

Her daughter continued to scowl as she moved slowly into the kitchen, coming back with another platter.

Mara took a couple of the bites and waited for the others to serve themselves.

Aaron joined in. 'Before you sit down, Peggy, could you also bring the platter of cheese in, please? Save your mother a trip after she's put the food together for us.'

To her surprise Mara saw Peggy scowl and move back towards the kitchen at a deliberately slow pace. More childish behaviour. To hide her disapproval, she nibbled one of the pieces. 'Mmm. These are delicious. I can't quite figure what's in them, though.'

'Whatever veggies and leftover meat I have handy with a special spicy sauce I make myself, then all wrapped in filo pastry. I'll give you the recipe if you like. It's easy to make in advance. Thanks, Peggy.'

Mara chewed another mouthful with relish. 'I'd like the recipe very much. Dad and I love spicy food.' She watched Peggy put the cheese platter down without offering it to her, then sit, pick up her glass of water and take a sip. She made no attempt to eat anything. More fool her. The food was delicious.

Rufus's voice brought her attention back to the group. 'Is your mother a good cook, Mara?'

She shook her head. 'No. And she doesn't even try at the moment because she's not well. Recently we've been getting takeaways but Mum doesn't like the smell of them, so Dad and I just have them occasionally and we take it in turns to rustle something else up. She's very conservative in her ways.' Actually, her mother called the takeaways 'foreign muck' quite openly but they ignored that.

'She always went for plain food when I knew her,' Aaron commented.

Which was a good way of summing up her mother's approach to eating, she thought as she turned to Emma. 'I'll help out in any way I can while I'm here, but I'm not the world's best cook, not in your league if these are anything to judge by. I'd love to learn new dishes, though, if you have time. Curries are my best at the moment, because I used to share a flat with an Indian friend.'

'Then we'll look forward to an occasional curry night, as long as you keep them mild.'

'That much cooking will put you way ahead of Peggy,' Aaron commented. 'Since she came back home, she seems to have forgotten how to cook and has yet to prepare a meal for the whole family. Even a mere male like me can manage a barbecue from time to time.'

'Ma does it so much better than me.' His stepdaughter's voice was sharp.

'But she shouldn't always have to cook,' Aaron said. 'And you hardly eat anything. That's not healthy.'

Peggy glared at him.

Was she always so touchy? Mara wondered. Surely at her age she should be taking a share of the household chores without being told?

The atmosphere became easier once Rufus and Peggy had left to meet their friends. The three of them continued to sit outside near the canal, but no one forced conversation.

As it grew dark, Emma advised Mara to put on some insect repellent when a mosquito came buzzing around to investigate her, whining past her ear.

Aaron switched on a gadget on the wall which he said helped deter the little pests. 'Nothing gets rid of them completely, though, and mozzies seem to enjoy nibbling newcomers. What blood type are you?'

She was surprised at the question, which seemed like a non sequitur. 'O positive.'

'Like me. Some people say mozzies prefer O type blood. Emma and her two have B positive and they don't seem to get bitten as much, I must admit.'

'I never knew that.'

'If your bites swell, tell me. I have a great remedy. You dampen a chunk of rock salt and rub it on the bite every few minutes for the first hour or so. I'll put a piece in your bathroom tomorrow.' Emma waggled her glass at Aaron. 'Is there any fizz left?'

'No. I'll open another bottle.'

He'd poured more for Mara before she could stop him. She'd better keep count. It slipped down very easily.

He turned to his wife. 'Peggy doesn't seem to be coping all that well with her break-up. I've never seen her so grumpy.'

'No.' Emma looked across at their guest. 'She and her guy broke up recently. Turns out he's commitment phobic and doesn't want children. I think she was expecting wedding bells and she'd definitely been getting broody.'

'Frankly, she can do better for herself than him, so I'm glad to see the back of him,' Aaron said.

Emma turned to Mara. 'Do you have a steady guy? Tell me to mind my own business if you don't want to talk about it.'

Mara shook her head. 'I don't mind you asking. I don't have anyone now. I was in a relationship for a while but it didn't work out. It's been a couple of months and I'm well over him. It wasn't a great romance or anything, though he could be fun.'

'Was he commitment phobic? So many guys seem to be these days.'

'No, just delaying marriage till he's climbed a bit higher up the managerial ladders. The trouble was he didn't mind who he trod on to get the promotions, me included. I'm definitely not looking for a replacement guy. I need to sort my own life out first, get a new job and a new place to live.'

Emma let out a sudden gurgle of laughter. 'Be careful what you say. I'd given up men *definitely for ever* the day before I met Aaron. It didn't take him long to make me change my mind.'

It was as if a little of their marital happiness spilt out around them, making Mara smile. Once again she wished she'd grown up in a loving household like this.

When a sudden yawn caught her out, she gave the other two a rueful smile and said, 'I think my need for sleep is beginning to win over my enjoyment of sitting out here chatting to you and looking at the moon shining on the water. It gets dark more quickly here, considering you're coming up to summer.'

'We don't have daylight saving like the UK,' Aaron said.

'Ah. That explains it. I'd have found out more about Western Australia if the trip hadn't blown up so suddenly.'

Emma waved one hand dismissively. 'We usually shorten it to WA and you've done very well at fitting in with our time of day. If you wake up hungry during the night, just go and raid the fridge. There's plenty of fruit and some biscuits on the surface next to the fridge in the tin marked with that same magic word. Well, there ought to be. I'll check before I go to bed. Rufus does tend to raid them rather frequently.'

'Thank you.'

When she'd gone, Aaron looked at his wife. 'She seems a nice lass.'

'Bit old to be called a lass, but yes. Nice and with very good manners, but a bit shy or reserved, I don't know which yet.'

'I'm trying to tread carefully.'

She hesitated then said gently, 'Don't forget that it takes time to build up a rapport with someone, Aaron love.'

'It only took a few minutes with you.'

'That was a once in a lifetime moment.'

'Yes, wasn't it? Come on. I'll put a cap on the bottle. Time to go to bed, my darling.'

'I hope my two come in quietly, especially Rufus. It is a working day tomorrow, after all. He's been getting back rather late. You can only do without sleep for so long.'

'I think he's a bit taken with this Jenn.' He grinned at her. 'We must be getting old, watching the young ones start courting.'

'I don't mind. *Grow old along with me, the best is yet to be*,' she quoted. 'I adore Browning's romantic poems. He certainly understood what it was to love someone.'

'So did his wife. *How do I love thee, let me count the ways*. It must have been great for two poets to marry.'

They exchanged affectionate glances then Emma stood up. 'Come on. Peggy will probably say something scornful if she catches us being loving towards one another.'

'She's a bit hard to live with at the moment.'

'She's hurting about Mike and has gone into man-hating mode to hide it. I'm glad Rufus found Jenn. I think people were meant to live in pairs. Keep your fingers crossed it works out. I'd like to have grandchildren one day.'

'So would I.' Something else occurred to him: if Mara had indeed had children, they'd carry on his bloodline. That idea warmed something inside him that had been faintly sad for years.

Chapter Nine

Mara woke with a start the following morning, not knowing where she was for a few seconds then realising she was in Australia. Wow, she really was! She looked at a bedside clock and found it only just after five o'clock in the morning, getting light already. No need to rush getting up. Emma seemed very laid back about how the house functioned.

She lay there for a few minutes thinking over her first encounter with her birth father. Aaron seemed very nice but he clearly didn't know how to bridge the gap between them. Neither did she. It was such a yawning gap, thirty years. Where did you start catching up? What did you include or leave out?

Deciding she'd had enough of lying in bed, she got up and went to stare out of the window, looking along the side of the house. It furnished a tantalising glimpse of the sparkling blue water and the blue sky above.

How wonderful to live right next to water!

She decided on another quick shower then donned a casual skirt and tee, with flat sandals, leaving her legs bare. That felt great after a cold autumn and early winter where she'd been bundled in layers of clothes. The bad weather of the approaching winter had seemed to echo her own unsatisfactory personal and professional life.

What did you do when you were in the wrong type of job and couldn't afford to change tracks? Let alone, you had a mother who would make your life a misery if you even hinted at doing something different. Mara hadn't found working in IT fulfilling, though she was competent at what she did. She'd wanted to study art but her mother had hit the roof about that and after her mother's two breakdowns she hadn't liked to rock the boat.

What would Aaron say if she told him the truth? No, she couldn't. It might sound as if she was asking to be given financial support.

There was no one in the kitchen so she made herself a cup of coffee and took it outside to drink. As the door to the patio was still locked, she assumed she was the first to get up. Outside it felt pleasantly warm already and she sat watching a few gulls squabbling over who knew what morsels further down the canal.

She heard a door slide open and turned to look at the house, but there was no one around. A movement caught her eye next door and she saw that the sound had come from there. A tall guy of about her own age had just come out onto the patio, wearing shorts and a faded tee shirt. She felt like a voyeur because he hadn't noticed her. He too was carrying a mug and took a sip, standing staring at the water as if the sight were new to him.

Oh yes, she remembered now. Emma had said he'd inherited the house from his mother. He must have come from the northern hemisphere because he didn't have that slightly tanned look her father and his family did.

When he turned round, he noticed her. After a moment's hesitation, he raised one hand in greeting, so she did the same. But he clearly wasn't after any sort of conversation because he turned away from her again and moved towards the small table and chairs which were all his patio boasted by way of furnishings.

She watched in appreciation the loose-limbed grace of his movements. A man at ease in his own body, this, and quite good looking, with hair a dark brown, and a profile which would have sat well on a Greek statue.

That thought made her smile. She didn't usually stare at strange guys, but the two of them seemed to be the only ones up so early along this stretch of the canal and he couldn't see her staring, could he? She continued to watch him until she'd finished the coffee, then her stomach growled so she went back into the house in search of food. Emma had said to help herself so she picked up a luscious-looking peach from a pile in a fruit bowl, sinking her teeth into it with a low hum of pleasure.

She was disappointed to hear footsteps coming down the stairs, because she'd been enjoying the early morning peace. She was even more disappointed to see Peggy come into the kitchen.

The other woman stopped to scowl at her. 'Are you an early riser or just jetlagged?'

'Early riser.'

'So am I, but I don't like to chat till I've woken up properly. Nothing personal but I'm going to make a cup of tea and sit outside *on my own*, I hope.'

Like that, was it? Well, let Peggy keep her distance but Mara wasn't going to stop sitting outside whenever she wanted to.

More footsteps sounded soon afterwards and Rufus came into the kitchen. He nodded a greeting to Mara, then looked outside and added, 'Don't take it personally if she was grumpy. She's always been like that in the mornings.'

'Are you an early riser too?'

'Only on working days. I have to be at the office by eight a.m. and it's a forty-minute drive away.'

'That's an early start.'

'This is Australia. Everything seems to start earlier here than in the UK. Did Aaron tell you I don't usually live here? I'm just staying with them temporarily while I'm on a short posting to my company's West Australian office.'

He set about getting something to eat and Mara decided to let him go first in the kitchen. She went across to a bookcase and chose a thriller by an author she'd enjoyed before. When Rufus sat down to eat, she returned to the kitchen area and decided to grab a slice of toast to put her on until the others got up.

Her companion ate at breakneck speed, finishing before she could join him. He put his crockery in the dishwasher and vanished, presumably going up to his bedroom again.

By the time she'd buttered her toast, he'd come down again, in what she thought of as 'full office uniform': white shirt with subtly patterned tie and dark trousers. He was carrying a briefcase and the matching suit jacket.

He peered into the kitchen and called, 'Enjoy your day!' but left the house without attempting to say goodbye to his sister. There was the sound of his car outside then silence fell again.

Peggy was still gazing morosely at the water but after finishing her coffee, she came inside, dumped her empty mug on the surface and went upstairs without a word.

Mara was enjoying her second piece of toast and a banana as Peggy came back into the kitchen, also dressed for work.

She stared at the plate and shuddered. 'I don't know how you can eat that much so early in the morning. You're as bad as Aaron.'

'Is there something wrong about having a good breakfast?'

'It's how people, especially women, get fat.' Her sneering look said that she considered Mara to be overweight already.

'Well, I'll worry about that if I put any weight on. Mine hasn't changed for years and I'm comfy with this size.'

A disdainful curl of the lips said Peggy didn't approve. It was mutual. Mara considered the younger woman dangerously thin and she was very pale, didn't look at all well.

Peggy got out a tiny container of yoghurt and carefully cut a peach in half. She ate quickly, leaving half of the peach and the nearly empty yoghurt container on the plate and not attempting to clear them away.

She left the room with a mutter Mara couldn't decipher. It might have been a farewell, probably wasn't, though.

Mara followed Rufus's example and put her crockery in the dishwasher, then went to sit outside again with her book. She didn't pick up after Peggy. Why should she?

No one disturbed her for over an hour except for a pelican which flew down onto the canal then bobbed along majestically, looking at her expectantly. If it was expecting food, it'd not get any from her. Wild creatures needed to feed themselves, in her opinion.

Emma came down and called a greeting from the kitchen. 'Oh good, you found something to eat. Have you had enough or would you like something else?'

'I ate a quick snack a while ago and was going to see if I could find something else when you got up. I'm a hearty morning eater, I'm afraid.'

'Unlike my daughter.' She looked at the small plate with its half peach turning slowly brown and the empty yoghurt pot lying on its side next to it, and frowned. 'I presume that's the remains of her breakfast?'

'Yes.'

'I've told her before to pick up after herself. And it's not much food for someone who used to eat a proper breakfast. I blame that man she was living with. That's when she began avoiding food. He's scrawny too. Please don't put things away for her. I'm keeping track of the situation.'

Aaron joined them shortly afterwards, smiling at Mara. 'Did you sleep well?'

'Like a log.'

He too stared at the plate and mug that had been left on the table. 'Peggy's?'

Mara nodded.

Emma made two mugs of coffee and dumped one in front of him, then scowled at her daughter's dirty dishes. 'No, I can't leave them here all day for her to pick up tonight.' She stacked them in the dishwasher then got some eggs out of the fridge and a big frying pan out of a cupboard. 'Spanish omelette?'

'Yes, please. I'm ravenous.' He picked up a peach and bit into it with a loud sucking sound. 'Mmm. These are lovely and juicy now. Do you like Chinese food, Mara?'

'Love it.'

'Let's go out for a Chinese meal tonight then, eh?'

'Good idea. Would you like some omelette, Mara?' Emma asked.

'If you don't mind.'

'Why should I mind? I'm making one anyway and we've plenty of leftover veggies. It's no trouble to cater for all three of us. I forgot to ask last night whether you have any food problems.'

'None. I'm lucky that way. I like anything and everything.'

Aaron strolled over to the windows and pulled the fly screen across the open doorway, smiling at Mara. 'We prefer to keep the insects outside, so we keep the movable flyscreens closed. You'll have noticed the ones on the windows aren't made to be moved out easily.'

'I'll remember that.' She didn't say that it was Peggy who'd come in last.

'You weren't to know.' He glanced towards the left. 'The young guy next door looks like his mother, doesn't he, Emma? Should I go out and speak to him, do you think?'

'He waved at me this morning but turned away,' Mara volunteered. 'He didn't seem to want to chat.'

'Better leave him to himself, then. We'll invite him round for a drink once he's had time to settle in.'

He came back into the kitchen area just as Emma finished cooking the omelette.

She'd already put some plates and a crusty loaf on the table, then brought the omelette across, so he gestured towards the table. 'Come on, Mara. Let's dig in. I'm always ravenous in the mornings.'

'You're not bad at eating the rest of the time, either,' Emma teased, then smiled at Mara. 'Enjoy! That's home-made strawberry jam, by the way. Or there's Vegemite. Though Poms usually prefer Marmite.'

'I haven't tried Vegemite, but I'm not fussy about anything.' Mara took a forkful of omelette and murmured in appreciation. After she'd cleared her main plate, she followed Aaron's example and cut another slice of the crusty bread, slathering it with butter and jam and enjoying every bite.

'It's a pleasure to see you eat,' he said.

'We ought to discuss what you'd like to do today,' Emma said as they lingered over a second mug of coffee.

'Go for a walk, get some sun on my face.'

When they both shook their heads at this, Mara looked at them in surprise.

Aaron grinned. 'You're straight out from England. You'll get sunburnt if you spend too much time in the open. You need to acclimatise gradually. We regularly see recently arrived Poms who look like boiled lobsters.'

She grimaced at her arm, comparing it mentally to their golden tans. 'Instead of looking like pale ghosts!'

'Don't worry. In a couple of weeks' time you'll have a golden suntan, and without the skin damage.'

'We can go out in the car and drive you round the town, then up and down the coast, so that you can get a feel for the area,' Emma suggested. 'There are some lovely beaches round here. We may even let you out of the car for five minutes now and then if you put some block-out on your bare skin.'

'I shall enjoy looking round but please don't think you have to entertain me all the time. I have my laptop and I have a personal project I'm working on.'

'If you need to make any hard copies,' Aaron said at once, 'I've got a couple of printers in my home office. I'll show you them later. Feel free to use them.' He took Emma's hand and gave it an exaggeratedly sloppy kiss. 'I shan't be there a lot because I prefer to get under my wife's feet. Got to confess, I've never been into bashing little white balls around as you said your father does.'

'Mum wouldn't like Dad to be around in the house all the time. She's very pernickety, has to have everything just so.'

'Is she still like that? It must be hard to live with.' He clapped one hand to his mouth. 'Sorry. Rude of me to say that.'

Mara took a sudden decision to be open with them about the situation back home, in case she had to rush back for an emergency. 'Mum's always had a few problems but they've been getting worse. I don't know how Dad has put up with it lately, to be frank. He's a saint. Unfortunately she's refusing to seek help this time. I'm a bit worried about how he'll cope if she continues to get worse but he insisted it was more important that I come to meet you.'

'It's nice to hear you speak of him with such affection,' Aaron said suddenly. 'I only wish I'd been around for you some of the time, at least.' He broke off and gave a slight shrug of the shoulders.

Later they then took her out for a drive along the coast and allowed her one small paddle in the sea, stopping at a café with ocean views for lunch.

They were so easy to be with, she thought when they got back. She had no hesitation in confessing that she was finding it hard to stay awake, sure now that they wouldn't take offence.

'Jet lag. Why don't you take a nap?' Emma suggested.

'If you don't mind, I will. I could fall asleep standing upright at the moment.'

'Why should we mind? You're doing brilliantly for your first day here.'

'It's been interesting seeing what the town is like. I'll set my alarm for an hour, so that I stay close to local time.'

She lay on the bed, thinking about Peggy, for some reason. Could she have anorexia? That would be so sad.

There were few people who didn't have some problem or other to cope with, Mara had found. She hadn't realised how watchful she'd always been about her mother till she moved away from home. Phil had encouraged her to leave; her mother had sulked and been sharp with her for months.

Any other man would have left Kath years ago. She suspected he'd stayed partly because of her. He couldn't have been more her father in all the ways that mattered if he'd created her.

That wouldn't stop her getting to know Aaron, but if Phil ever needed her, she'd be there for him like a shot.

Mara woke just before her alarm went off, went downstairs again and sat chatting to Aaron out by the canal. He asked her about all sorts of things: school, boyfriends, sport, university, the job. When he asked why she hadn't travelled more, she explained that Kath didn't like going away on holiday.

Later, she thoroughly enjoyed the Chinese meal, which they'd decided to do as a takeaway, and chatting to Emma.

Once the sun had gone down, they took her for a walk along to the foreshore, which wasn't far away. There were lights, busy cafés and happy groups of people. And the calm water of the inlet to one side formed a lovely backdrop with the reflections of the town's lights seeming to bob gently about in it.

Back home she found that she and Emma shared a liking for the same TV series, so they watched it together. Mara had seen that episode before but enjoyed the older woman's comments on it. Sometimes the differences between Australia and England seemed more marked.

After it ended they said they'd watch the next programme, if she didn't mind. She went to sit out by the water, couldn't seem to get enough of the peaceful atmosphere there.

A boat went past, carrying a group of noisy revellers, and she was glad it didn't linger. The canal water settled down again, with gentle fractured reflection of lights from some of the houses and gardens along its sides. There were faint voices but no one was playing loud music or making a lot of noise.

When she started to feel sleepy again, she went

inside the kitchen and found her father there, getting a pan out. 'Cocoa? Health warning: it's the old-fashioned sort, made with full fat milk.'

'I'd love some.'

'I wanted to say how sorry I am that you've walked into the troubles with Peggy. It's a recent thing and if she gets any thinner, we may have to deal with it and that will cause a few rows, I'm afraid.'

'If things get bad and you want me to go into a hotel for a few days . . .'

'No, of course I won't want you to do that. Definitely not. I really do want to get to know you, Mara. I'm not trying to take your stepfather's place or come between you and him. I just – you know, would like to make my own place in your life.'

He was so obviously sincere, it made her feel good. 'Phil says there's no law against a person having two fathers.'

'That was kind of him.'

'He's a very kind man. Did it upset you when Mum wouldn't come to Australia with you?'

'No. I knew she probably wouldn't. But the more I found out about this country the more I wanted to come here. I had no idea she was expecting, though. I don't know how that happened. She'd been on the pill. I suppose she missed taking one and didn't realise it put her at risk.'

Mara didn't say it but it occurred to her that her mother might have thought a pregnancy would be the way to stop him going to Australia. If so, why hadn't she told him she was expecting?

'After a few years here I met Emma and that was it. I fell in love with both the country and the woman.'

'I can see how together you are.'

He poured the hot milk into two mugs and stirred the cocoa. 'Let's go mad and have marshmallows in them.'

'I've read about that but never tried it.'

'You'll like it.'

They didn't say anything of great importance as they sipped the cocoa but it was the most comfortable she'd felt with him. And anyway, family life was made up of small moments and interactions, wasn't it?

When he'd finished, he yawned, stretched and stood up. 'If you'd like to sit out a bit longer, would you please be careful to lock the sliding door when you come in? People can get burgled by boat here.'

'You don't mind if I stay out a little longer? It's not bedtime yet in my head. I don't need a lot of sleep. My mother needs ten hours a night, always has done.'

'Stay out as long as you like.' He chuckled. 'This isn't a boarding school with regimented hours, you know.'

'I'm just trying to be a polite guest.'

'You're succeeding too.'

'Good. I love sitting out by the water. I haven't relaxed this much in weeks.'

'Good.' He hesitated then said simply, 'I'm glad you came, Mara.'

'Me, too.'

She was still smiling after he'd gone up to bed. It'd be hard to go back to grey streets and houses sitting cheek by jowl with one another after this.

Chapter Ten

The following morning Mara was again the first to get up. She didn't see any sign of Peggy but Rufus rushed down soon afterwards to grab a quick breakfast, looking tired but happy.

'Peggy not around?' he asked between mouthfuls.

'No.'

'What time did she get home last night?'

'She wasn't home by the time I went to bed and your parents had already gone up by then.'

'Oh.' His voice was flat.

'Is that a problem?'

'Could be. I saw her having a drink with her ex. If she didn't come home, it's my bet she slept with Mike.'

'Getting back together, do you think?'

'Hell, no. I told her what he'd done before but she wouldn't listen. Someone had warned me, you see. They said he'd used other women he'd broken up with occasionally afterwards until he found another steady girlfriend. He must be brilliant in bed, that's all I can say, or else the best actor on the planet.'

He waited a minute and when she didn't comment, he asked, 'Would you go to bed again with someone who'd broken up with you for no real reason, except that things had "grown rather stale"?'

'No way. But I did live with a cheat for a while without realising what he was like, so I can't pretend to be particularly good at judging relationships, my own or other people's.'

'Who is a perfect judge? Dad's been telling me for years that I'll know for sure when I find *the one* I want to spend my life with. I haven't gone for the live-in partners stuff before because my job had me moving around a lot as part of the management training process, to other countries as well as round Australia, and it didn't seem fair. Plus I hadn't met anyone that special. I've never cheated on anyone I was seeing regularly, though, and never would.'

He hesitated and added in a softer voice, 'This time it is different, though, I will admit. I'm wondering whether I might try moving in with Jenn.'

'You like her that much?'

'Oh, yes. Very much indeed. I've never met a woman who's so easy to be with.' He coloured slightly. 'And one who can put up with me. I'm nowhere near Mr Perfect but she just tells me if she doesn't like something I do and then lets it drop. Says I have to tell her if she upsets me. Only she doesn't.'

'Then good luck to you.'

'Thanks. I may—'

A phone rang loudly and harshly somewhere in the house and he stopped abruptly. 'That's Dad's business phone. It sure catches your attention, doesn't it? Be warned. Sometimes he has to drop everything and fly off to sort out a problem. He may have semi-retired but he hasn't yet managed to sell the business so he can't afford to ignore trouble. Oh hell! Look at the time. I have an important meeting at 8.15 today.'

He crammed the last of the toast into his mouth, shoved his crockery in the dishwasher and rushed out.

Mara made herself another cup of tea, worrying that there was still no sign of Peggy. And what if Aaron was called away? Would she be able to stay here or what?

Emma came down for breakfast shortly afterwards and looked round the surfaces. 'Did a miracle happen and Peggy put her dishes away today, or didn't she eat anything?'

'I haven't seen her this morning.'

Aaron had finished his phone call and come into the kitchen in time to hear this. He and Emma exchanged glances, then she said, 'I'd better nip up and check that she's all right.'

She came down the stairs a lot more slowly than she'd gone up, looking upset. 'Peggy isn't there and her bed hasn't been slept in.'

'Ah. Right. Well, she's twenty-five, love. We can't

stop her doing what she wants, even if that includes sleeping around.'

Mara hesitated then told them what Rufus had said about his sister's ex.

'Damnation! That's all we need,' Aaron muttered.

Emma took Mara for a drive and a short walk on a sunny beach, complete with block-out and broad-brimmed sun hat, then they did some shopping. But she kept frowning and falling silent.

When they got back they could hear Aaron in his office, talking on the phone again.

'There's some business crisis, I'm afraid. On top of Peggy,' Emma said.

'It's only natural you'd be worried about her. She doesn't look well to me.'

'She's just about stopped eating.'

'I'm quite happy to sit around, you know. I can always entertain myself. I have some part-finished sewing I can get on with now and then, if you don't mind a bit of a mess. I'll clear up after myself, I promise.'

'Why should I mind?'

When she brought her sewing bag down, Emma watched her. 'That looks like a serious sewing kit and must be important if you'd bring it all the way to Australia with you.'

Mara took out her project.

'Is that what I think it is?'

'A teddy bear? Yes. It's a hobby of mine, designing and making soft toys – at the designer end of the market, not the cheapies.'

'That one's really cute. Did you buy a pattern or do you just make it up as you go along?'

'I make my own patterns. I'm thinking of selling kits with variable outfits and finishes, only it'd cost quite a bit to set myself up, do the advertising and so on. When I lost my job I had to postpone my start-up because it'll be a while before it'll support me – if it ever does support me fully. Meet Clarissa.' She held out the bear, whose fur was a subtle shade of pink. 'Hold her. See how she feels to cuddle.'

Emma took the toy and smiled instinctively, then ran her fingers up and down one of its arms. 'It's lovely material, so soft. You have her in underclothes, pretty ones too. What's the top layer going to be?'

Mara took out the sketch of the clothes she was planning to make for Clarissa, which included a little hat with flowers on it, not the usual bonnet.

'Oh, that's going to be lovely. Those clothes will add just the right touch.'

'Yes. I'd have to charge a lot for a one-off like this, but some people will pay a lot once the maker gets a reputation.'

Aaron came in, looking annoyed.

'What's wrong?' Emma asked at once, dropping the sketch.

'Karen Danson has quit on us and we've been drawing up adverts for her job. We can start advertising it from a distance but you can't gauge what a person is really like till you've spent some time with them.' He spread his hands in a gesture of helplessness. 'I may have to nip across to Sydney, or wherever is the best place to conduct the interviews.'

'Can't you bring applicants over here to the west?' Emma glanced towards their visitor.

'There are more people than me involved, most of them in Sydney. I've still got that studio flat over there. Of all the times for Karen to quit on us, though!' He wandered back towards his office.

Emma let out a growl of frustration. 'The sooner he sells that damned business the happier I'll be.'

Mara didn't say anything but she was beginning to feel that fate was messing her about again. Yes, it was nice to be here, but most of all she wanted to get to know her father and if he wasn't going to be around what was she going to do with herself? She liked to keep busy.

For the rest of the afternoon, Aaron was in and out of the office, apologising to her a couple of times and trying to chat, though his mind was obviously elsewhere.

She didn't get a lot of sewing done, but having it on her knee as she sat outside made a good smokescreen and stopped them worrying about entertaining her, at least.

It didn't stop her worrying about being left here without him, though. It'd be awkward to say the least, especially with Emma anxious about Peggy, who still hadn't shown up.

* * *

Hal admitted to himself that he was still procrastinating about going through his mother's possessions and he'd been here in Mandurah for a few days now. He kept walking into the various rooms then coming out again without starting the jobs necessary to clear the place out.

Apart from anything else, he was, he admitted to himself, recovering from a period of intense stress winding up his business. Lazing around seemed to suit his current emotional needs, so he gave in to it. His deadlines were self-imposed after all.

He enjoyed several leisurely drives up and down the nearby coast, parking a few times simply to sit and watch the sea and the holidaymakers frolicking on the shore.

In the evenings he sat out on the patio, careful not to face the neighbours because he wasn't in the mood for social chit-chat. He had to give them credit for not pushing a conversation on him; indeed, they hadn't intruded in any way.

He'd seen no sign of anyone on the house at the other side. It looked shut up with roll-down shutters covering each window. The garden was a sere wilderness of rocks and coloured pebbles. What was the point in owning a house in such a wonderful position on the water if you never came here?

At least his mother had enjoyed this home, though it was really far too big for one person. He'd get a cleaner in to go through the place once he had finished clearing out her things and in the meantime the parts he wasn't using could stay dusty.

When he went indoors later in the evenings he either watched TV or read books from his mother's wall of what were clearly well-loved romance novels. To his surprise he found himself enjoying the stories, especially the happy endings, which left him feeling good.

He should be so lucky as to have a romantic ending like that in real life!

He selected tonight's tale because he liked the heroine's face on the cover. It'd be another gentle story. He couldn't even imagine his mother reading a murder tale or anything gruesome.

He'd switched the news on the TV automatically, following a long-time daily habit. As he got up to go to bed, he realised that he hadn't taken much in about what was happening in the wider world, not tonight and not since he'd been here.

However, he got up the next morning feeling better enough to want more out of life than idling around. He was starting to feel a sense of physical well-being again, thank goodness.

He ate a hearty breakfast for the first time and sat thinking about what to do. It seemed clear that before he could build a new life for himself, he needed to do as his mother had asked and clear out her possessions, so that was where he'd start. And he *would* start today.

He might get someone from a charity to come and go through her clothes but he was the only one who could or should sort out her office. Before he could change his mind, he marched into that room and switched on her computer.

Of course it wanted a password before it would let him in and for a moment he couldn't think what to do. Then he remembered the lawyer giving him a piece of paper with various bits of essential information on it. Old-fashioned, that lawyer. He could have sent him this information in a digital file, or even emailed it.

It took him a while to find the paper, which was crumpled up in a drawer next to his bed. Why on earth had he put it there?

He scanned it rapidly, relieved to find the password. It made him smile. It was the name of a toy dragon he'd been very fond of as a child. He'd have no difficulty remembering it from now on.

'Good idea, Ma,' he said aloud, took a deep breath and started investigating what was on her computer.

She couldn't have spent a lot of time exploring online, he decided quite quickly. Well, he knew she'd usually done the first drafts of new poems in pencil on the little pad she carried everywhere. She didn't seem to be in any social media group, but had sent emails regularly to him and a few old friends whose names he recognised, and to her editor. There didn't seem to be any new friends among them, though.

He'd taken a fresh notepad from her stationery stash and now started his own list of 'To do' tasks. First, contact those friends and make sure they knew she'd died. Surely they would by now? It had been mentioned in some newspapers, just a paragraph or so.

It was no surprise that she had quite a lot of document files. He opened the folder labelled 'Published poems' first of all, finding the master files for all her books there. He sent them to his own cloud storage straight away, just for safety.

Then he opened a folder labelled 'Works in progress' and found files containing sets of poems or partially completed poems, grouped in similar topics. Then there were some 'ideas' for future poems for her next collection. It was to be named, appropriately, *Final Thoughts: A Personal View of the World*. Only she hadn't lived long enough to finish it, sadly.

He took a deep, painful breath and opened a folder at random. 'Older subjects'. There were quite a lot of poems there, ones he hadn't seen before.

He started reading and soon realised these were simpler poems than most of the ones in her other books. They seemed to be offering her views on life or describing people and everyday scenes.

One entitled 'Old Friends' was particularly moving because it reminded him of a dog they'd had when he was a child. He'd taken that dog for some of her final slow walks himself. Such a lovely dog, Ellie.

We pace the streets of suburbia
My four-legged friend and I
In a leisurely way
For we've both had our day
And we study the world we pass by.

We envy the young folk their running,
My stiff-legged old pal and I
So I pat him and say

'Well, we once used to play
Now we'll just watch the others trot by.'

He read it to the end, liking the way the rhythm of the words seemed to echo the slow paces of the two elderly characters moving along the street. He had seen old people walking their dogs in just this way, both owners and pets stiff with age.

'Claudia, you can still touch my heart,' he said aloud. He'd started calling her by her first name when he turned eighteen. It had seemed more appropriate, somehow. The first time he did it, she'd looked at him, head on one side, and nodded. It wasn't that she'd not been loving, just not in the usual motherly way.

Ah, well . . .

He blew his nose vigorously, checked the printer and made a copy of that old dog poem. He could see the scene so clearly and was going to make a sketch to go with it. He didn't discuss his sketches with anyone. Only his mother had known how much his hobby meant to him. She'd tried to persuade him to follow his creativity instead of going into business. But they'd been short of money when he was young and once it came to choosing a career path, he'd wanted security more than anything else – for both himself and her – so had chosen to study economics and, later, personnel management.

The habit of sketching had refused go away, though. It had been easily portable whenever he travelled, a way of relaxing in his rare moments of leisure, an activity for the precious quiet times on his own when he'd not been caught up in anything.

Since he'd come here to Mandurah he hadn't even got out his sketching materials, had only unpacked a few clothes. He would unpack the rest of his things later today. It felt as if that would be putting down a few tentative roots. Only time would tell whether he could thrive here.

Whatever happened, there was nothing to stop him setting up one of the spare rooms as a studio. He'd buy some oil and acrylic paints as well as paper and other essentials. He'd tried painting a few times, but it was too messy to take the paints with him when he travelled, so only the sketching materials had gone with him.

Enough thinking about the past! he told himself and went back to reading his mother's poems.

They were rather different from her early collections, but it was still her voice, her perceptive views of the world around her.

This last year she seemed to have been painting the everyday world in simple words and beautiful images, captured like soap bubbles drifting along on the breeze.

He smiled as he sat and ate his lunch. It felt good to have made a start on her office.

Then he unpacked his sketching materials. He'd need to buy a lot more 'stuff'. And set up her office with the right sort of desk and maybe an easel.

Not a long-term life plan, but a beginning at least of new patterns of behaviour.

Chapter Eleven

When Peggy did eventually come home that evening, she looked heavy-eyed and had a bleak expression. That changed to anger when she saw her parents get up hurriedly and come into the house towards her.

Glaring at them, she made a movement with one arm as if to fend them off. 'What is this? A welcome home committee?'

Mara had started to get up too, but sat down again and stayed out on the patio. They'd be better off without her around if they were going to quarrel with Peggy.

'We were worried when you didn't come home last night,' Emma said.

'You should have phoned,' Aaron added.

'I'm an adult. I can do my own worrying, thank you very much. Now, I had a late night yesterday, so I'm going straight up to bed. And no, I don't want anything to eat.'

She hurried out of the room and ran up the stairs. After her bedroom door had slammed shut, Mara saw Emma go straight into Aaron's arms and burst into tears.

It was a while before Emma went upstairs and then Mara's father came out again to join her, giving a helpless shrug as he sat down.

'I'm so sorry you walked into this situation, Mara. It's blown up quite suddenly. She was living with that horrible fellow and seemed happy, most of the time anyway, then suddenly she was knocking on our door, needing somewhere to live, saying he'd thrown her out. We couldn't say no, could we? Bad timing, though. I'd wanted things to go more smoothly for you and me.'

'It's usual for families to have problems.' She was an expert witness to that. Her mother hadn't once responded to her emails about what Mandurah was like. Her father sent her a message every day, not saying anything about her mother. 'I'm sorry Peggy is being so difficult, Aaron, but it won't make any difference to how I feel about you.'

'Would you give me a hug then? I'm mostly the one dishing out the hugs at the moment.'

Feeling shy, she walked into his arms – and felt suddenly at home there, as she did with Phil, so it turned into a proper hug.

When he moved away, Aaron blew his nose and said in a husky voice, 'Thanks. That really helped.'

Shortly afterwards Emma came downstairs again. 'Peggy won't even speak to me. It's time for the late-night news. Let's watch it together.'

But Mara could see that Emma was finding it difficult

to settle and wasn't surprised when she got up as the weather map came on the screen and said, 'I'll just leave a small plate of salad for Peggy. She might – you know, want a snack later.'

She put some leftover salad from the evening meal on a plate, arranged it artistically and covered it with cling film. Then she put it on the kitchen surface with 'Peggy's snack' on a piece of paper in big, dark writing.

She and Aaron went up to bed shortly afterwards.

Mara went back out to sit by the canal. She was getting rather bored with sitting here by herself. She hadn't liked to go out for a long walk after the dire warnings about sunburn, so had confined herself to strolls round the nearby streets, which seemed mostly deserted during the daytime.

Just as she was thinking of following the rest of the family's example and going to bed, she saw Peggy come down into the kitchen. With a sigh, she again stayed where she was to avoid a confrontation.

Peggy made herself a cup of tea, took the covering off the salad and fiddled with it. She ate a couple of pieces of tomato, then muttered something and scooped the rest up and put it into the rubbish bin. She frowned down at it then covered it up with a crumpled sheet torn off the daily newspaper. After that she went back up to bed, her movements slow and weary.

Mara wondered whether she should have spoken to her about how upset her mother was and how dangerous it was to go without food for long periods.

No. It'd have done no good. She was a newcomer

here, should stay right out of their quarrels. The trouble was, Mara had once worked with someone whose sister had died of anorexia and it had been a horrible, long-drawn-out experience for her friend and the family. Looking on from the sidelines had been painful. And now it was happening in her own family.

She stayed there worrying for long enough to see the guy next door come out and throw himself down on one of the cheap plastic chairs. He looked sad. Well, his mother had died recently, hadn't she? There would be something wrong if he wasn't sad.

He didn't glance towards Mara and she tried to go into the house silently.

She was tiptoeing round everyone here, not what she'd expected at all.

The following morning, Emma got up earlier than usual and went downstairs to see whether the plate of salad had been touched. Surely her daughter would have got hungry enough to eat some of it? Her hopes began to rise when it wasn't there or in the fridge.

She looked across at Mara, who was on her way outside with a mug of coffee, and saw her flush and look hastily away as if feeling guilty.

Something had clearly upset her and Emma wondered whether it might be connected with Peggy and the food. Emma had heard Peggy creep downstairs before Mara came up to bed.

It'd be unfair to expect their guest to tell tales about her daughter so on the off-chance that she'd guessed correctly, she looked into the rubbish bin. Thank goodness! There was no sign of the salad, just some crumpled newspaper. Then she realised it had yesterday's date on it. She definitely hadn't thrown that newspaper away because Aaron liked to keep them for a few days.

She looked in the bin again. Where were the food scraps she'd dumped in there after making their meal last night? They'd formed such a brightly coloured collection of bits and pieces that she'd felt smug after reading recently that it was healthy to eat as many vivid coloured fruits and vegetables as you could.

Taking a spoon, she poked around, her heart sinking as she found the salad she'd left for Peggy wrapped in the thin plastic film. It didn't look as if any of it had been eaten.

Aaron had followed her downstairs and came across to see what she was looking at. 'Was that Peggy's salad?'

'Supposed to be.'

'Is she eating anything at all?'

'Not that I've seen. I can't let this go, Aaron. Anorexia can be a life-threatening illness. Can you two go out somewhere this morning and leave me to have a quiet chat with Peggy?'

'Yes, of course. Good idea. We'll go out for a drive.'

But before he could invite Mara to do that, they heard someone coming down the stairs. There wasn't even time for him to get out to the patio without being seen.

'Oh, hi, Peggy. Excuse me, I'm expecting an important message from the UK.' He went across the hall into his home office.

Peggy stood by the door, rubbing her forehead as if it ached and frowning at her mother.

Emma waited, watching her daughter realise she was standing near the open waste bin. 'Was something wrong with the meal I left for you yesterday?'

'Of course not. I just – wasn't hungry.'

'Then why waste it? You could have put it in the fridge for someone else to eat.'

'I didn't want to upset you. A group of us had been to a café and I had something to eat there.'

Emma folded her arms. 'I can still tell when you're lying to me. Did you have anything at all to eat?'

Peggy shrugged. 'No one else was eating and I wasn't hungry. Food makes me feel nauseous lately.'

'No wonder. You're hardly eating enough to keep a cat alive. Talk to me, Peggy. Come and sit down. Tell me what I can do to help.'

Her daughter stiffened visibly. 'I'm *not* going to force food down just to please you when I'm not feeling hungry. And I'm twenty-five, thank you very much, not five, so I'll manage my own food intake.'

'You're acting more like a five-year-old at the moment.'

'Being fat isn't healthy.'

'Being skeletal isn't healthy, either. Nor is it attractive to normal men. You've lost a lot of weight lately.'

'Well, Mike prefers slender figures.'

'You're going back to him?'

Tears filled Peggy's eyes. 'I thought – he said he'd missed me, so we went back to his flat. Then later, he said he was sorry, it still wasn't working for him and I should go home.' She gulped back a sob, struggling not to weep.

Emma's voice was flat. 'So he took you for a sucker. It was just sex he wanted.'

'I wanted it too.'

'Ha!'

'OK, I wanted *him*. You've no need to pull all the grubby little details into the open and hang them out to dry. I shan't give in to him again, believe me.'

'I should hope not. At least show a bit of pride.' She waited and then as the silence continued, she said, 'Could you just have something small to eat? *Please*.'

'I'd throw up if I tried. I've thrown up once already this morning.' She whirled round and yelled over her shoulder, 'Leave me to sort out my life myself.' She ran out of the house and shortly afterwards there was the sound of a car door slamming.

When Peggy had roared off down the street, Aaron came out of his office. 'I heard what she said.' He put his arms round his wife, who sobbed against him.

He pulled her towards the stairs but she resisted and gestured towards the patio. 'You have a guest.'

'Come up and sit on our balcony. No one will bother us there. Mara won't take offence if you and I take some time for ourselves, I'm sure. She'll have overheard your quarrel with Peggy, just as I did. You need me much more than our guest does at the moment.'

He looked towards the patio and Mara made a shooing gesture, so he guided his wife towards the stairs, holding her hand.

A few minutes later he came out onto the patio to tell Mara he and Emma were going for a walk on a nearby beach. 'Do you mind us leaving you? There's nothing as relaxing as the beach when you're stressed and it's going to be thirty-four today, too hot for you to spend long in the sun. That's centigrade, not Fahrenheit.'

'Of course I don't mind.' When they'd gone she pulled out the soft toy and tried to get on with the sewing, but found it hard to settle.

The neighbour came out, saw her and looked as if he wished she wasn't there. He hesitated, then raised one hand in a brief greeting and turned away as usual.

She didn't respond in any way.

This wasn't at all what she'd expected from her visit and she was beginning to wonder whether she'd upset her mother unnecessarily.

She reminded herself that it wasn't anyone's fault, had just happened, but it didn't make her feel any better.

Shortly afterwards Rufus came home and joined Mara in the kitchen where she was about to make herself something to eat.

'Hi! I'm spending the night at Jenn's so I came to pick up my night gear and my clean work shirt for tomorrow. I see Dad's car has gone. Has Mum gone out too?'

'Yes. They went to walk on the beach.' She hesitated.

'What's the matter?'

'There's been some more trouble with your sister. She really needs professional help.'

'Oh, damn. Well, she'll go her own sweet way; she always does. Mind if I join you? I'm going to grab a quick sandwich.'

When he was sitting at the table with her, he asked, 'What actually started off today's row?'

'Peggy threw the meal Emma left for her last night into the kitchen rubbish bin, covered it up and pretended she'd eaten it.'

'She's getting worse.' He took a bite of the sandwich and followed it with a swig of water. 'It's all because of that scumbag she used to live with. I've been working over in the eastern states for the past year, so I've only seen or heard about her big love affair intermittently from a distance, but I wasn't happy about it being him and I guessed she was heading for a fall.'

Mara murmured encouragingly, wanting to find out more, waiting for him to chew and swallow another bite. 'Go on.'

'He's treated other women the same way: all over them for a few months, then suddenly dropping them. I did warn her, but you can't get through to someone with stars in their eyes, can you? The dazzle gets in the way of the real picture.'

'It's hard to see clearly when you first meet someone because you're both on your best behaviour.' She glanced down at herself. 'I could never give up eating to please a man, though.'

'What did your guy do to upset you?'

'He pretended to be interested in me partly because I got on well with the boss, I reckon. Then he realised I was writing a computer program and assumed it was to do with work. It wasn't. But he must have used it to score over me and told lies about me stealing work I'd done in company time, because he got to stay and take over my revamped job and I got made redundant.'

Rufus let out a soft, low whistle.

'If Darren's claim that I'd been writing the program at work had been true, the rights would have belonged to my employer. They took his word for it without even asking me and sent me a lawyer's letter claiming ownership. Only I hadn't done any of it at work and what's more, the program had no connection with my job. I heard yesterday that my dad and his friend George have sorted it out for me. Dad says my old manager was very upset about me being accused falsely. But Darren still has my job.'

'Tough on you. What was the program about?'

'It was to help me market luxury toys, the sort adults sometimes buy or collect. And kits to make better quality toys yourself. It's nearly finished but I can't use my savings to start up the business, as I'd planned, not until I have another job to earn my living with during the early days. I need a roof over my head and, as they used to say in the old days, I need to put bread on the table.'

'You don't seem to be languishing about losing your partner, though, like Peggy is about Mike.'

She shrugged. 'I'm older than her and I've got a bit

more sense than to languish over anyone I only went with for less than six months. I'm angry with Darren, more than anything, and my biggest worry now is him bad-mouthing me so that I get a bad reputation in the industry.'

He shot her an amused glance. 'You look really fierce when you talk about him. Remind me never to make you angry.'

'Actually, I didn't enjoy living with him nearly as much as I'd expected, because he was a lazy slob and I wasn't going to turn into a housemaid after I got home from work. I don't think I'm cut out for marriage and all that stuff. I've seen too much of the downside.'

His voice grew more gentle. 'With your mother? I heard Dad say she had certain, er, problems.'

'Yes. You can't blame her exactly. Mental problems are an illness just like any other. But I've never seen signs of love between her and Phil, like I see all the time with your parents.'

'Yeah. I love seeing those two together.' He smiled into the distance for a few moments, then glanced at his watch. 'I'd better get going. I have an appointment in Mandurah this afternoon.' He studied her, head on one side. 'You know what?'

'What?'

'I thought I'd dislike you, but I don't. Jenn told me to look at your eyes and you haven't got mean eyes. In fact, yours seem to smile gently out at the world most of the time. It's nice to see.'

And with that unexpected compliment he went out

to his car. It had been the sort of compliment she really appreciated.

As she stood up to put her plate away she noticed he'd dropped some papers which had wafted under the table, so she picked them up and ran after him.

She caught him just as he was opening his car door. 'You dropped these.'

'Wow! Thanks. I'd have had to come back for them.'

There was the sound of a garage door whirring open and a car starting up nearby. Both of them looked round.

'It's our new neighbour going out,' Rufus said.

She thought the man driving the car was still looking sad from the way he was slumped in his seat. 'Must be awful to have to clear out your dead mother's house.'

'Mum says he hasn't made any attempt to chat, even to comment on the weather. He seems to be as aloof as his mother was. She didn't mix socially, just chatted occasionally to my parents.'

'Well, perhaps she was already ill when she got here. What a waste of talent for her to die so young! She was a brilliant poet.'

He looked surprised. 'Was she? Come to think of it, Ma said something similar, but I'm not into poetry so it went in one ear then out the other.'

He got into the car, dropped the papers on the passenger seat and left with a cheerful wave.

She went back into the house, glad she'd had a proper chat with Rufus. It had been nice to be told he liked her, but she wondered how Peggy might take that news. She might have preferred her brother to take a dislike to

Mara, as she had done, for no reason that anyone could figure.

Mara got herself a peach with some cheese and biscuits. She'd only had a light lunch because of chatting with Rufus.

Perhaps it'd be a good idea to hire a car, then she could go out on her own and not be such a burden on a family which had such serious problems happening. It was nice sitting out on the patio looking at the water, but she didn't want to spend all her time down under doing that.

She wanted to see something of Western Australia as well as getting to know Aaron. The tourist guides she'd seen online mentioned a wine growing district not too far south from Mandurah, then there was the capital city itself and Fremantle, its port. Oh yes, lots to see.

Chapter Twelve

Hunger satisfied, Mara lingered to finish the chapter of the book she was reading, forgetting where she was and reading on till a slight cramp in one leg made her suddenly realise she'd been sitting there for a long time and needed to move her body. Good books could do that to you, make you forget your surroundings.

She picked up her plate and took it inside to the dishwasher. When she heard the sound of an engine outside on the canal she couldn't resist turning to see what sort of boat it was. Such sights were still a novelty to her.

A smallish motorboat containing two men cruised slowly past and turned round at the end of the canal, slowing down and pulling up by the sea wall of the house next door. The one who stood up in it gave a furtive glance round – yes, definitely furtive; there was no other way to describe it. That caught her attention.

He stepped up onto the edge of the boat and clambered up the jetty. To her surprise, he immediately began to take photos of the house and garden. His companion kept the boat in place by holding on to the ladder with a boat hook, but made no attempt to tie up properly.

What on earth was going on? She'd seen the guy next door go out earlier, so what was this chap doing here? A little worried, she waited till he was looking in the other direction and moved quickly across the room to a closer vantage point behind a huge potted plant near the window.

He took a few more photos then looked towards her house as if checking that no one was around. Once again the word 'furtive' came into her mind. Slinging the camera round his neck, he moved forward to peer through the nearest window.

After staring into the house, he glanced from side to side yet again, before edging across to the sliding door and trying it. When it moved easily, he grinned and raised one thumb to show the man in the boat things were going well.

As he tugged the door fully open she knew she had to do something. She couldn't just stand by idly and watch an intruder break into a neighbour's house.

She crossed to the door leading out onto the patio and slid it open as noisily as she could, pretending to call to someone in the house, 'I'm just going to sit outside for a while, Aaron.'

She was ready to jump back into the house and lock

the door if they threatened her in any way. But by the time she got outside the intruder was running back towards the boat.

He kept his face turned away from her, calling to the man in it, 'No one at home. We'll come back another time.'

Who did he think he was fooling? Any watcher could tell he'd been about to break in. He must be totally stupid. Well, she'd seen his face clearly and she'd remember it.

Within seconds of him clambering down into the boat, it set off, both men still trying to hide their faces. Unfortunately she hadn't seen the face of the one driving it but he looked from the back like a much older man.

She'd seen the boat's name as well and wished she'd had her mobile phone with her to take photos of what was going on.

As the boat had now disappeared into the main canal, she felt safe to clamber over the low wall to the next house and shut the door the intruder had left open.

What the hell was going on? Had she really just foiled a burglary?

'You're a heroine, Mara Gregory,' she told herself, smiling.

This was proving to be a very strange sort of day. In fact her whole visit so far had not been at all what she'd expected. Clearly not what her birth father had expected them to be doing, either. Poor Aaron.

What on earth would happen next?

* * *

She made herself a mug of coffee and sat down outside. She'd shut the door for the neighbour but his house was still unlocked and she was worried about leaving it open to another invasion. Surely the sight of her sitting here would put those two off if they did think of returning?

The trouble was, she couldn't settle to reading and there was nothing else to watch. These side canals could be very quiet sometimes and dimly lit when the houses weren't occupied. There was much more to-ing and fro-ing along the main canals. She could often hear boats because sound carried further on water, but she couldn't see them very clearly from here.

It was over an hour before she heard the sound of a car in the street and then a garage door whirring open.

Surely that was – yes, it was. She saw lights come on and the owner moving about next door, so clambered over the low wall dividing the two properties and walked across to the sliding glass door, rapping on it.

He spun round, looking surprised when he saw who it was.

'I'm staying next door,' she said.

'Yes, I've seen you.'

'Look, did you book someone to take photos of your house tonight?'

'What? No, definitely not.'

'Well, about an hour ago, a boat stopped and a man got out and started taking photos of your house, or maybe he was just pretending to. Then he went to look in through the windows, and since the sliding door wasn't locked, he opened it and was about to go inside. So I came outside, pretending to be talking to someone in our house, and he ran back to the boat, which took off.'

He gaped at her as if he couldn't believe what he was hearing.

'I thought I'd better warn you to be sure to lock your doors next time you go out. And if you have a security system, switch that on too. I should think these houses are more at risk of break-ins since they can be approached from the water or the street side.'

'Good heavens! How could I have been so careless? Thank you so much.'

'That's all right. I'll leave you in peace now.'

'No, don't go. I'm really grateful to you for intervening.'

'It's what neighbours do.'

'The good ones. Can I offer you a glass of wine as a thank you?'

'You don't have to.' But she was tempted. He had such a nice smile and she was fed up of being alone.

'Actually, it'd be good to have some company for a change. Like me, you seem to spend a lot of time on your own. If you'd rather not join me, just say so. Otherwise, I have a very nice Australian Chardonnay I'd be happy to share with you.'

She'd love some company too.

As if to emphasise her lack of social interactions, there was a sudden chorus of voices yelling 'Surprise!' and an outburst of laughter and applause. It came from near the far end of their canal and people had suddenly crowded out of the house onto the patio after a boat pulled up. A huge sign saying '60 Years Young' had been unfurled from an upstairs window.

'Someone must be holding a surprise birthday party,' he said. 'If there's no one else at home next door, you may as well stay for a while, because from what I hear, we'll get no peace till the party ends. My mother said once or twice that parties were the main downside of living here because of the noise.'

As if to prove him right, loud music started up, thumping away, and he rolled his eyes. 'If it's late enough for a party, it's definitely late enough for a drink. I'm having one whether you join me or not.'

She gave in. 'I don't know how late that needs to be, not being Australian, but I'd certainly enjoy a glass of wine.'

'Good. I'm Hal Kendrell, by the way.'

'Mara Gregory.' She took the hand he was offering and a shiver ran through her. He was, after all, very attractive. No, she shouldn't even think about that sort of thing. She was only here for a few weeks and he was recently bereaved.

'Do please sit down and I'll open the wine. I feel like celebrating anyway.'

'Did something nice happen?'

'Not exactly. But I started clearing my mother's office today. I've been avoiding it since I got here a few days ago and feeling guilty about that, but I managed to get my act together today at last.' He stared into the distance. 'It side-swiped me, my mother dying so suddenly. I didn't know she was ill, even.'

'Maybe she wanted to be on her own. Some people do.'

'Knowing her, she probably did, but I'm an only child and I'd have liked to say a proper farewell to her. She even had the funeral without me, if you can call it a funeral with only her lawyer present to supervise the cremation.'

'That must have felt hurtful.'

'Yes. Though it's typical of her. She's never conformed to other people's ideas of what's right.'

'Neither has my mother. It can make life difficult.'

'You might have heard of my mother – Claudia Kendrell, the poet.'

'I was going to say I'm sorry about your loss, and I am, but it's the world's loss, too. I absolutely love your mother's poetry, especially the *Winter Days* collection.'

He beamed at that. 'You've read it?'

'Yes. I own all her books.'

His voice became choked with emotion. 'That's wonderful. What's more you're reminding me that something of her will live on.'

'Definitely. She was a wordsmith of some note. You must have been very proud of her.'

'I was – am, I mean.'

He poured more wine, trying to wipe his eyes without her noticing, which made something warm twist round inside her. He came across to hand her a glass then went back and fumbled in the cupboard, producing a packet of crisps. 'I don't have any fancy nibbles to offer you, but we ought to put something in our stomachs.' Then he grinned. 'Besides, I love salt and vinegar crisps.'

He tipped them into a pretty glass bowl and put it on a small table between them. '*Voilà, madame.* Your gourmet snack.' Then he picked up his glass and held it out towards her. 'Cheers.'

She clinked hers against it. 'Cheers back at you.'

The wine was smooth and left a nice aftertaste. They both sat quietly while noise from the party continued to echo across the water. It didn't seem desperately important to rush into conversation; it was nice simply sitting with someone congenial.

He leant back in the chair. 'I have another thing to celebrate: I've just retired.'

'You're a bit young for that, surely?'

'Well, it's been part of my life plan to semi-retire quite young, so I've been concentrating on making money. I'm not rich, mind – you need far more than I have to call yourself rich these days – I've just got a sound basis for a quieter life. I was going to take a sabbatical for a while and work out what to do with myself during the next stage, but as I now have what my mother left me as well, I won't have to work at all if I don't want to. Imagine that: I can do exactly what I want for the first time I can ever remember since I left university.'

'I envy you that lack of financial pressure.'

'What do you do for a living?'

She shrugged. 'Nothing at the moment because I've recently been made redundant. I used to work for a toy company, on the IT systems and so on.'

'Sounds interesting.'

'It had its moments, but I didn't always agree with what they did and the illustrations they've been using recently from a new artist were bizarre, if you ask me. Why the new man always has to make the characters look like ugly caricatures of human beings I do not understand. Why can't they offer kids beautiful scenes and people sometimes?'

She tried to take another sip and was a bit embarrassed to realise that her glass was empty already.

He picked up the bottle, gestured with it and, at her nod, refilled both their glasses. 'Are you related to the Buchanans? You have a distinct resemblance to Aaron next door.'

She felt comfortable enough with him to tell the truth. 'He's my birth father. We just found one another. My mother had always told me he was dead.'

'Wow. Truth can be stranger than fiction sometimes, can't it?'

She sipped again, relaxing, finding him the easiest person to chat to that she'd met in ages. She'd not expected that with this neighbour because Emma had said he seemed as reclusive as his mother. 'I hope I'm not taking too much of your time?'

'No. I'm enjoying your company. You don't fill the silences with meaningless chattering.'

'I like that about you, too.'

The party noise erupted again and they both grimaced. Then it died down and he chuckled suddenly. 'The silence probably means they're feeding their faces now. Food usually shuts people up.'

She laughed too. 'You're so right. And I'm as guilty of it as anyone. I enjoy my food.'

'What's your favourite cuisine?'

They discussed that and agreed that they were both addicted to various sorts of Asian food, then they enjoyed another few more moments of silence.

She was sorry when she heard noises next door. 'Ah. I think Aaron and Emma are back. They'll wonder where I am.'

'Do you think they'd like to come in for a drink?'

'Not today. They're having trouble with their daughter.'

'She certainly shouts a lot, doesn't she?'

'Tell me about it. The atmosphere has grown very fraught at times.'

'You, on the other hand, are one of the most peaceful people I've met in ages.'

She immediately felt guilty. 'I shouldn't have stayed so long, though.'

'On the contrary. There aren't many people I feel comfortable sitting quietly with, but you definitely haven't outstayed your welcome.'

'I've enjoyed your company too.'

'We should do it again sometime. Um, how about you come out for dinner with me tomorrow evening?'

She looked at him in surprise. It was the last thing she'd expected. 'Well, if you're sure? I don't need paying back for helping you, though.'

'I'm sure I want to take you out and spend more time with you. Our outing won't be to pay you back for your help, though, I promise.'

'Then I'd love to come.'

'Do you prefer to eat early or late?'

'Early by choice, but I'll fit in with you, Hal.'

'I like to eat early too. Do you have any food problems?'

'None at all.'

'That's great. I know people don't get food problems on purpose but they do make social life difficult when you first get to know them.'

'Yes. Till you understand their needs. Then it's OK. I blame it on the chemicals that seem to be added to nearly every foodstuff manufactured. The first time I found out that strawberry flavouring had no connection whatsoever with strawberries I felt absolutely outraged.'

'You'd have got on well with my mother. She felt very strongly about that sort of thing.'

'I'm sorry I never met her.' Mara turned her head as Aaron called her name and stood up, calling back and waving to him. 'I'd better go.'

'Rendezvous outside my garage around six p.m. tomorrow?'

'Yes, kind sir.' She gave him a mock curtsey then went back home. Only it didn't feel like home. Her parents' house hadn't either. She still missed her cosy little flat, or maybe it was just the peace and quiet she'd had there.

Oh, get over it, she told herself. *You haven't got a home at the moment but you do have a very elegant roof over your head and a second father – not to mention a rather attractive neighbour.*

She even had a date for the first time in ages. And with a man she fancied greatly.

Aaron and Emma looked relieved to see her.

'Sorry we're late home. We met some friends and had a drink after our walk. We tried to phone you to let you know, but there was no answer. No wonder, if you were schmoozing next door. What's he like?'

'Charming.' While Emma put together a quick salad, Mara told them what had happened. They were astonished at the near break-in.

'Well done for stopping it,' Aaron said. 'We'd better be even more careful about locking up our place in future, then.'

'It's usually Peggy who forgets,' Emma said. 'Oh dear, that's yet another thing that's going to cause trouble between us.'

Mara couldn't see why locking up carefully should upset anyone, but kept her thoughts to herself. She'd been brought up to lock every external door in the house carefully, even when she was pottering about at home, and never, ever to leave a window open when she went out.

That reminded her that her father still hadn't replied to her emails, which was starting to be a serious worry. Her mother only used email intermittently and it sometimes felt as if the real mother had vanished a couple of years ago, which was when the latest changes in behaviour started.

By the time they finished their meal it was quite late, but there was still no sign of Peggy.

Emma made a poor job of hiding her concern about that, saying valiantly, 'We won't wait up for her, and Rufus isn't coming home, so it'll just be us three tonight.'

To distract them, Mara got out her laptop and shared some of her childhood photos, transferring a few particularly good ones to Aaron's system.

As they sat chatting afterwards, Emma said thoughtfully, 'You know, I thought Rufus was just amusing himself with Jenn, but he's been seeing her nearly every day and now he's spending the night with her, so maybe he's getting serious.'

'Well, good luck to him,' Aaron said. 'She's a fine figure of a woman, reminds me of Sophia Loren, who was my ideal woman as a young lad. At least that makes one of them whose love life we don't have to worry about – for the moment at least. What do you think, Mara?'

'He does sound to be smitten when he talks about her. His voice goes softer.'

'Good. We're more than ready for grandchildren, aren't we, love?'

There was a big jump these days from sleeping with someone to settling down and starting a family, but Mara didn't point that out. Let them dream.

'I wish Peggy would phone,' Emma said out of the blue a little later, proving that she'd moved back to worrying about their daughter.

'She won't. And she'll not be in till late,' Aaron said. 'She's avoiding us.'

It was Mara who went up to bed early this time. She felt the other two needed releasing from the need to entertain her.

She didn't know what she needed. More than this dawdling life, that was sure. But at least she had a date with Hal to look forward to tomorrow.

If this continued, she'd have to find something more interesting to do with her time in Australia. And then, after she got back, she'd have to deal with her mother somehow and find a job, any job as long as she could afford her own place and make a new life for herself.

Her mother had said bluntly that she was expecting her daughter to stay at home permanently from now on and get a job nearby. No way was Mara going to do that. Unfortunately that would leave poor Phil on his own, and with Christmas coming up in a few weeks perhaps this wouldn't be a good time to make the break. Could she bear to hang on till after the festivities? Maybe. For her father.

She wasn't sure of anything lately. Life was so much easier when you had money coming in regularly. Her mind churned round and round, hemmed in by what felt like the high walls of this dilemma. It was a long time before she fell asleep.

In England, Phil was keeping a careful eye on his wife. Kath had been getting quieter and quieter since Mara left, hardly saying a word to him and rubbing her forehead as if it ached. He was seriously worried and nothing would persuade her to see the doctor.

The rigid weekly routines were still to be adhered to but she wasn't holding anything like a proper conversation, just firing orders or refusals at him from time to time.

In the end, after a sleepless night, he decided to have another attempt to make her face up to reality. He waited till they'd finished tea, but for once she didn't eat hers, just pushed it around her plate.

'We need to have a serious talk, love.'

She looked at him warily.

'I heard from Mara today. She says Aaron is very nice and so is his wife.'

Kath picked up a magazine and stared down at it, rustling its pages loudly, making no attempt to reply.

'Their house is beautiful, apparently. It's large, detached and right on the water, with boats going past and dolphins sometimes too.'

The magazine sailed through the air and the edge of its spine hit him on the ear.

'Ouch! That was a stupid thing to do.'

The next thing he knew, a vase followed it across the room, showering him and the carpet with water and flowers. It was followed straight away by an ornament, which smashed against the wall to one side of him, then another followed and hit him on the side of his head. He could feel blood trickling down his cheek and was so astonished that for a while he could only stand there, yelling at her to stop.

She didn't. Instead she speeded up, tossing anything that came to hand at him. As he tried to duck, broken glass crunched underfoot but she didn't seem to notice.

Then she stumbled and fell, lying there screaming, on and on. He couldn't work out why. She didn't seem to have cut herself. He was the one who was bleeding or bruised in a few places now.

It had gone way beyond reason, so he stopped trying to reason with her and ran out of the room, tugging open the front door, intending to run next door and call for help.

She was not only way out of control, but a danger to herself and to others.

But as he left the house, the world seemed to explode around him and he could feel himself falling, down into a dizzy spiral.

When he recovered consciousness, it took Phil a few moments to work out that he was in a moving vehicle, an ambulance, and his head was throbbing painfully.

'Can you please try to lie still, sir?' The man sitting next to him was a paramedic, judging by his clothing.

'What – happened?'

'You were knocked unconscious and your neighbour

phoned for the emergency services.'

'My wife?'

'She's in another ambulance. It's a good job the police were there because she needed restraining, I'm afraid. Has she behaved violently before?'

'Yes.' And suddenly Phil was tired of it all, not to mention downright exhausted. He'd done his best for years, his very best, and it hadn't been enough. He had nothing left to give now, nothing at all. He felt utterly boneless, empty and more weary than ever in his life before.

He closed his eyes and let them get him out of the ambulance and into the A&E department at the hospital.

They treated him gently, which he appreciated. They spoke softly, letting him take his time to answer – when he could find an answer.

At one stage another doctor came into the cubicle and asked various questions about his wife, scribbling down the name of the medical practice his family used and the dates of her other serious incidents.

'And she's been all right living at home since her last episode, taken her medication and so on?'

'Yes, well, sort of. Lately, she hasn't always taken it and she's been getting worse. I can't manage her. I just can't do it any longer.' His voice broke and he felt tears trickle down his face.

A woman took his hand. 'We'll look after her for you, then, shall we? I think you need a good night's sleep more than anything at the moment, Mr

Gregory, and we need to check your heart properly in the morning. Your blood pressure's far too high, for a start. All right if we admit you tonight, just for observation?'

'Fine by me. I'm so very tired.' It'd be good to have someone else to look after him – and after Kath.

Another nurse took down the name of Sally next door, who had a key to their house. She told him she'd pass on the information to the police, who would contact Sally and make sure his house was locked up safely.

Phil thought he'd said thank you, hoped he had, just wanted to close his eyes and sleep for a very long time.

When Phil woke up, bright sunlight was streaming in through the window, but this wasn't his own bedroom. He tried to sit up but found that he was hooked up to a monitor which had started beeping loudly.

A nurse hurried into the room. 'Awake at last, Mr Gregory?'

He stared at the kind young man as the pieces of the puzzle clicked into place. 'I remember now. How is my wife?'

'I don't know, but I can ask the person in charge of her area. Let's make you comfortable first, eh?'

When he'd done that the nurse said brightly, 'The doctor will be in to see you soon. Try to rest till then.'

It seemed a long time till the doctor arrived. She looked at a chart, listened to his heart then said gently, 'Well, you've had a lucky escape, Mr Gregory. If you'd tried to carry on any longer without help, you might have done yourself some permanent damage.'

'My wife?'

'She's had a sort of seizure, I'm afraid, and is unconscious. It happened just as we were going to take her to a secure ward at a nearby psychiatric hospital.'

'Oh, dear.'

'We're not sure exactly what happened and she's still being assessed. She's in the best place here to get whatever help she needs, believe me.'

'She's been acting strangely for a while and I couldn't persuade her to see anyone. She always said she was all right, but I could see she was getting worse.'

'She'll be carefully looked after, I promise. It's you we have to worry about at the moment. You're in desperate need of a good long rest. At your age, there's a limit to how much you can or should do.'

They didn't let him go home till the following day, by which time they'd run tests, put him on blood pressure pills and made him promise to take it easy. It was a promise he'd find easy to keep. He was still feeling exhausted.

The man who had driven him home in a sort of minibus helped him into the house, then left him on his own.

Phil could feel that Kath wasn't around. She always seemed to generate an air of tension. At the moment the terraced house he'd worked so hard to buy was just a quiet little house in a quiet street. And that was what he needed most of all, peace and quiet.

He couldn't go back to living with Kath, just . . . couldn't do it any longer. Even if she did recover. Only, they weren't sure she would. They'd told him not to make any alternative plans for her till they'd found out what was wrong.

What would Mara say about all that? Would she despise him for abandoning his wife? She had a new father now, a rich man by Phil's standards. Would she choose him over the adopted father who'd raised her and loved her so very dearly?

No. He didn't think his Mara would do that.

He was too tired to contact her now. He was going to follow instructions from the doctor to the letter: eat healthily, maybe watch a little television, do a few crosswords, read a book or two and have a good long rest. Most of all, avoid stress.

Tomorrow he'd think about the future. Or the next day. Whenever his brain resurfaced properly from a very dark abyss.

The house was cold so he turned up the central heating.

Someone knocked on the door and with a sigh he went to answer it, relaxing a little when he saw it was Sally from next door.

She held out a covered dish. 'I won't disturb you, Phil, but I brought you a casserole.'

He shivered. 'That's so kind of you. Why don't you come in for a moment? We don't want to let out all the warm air.'

'I'll make you a nice cup of tea, shall I?'

'Make one for both of us. Um – was it you who called the ambulance?'

'Yes. How's Kath?'

So he said it out loud, to make it seem more real. 'She's had a sort of seizure. They were going to take her into the psychiatric hospital but she's unconscious so they don't want to move her till they find out why.'

'She's been a lot worse lately, hasn't she?'

Her tone was so understanding, he nodded. 'I coped for as long as I could, truly I did, but I'm not a young man and she – well, she needs more help than I can give her.'

'You were wonderful with her,' Sally said. 'I don't know how you managed to do it for so long.'

That made him feel slightly better because Sally couldn't lie to save her life.

She stirred the tea in the little brown teapot. 'Have you heard from Mara lately?'

'Not for a day or two.'

'Give her my regards next time you speak to her.' She poured them mugs of tea and sat down near him, chatting of this and that.

As he finished his tea, he said something he'd wanted to tell her for years. 'Eh, you're a kind woman, Sally. I wish I'd had a wife like you, I do that.'

'Well, you've still got a friend and neighbour like me. I get a bit lonely at times since my Donny died, I must admit, and you've helped fill that lack.'

'I've been lonely for years. I don't know what I'd

have done without you.'

She stood up and patted his hand. 'I'll leave you in peace now, my dear friend. You look like you could do with a nap.'

'Yes. But it was nice seeing you.'

She moved towards the door, and he'd normally have stood up and escorted her out, but today he felt too tired to move.

She turned at the door to say, 'I nearly forgot. I'm going shopping tomorrow morning so if you need anything just let me know before ten o'clock. I can easily pick up a few things for you.'

'Thanks. I'll have to check what's in the fridge.'

'You can buy some ice cream now. Goodness knows why she took against it.'

'Said it made her head ache.'

'Well, you make a list. Tell me what your favourite flavour is.'

'Plain vanilla. Like me. I'm a very ordinary sort of chap.'

'No, you're not. You're interesting to talk to, always have been.'

He stayed where he was after she'd left, feeling weak and tired, but her kindness had helped. Yes, it definitely had. It'd reminded him that there were kind people in the world and he didn't have to struggle on his own. Not any longer.

The beef and vegetable casserole was still warm so he ate some of it, suddenly hungry. Then he put the rest in the fridge and sat on his big recliner armchair watching the local TV news.

When he woke it was nearly teatime and a different woman was talking on the TV. He switched the sound off, because she had one of those croaky voices that seemed to be fashionable among the younger generation. It made his throat ache to listen to them and he and Mara had joked about sending one particularly croaky young woman a packet of throat lozenges as a 'present from a viewer'.

He was starting to feel he could cope. He *would* cope – with whatever happened. He wasn't having Mara rushing home before she needed to and if a miracle occurred and Kath recovered, he wasn't having his lass give up her life for a woman who was incapable of being anything else but selfish. Nor was he giving up any more of his own life.

Poor Kath. She'd been dealt a bad hand in life and had got slowly worse as the years passed. He'd had a hard time of it, too.

One day they'd probably be able to cure people like her but at least they didn't lock them away or chain them up as they had in the past.

He watched what he wanted on TV, feeling guilty when he laughed aloud at a comedy show. It felt good to be able to do everything at his own pace, leave his mug on the small table beside his chair till the next time he got up.

He'd choose when to eat his meals, go out for strolls, just relax.

He slept like a log, not stirring all night. Wonderful, it was, to wake up and not have to get up straight away and make the bed.

Chapter Thirteen

The following morning Mara checked her emails and frowned. Nothing from her dad again. She hadn't heard from him for a few days. Something must be wrong. She sent him another email straight away asking if he was all right.

Usually he'd have replied quite quickly but once again she didn't hear back. If her mother had got worse, he'd have let her know, surely? So it couldn't be desperate. Could it?

She decided to set her mind at rest by phoning just before she went out this evening. It'd be morning in the UK and he'd surely be around then. Since coming here she'd found out that the time differences between the two countries could be a nuisance, slowing down communication when one or the other of you was asleep.

She really needed to reassure herself that things

were all right with her dad.

In the meantime, there was this evening to look forward to. And that thought made her realise that she hadn't told Emma she'd been invited out for a meal by Hal Kendrell. She finished the last of her late breakfast and told her.

Her kind hostess beamed at the news. 'How nice for you! Have you read any of his mother's poetry? I keep meaning to but then I don't get round to it.'

'I own copies of all her books and I read her poems regularly. I even know a few of them by heart. I love how simple they can seem and yet she somehow gets to the heart of Life with a capital L. Real life I mean, not just writing about raving beauties, battles or pushy over-achievers.'

'Wow. I must get round to buying one of her books if they light you up like that.'

Mara didn't think Emma would buy one, or if she did, she wouldn't read most of it. The older woman was what Mara thought of as a do-er, someone always busy doing something, not sitting around reading books. And the world needed them as well as poets. 'Um, has Peggy got up yet?'

'Got up and left before we even stirred.' She sighed. 'Didn't leave us a message. There's nothing we can do about that.'

The words were out before Mara could stop herself. 'That's so selfish. She must know how worried you are.'

Emma blinked her eyes a few times in a vain attempt to hold back tears, then gave up trying to conceal how upset she was. 'She hasn't been the same since she met that horrible man.'

Aaron came across the room, gave his wife a quick hug and began making a cup of coffee, hovering nearby protectively as he waited for the kettle to boil.

After a few moments, he asked casually, 'Had any luck getting hold of your father, Mara? Well, keep trying. Don't worry about using the phone.'

'Thanks. How's the business crisis going?'

'We've drawn up the adverts for the job and my deputy will go through the applicants and make arrangements for me to see anyone suitable. Fortunately the woman isn't leaving straight away.'

Later, when Mara was ready, she tried to phone her dad and got that disembodied automatic voice. Her mother was probably at home, but if she was still angry she'd not be answering, could even be deleting the messages from Australia. Mara would have to try again later.

She went downstairs to wait for six o'clock and her rendezvous with Hal. She'd put on one of the two skirts she'd brought with her, a full-skirted maxi in a flowery print, together with a matching top in a subtle dusky pink, one of her particular favourites.

Aaron whistled softly and held up his thumb to show his approval of her appearance.

Rufus came home from work just before she left.

'Did you have a good time last night?' his mother asked.

He beamed at her. 'Yes. Jenn's such good company, so easy to be with.'

'You keep saying that.'

'Well, this time it was as a prelude to telling you that I'm going to move in with her, Mum, so you won't have to put up with me any longer.'

His mother gaped at this announcement. 'Wow! That's a first for you.'

'What's a first?'

Mara turned to see Peggy, who must have come into the house quietly while they were chatting.

'Oh, hello, love.'

Rufus turned to his sister. 'I'm moving in with Jenn. Doing it tonight, actually, if you don't mind, Mum.'

'I shall miss you but I do hope you'll be happy.'

'Heaven help the poor woman living with you,' Peggy scoffed.

Rufus stiffened and scowled at her. 'Fond sister you are *not*!'

She shrugged, caught her mother's eye and said quickly, 'I was just joking.'

'Come and sit down,' Emma said quietly.

She shook her head. 'I've got something to do. And before you ask, I'll get my own meal later, thanks.'

Emma opened her mouth, looking about to protest, but when Aaron gave her a quick poke in the side, she shut her mouth again.

Mara couldn't help envying Rufus his happiness. Then she glanced at her watch and felt cheerful anticipation welling up. 'Time for me to go. See you later.'

'Just a minute.' Aaron handed her a key. 'In case we're in bed when you get back. After what you saw yesterday we're not leaving any doors unlocked.'

'What did she see?' Peggy asked sharply.

Emma waved her hand in a shooing motion. 'I'll tell her. You get off and have a lovely time, Mara.'

She turned to her daughter and explained what had happened.

Peggy blinked at her, for once not ready with a snippy answer, then asked, 'Where's Mara going? I thought she didn't know anyone in Australia.'

'She didn't when she arrived but she got on well with Hal yesterday, and he must have liked her too, because he's invited her out for a meal.'

The cloud descended quite visibly on Peggy's face. 'Lucky her!' She swayed a little and grabbed a chair back to steady herself.

'Are you all right?' Emma asked.

'Of course I am.' She turned to go upstairs, but had only gone a couple of paces when she let out a gasp, crumpled and fell. She lay still, not moving.

Aaron rushed across to kneel by his daughter, feeling her pulse. 'She's taking a long time to regain consciousness. Call an ambulance, Emma!'

'She won't want that.'

'She's not getting a choice. Besides, this is a chance to get her some much-needed medical attention.'

Unaware of what was going on in the house, Mara got outside just as Hal's garage door rolled upwards. As he reversed the car out another, much larger vehicle drove up behind him, blocking his exit.

A well-dressed woman got out and approached his car. 'Could you please spare a minute, Mr Kendrell?'

'No. I'm about to go out.' He gestured towards Mara.

'Oh, sorry. It's just that I have a suggestion to speed matters up for you. I was thinking you'd need to clear the house and I could help you with that. I've done it before and can work quickly. It'll save you time so that you can get on with your own life.'

He glared at her. 'I am getting on with my life and as I've already told you, I don't want to sell my house at present. What's more, if I ever do sell it, it won't be through someone who pesters me. Now, please leave.'

She hesitated, then shrugged and said, 'Don't hesitate to call me any time. My client is still very eager to buy this house.'

As she started to get back into her car, she paused for a moment to study Mara, giving her a sneering look as if finding her lacking in something.

Mara moved towards Hal's car. 'What's that about?'

'Estate agent trying to persuade me to sell the house. Second time she's turned up out of the blue.'

'Are you going to sell it?'

'I don't think so. I really like living by the water.'

He pressed the button that rolled his garage door down. 'I'll wait to see that it goes fully down before we leave. I'm being doubly careful from now on about security.'

'I should think so, too.' She looked along the street and saw that the estate agent had stopped to watch them.

As the door clicked into place, he turned to smile at her. 'Never mind about her. Tonight is for you and me. You look lovely.'

She could feel herself blushing as he set off. 'Oh. Well, thank you. So do you.'

He chuckled. 'I'm supposed to give you compliments, not vice versa.'

'I'm not fishing for praise.'

'I can't help complimenting you. You *do* look lovely, a real woman not a scrawny model type like the person who just left. Did you overhear what she said?'

'Yes. Her voice is quite, um, penetrating.'

'Got a horribly shrill edge to it. I don't like women of that type. You've got a nice low voice with a soft timbre.'

He gave Mara another of those approving looks which made her feel flustered. 'Right. Good. Thank you for your kind words, Hal. Now, enough of the compliments. Where are we going?'

'You said you liked Indian food so I found a place in town by looking online and booked a table. I don't know what the food will be like but the menu made my mouth water.'

'Ooh, good.'

When he didn't give her any more compliments she calmed down and by the time they arrived at the restaurant a few minutes later, she was feeling more herself again.

'There's no trouble finding parking when you go out early.' He locked up the car and offered her his hand.

She took it without thinking and didn't like to pull away when he kept a firm hold of it. Besides, she loved the warmth of his firm grasp as they strolled together towards the entrance to the restaurant, hand in hand.

They were shown to a table in one corner and an attentive waitress offered them menus, asking if they wanted poppadums and mango chutney to nibble on while they were sorting out what they wanted.

Hal raised one eyebrow at Mara and she nodded. 'Yes, please.'

'I'll go and get them while you look at the menu, sir, madam.'

'Do we share dishes or do you prefer to get your own, Mara?' he asked.

'I'd rather share.'

'So would I.'

It was fun choosing a range of dishes and by the time they ate the last of the poppadums, their starters were arriving.

The food was excellent, but the conversation was the thing she was enjoying most, she decided as the evening progressed. He'd led a far more interesting life than she had and was happy to talk about the countries he'd lived in. He didn't gush over what he'd seen like a tourist guide, but commented on the differences in how people lived, both the good and the bad aspects.

When she'd finished sharing a dessert of gulab jamun, she leant back and smiled at him. 'That was wonderful. I ate too much but I don't regret a mouthful.'

'Neither do I. It's great to see a woman who enjoys her food. I'm going to take the leftovers home. They're too good to waste.'

'I don't like to waste anything, ever.'

'Me neither.'

He looked at her as if wondering whether to say something.

'Go on,' she encouraged.

'Well, I wonder if I could ask your help with something I simply can't face doing. It was talking about waste that reminded me.'

'I will help if I can. What is it?'

'Clearing out my mother's clothes. I know it's a bit of a cheek but could you help me with that? I don't know enough about women's clothes to figure out what to do with them and which would be worth saving, but many of them seem hardly worn.'

'Yes, of course I'll help you. You're right not to chuck them away.'

'How can we tell whether anything is reusable?'

'You might not be able to, but I would. I volunteer, no, volunteered, past tense, because it was in London, at a charity shop. I've helped a few times with house clearances that people couldn't face when they lost a loved one. I don't know the situation here as well as I would in the UK, but we can check with a charity shop and find out what's sought after and what isn't.'

'Would you really do all that?' He took her hand and raised it to his lips. 'You just get nicer with keeping.'

Shivers ran through her again. 'Stop it! People are staring at us.'

'Let them stare.' He gave her one of his nice, earnest looks. 'Thank you for your offer, Mara. I'd really appreciate your help. You're an absolute treasure. And what I said about not wasting things goes for this evening as well. It's still quite early, and I'm having too good a time to part company yet. I hope you don't want to go straight home. We could have nightcaps at my place.'

'Fine by me. Then you can walk me all the way home.'

They both chuckled at that and the tension ebbed. When they left with the remaining food boxed up, he held her hand again for the short distance back to the car.

She'd have been disappointed if he hadn't done that. In fact, she marvelled at how well they got on as she settled in the car. He hadn't put a foot wrong tonight as far as she was concerned and she'd not been bored for a single minute. He was almost too good to be true. What a pity she hadn't met him in England. She'd be leaving here in a few weeks, so she mustn't get too involved.

And how silly was it to start thinking like that on their first date! He might not even invite her out again.

Mind you, if he didn't, she could always invite him out. She was a liberated modern woman, wasn't she?

Mostly.

Only she'd prefer it if he invited her.

It felt to Aaron as if it took for ever for the ambulance to arrive but at last it turned up. Although Peggy had regained consciousness by now, she still seemed spaced out. She hardly responded to the paramedics' questions when they came inside to check how she was.

One of them whispered to her parents that something wasn't right and she should definitely be taken to hospital and checked by the doctors there.

Normally Peggy would have asked to be told what they were saying about her, but she didn't even seem to notice what was going on.

Emma sat in the ambulance with her and Aaron drove behind them in his car. He didn't forget to lock up but it didn't occur to him to write a note to Mara till he was nearly at the hospital.

All he could think of was being with Emma to face whatever was happening to their daughter together. Peggy was so pale and quiescent, only seeming half-conscious. That was so unusual for her it had him terrified.

He found a parking place, queued impatiently to buy a parking token, then slipped it into his car and ran towards the A&E entrance.

He saw Emma standing near the counter looking lost and put one arm round her shoulders. 'What's going on?'

'They took her away, said I should sit down out

here and wait to be called.'

'Was she still conscious?'

'Only in the same way as before. She didn't try to talk, didn't seem fully aware of where she was or what was happening.'

He looked at her and though he didn't say it, he knew they were both fearing the worst, the very worst that can happen to any parent.

It was a while before someone called, 'Mr and Mrs Buchanan.' The woman at reception had to call out the name twice and beckon to them before they became aware that they were wanted.

'If you'll go around to that side door, I'll let you in.' She pointed to one side.

'How is she?' Emma asked.

But the clerk had already set off, so they hurried across to the door she'd pointed out.

She opened it from the other side and locked it carefully after they'd gone inside. 'Come this way. The doctor wants to see you.'

They were shown into a sort of waiting room which contained only a few chairs and a small table. A moment later a man in a white coat joined them and introduced himself as a doctor.

'Did you know your daughter wasn't eating properly?'

'Yes. We tried to persuade her, but to no avail.'

'What exactly happened today?'

'She refused to eat anything, as she has done when she's come home from work for the past few days, then all of a sudden she fainted. She looked ill, was slow to

recover and then still seemed out of it, so I called an
ambulance.'

'Good thing you did. Do you know anything about
anorexia?'

'We've been researching it.'

'Then I don't need to explain how serious it can be.
And in your daughter's case, combined with pregnancy—'

'*What?*'

He looked surprised. 'Didn't she tell you? Oh dear. It
showed up in one of our tests and I just assumed . . . With
a bit of luck, if we can build her up again physically, the
baby may be all right. Does its father know she's here?'

And Emma didn't think twice about telling a lie. 'We
don't know who the father is. She broke up with her
former partner a while ago, so I doubt it's his.'

To her relief, Aaron didn't contradict her or give
anything away. The last thing she wanted, the very last,
was to get that selfish pig of a man involved with Peggy
again. He might have a good-looking face but he was
rotten inside, rotten to the core.

'I see. Well, we've got her on a drip and we're going
to try to feed her small amounts of a special food. You
can take a quick peep at her, then I'm afraid you'll have
to wait outside again. I've just called in one of our nurses
who specialises in that problem.'

They looked at him mutely, not knowing what to say
or do for the best.

'Actually, you should go home and phone when you
get up in the morning to see if we're allowing visitors.
Check that the admissions clerk here in A&E has your

contact information before you leave.'

When he'd gone, Aaron said, 'I think we should do what he suggested and go home, love. If they aren't letting us go near her, there's no point in staying. We need to be clear-headed before we see her tomorrow.'

They said very little until they got into the car, then he asked, 'Do you think she knows she's pregnant?'

'I doubt it. I bet she forgot to take the pill and if she's anything like me, that was enough to put her at risk.'

He groaned. 'Pregnant. What the hell will she do next?'

'Whatever it is, it won't be half as dramatic as tonight. I don't think anything could top that!'

'Good, because I don't ever want to have to face that again. I thought she'd died.'

She shivered. 'So did I.'

'Well, whatever it is, we'll find a way to help her.'

'If she'll let us.'

They both sighed at that.

Chapter Fourteen

When Mara and Hal went into his house, the relaxed pleasure of the evening was spoilt abruptly because they found that someone had smashed one of the big canal-side windows. It was badly crazed from what looked like repeated blows.

'Stay back!' he called out as they took in the damage.

She studied the broken window. 'Did they actually get inside? There isn't a hole in it.'

They both studied the area, then he said, 'I don't think they did, but I'll just check the other rooms to be sure they didn't break in some other way. Be ready to run outside and yell for help if I find anyone lurking. I warn you now, I'm not the world's best fighter.'

He was brave enough to take on the dangerous job of searching the house, though, she thought, praying he'd be safe.

He called out as he moved quickly in and out of the downstairs spaces. 'All clear here – and here. No sign of entry or damage downstairs. I'm going upstairs. Yes, all clear here as well.'

Then he rejoined her. 'You were right. They don't seem to have got inside. Mum said when she moved in she'd had the security beefed up. I wonder if she had special toughened glass fitted or a film put on it, or whether it was like that already. Whatever, it looks as if it did its job. I think I'd better call the police.'

'And we shouldn't touch anything.'

They were told to wait for some officers to arrive. He put the phone down and looked at her ruefully. 'Damn! I was looking forward to kissing your socks off.'

The thought of that made it hard for her to breathe evenly for a few seconds. 'Another time, maybe.'

'Definitely.'

She glanced out towards her own house. Something had been bothering her and she suddenly realised what. 'That's strange.'

'What is?'

'There are no lights on next door. I know Aaron and Emma weren't planning to go out because earlier on they were discussing which film to watch tonight. And it's far too early for them to be in bed. I might just nip across and see if everything is all right.'

He grabbed her arm. 'Not on your own, you won't. In fact, you and I shouldn't do anything till after the police have had a look round, both inside and out. Apart from your own safety considerations, you might disturb some evidence out there.'

She stilled, still worried, but he was only being sensible. She'd never had anything to do with a break-in before and now she'd been involved in two attempts.

When she nodded, he let go of her arm and she stayed where she was.

She hated the thought of someone invading another person's home and stealing their possessions. Didn't such thieves realise how cruel they were being towards their victims? Or were they so horrible they didn't care? If so, they were only half-price humans as far as she was concerned.

All she could do as they waited was keep looking next door in case Aaron and Emma had come back. And each time everything was still in darkness. She was getting to know their ways and they'd have plenty of lights on by now if they were home, even though it wasn't fully dark, because Aaron hated dim lighting after dusk.

Once the hospital had found Peggy a bed in a special unit for people with eating disorders and installed her there, the doctor came in to check her properly. He was glad to see that his favourite nurse was in attendance. He hesitated, then decided to step back a little and let Sarisha try to work her magic, though he'd keep an eye on the situation, of course. He'd known this particular nurse persuade patients to do what was needed when everyone else had failed, himself included. No one succeeded in helping everyone, but she had a higher rate of success than most.

'Let me tell you what's wrong with her.' He took her out of earshot and gave a quick run-down on not only the patient's condition but what the parents had said about her. 'Will you see if you can persuade Peggy to eat some of our special food, Sarisha? It won't be easy but if anyone can do it, you can. If we're to keep that baby healthy we don't have time for weeks of counselling.'

'I'll do my best.'

'If she refuses to eat, call me, but I think softly, softly is the best way to nip this in the bud, and you'll be around more often so will be able to do that better than I would. At least this woman hasn't been anorexic for years, only apparently for a few months, after falling for a man who prefers scrawny women.'

They both grimaced at that then the nurse gave him a motherly smile. 'I'll certainly try my best. There are no guarantees, but having four daughters of my own has taught me a lot about young women and their desperate desire for a mate. Or, as time goes on, there can be a longing for a child.'

When someone insisted Peggy sit up, helped her to do it then held out a spoon to her, she shook her head automatically. 'Not hungry. Um, where am I?'

'You're in hospital because you fainted and you're still drifting in and out of consciousness.'

'I don't want to be here.'

'Of course you don't. No one wants to be in hospital. But there are complications in your condition that make it necessary, I'm afraid.'

That caught Peggy's attention. 'What do you mean by "complications"?'

'They did tell you but I don't think it sank in. Please listen very carefully for a minute or two, then think twice before you push the spoon away again.'

She glared at it. 'I'm *not* hungry.'

'The main complication is that you're pregnant.'

Peggy felt the room whirl round her. 'What?'

Somehow she couldn't ignore that gentle but firm voice. This wasn't a young nurse; this was an older woman, one who seemed to exude authority – and motherly kindness too.

'Weren't you taking precautions, Peggy?'

'I'd stopped taking the pill, but the pregnancy could only just have happened.'

'Well, we'll have to do something about your other problem now, for the baby's sake. According to your parents, you don't seem to be eating. Anorexia won't give your baby the nourishment it needs to develop properly.'

'I'm not anorexic, just looking after my health.'

'This isn't healthy.' She held up Peggy's arm. 'Compare it to mine.'

Peggy looked at it. Her arm seemed thinner than usual and there was a drip in it. If only her head would stop aching. She couldn't seem to think clearly.

'If there are no complications, why are you here?

We're short of places in hospitals. The last thing we want is unnecessary patients. As I said before, you fainted and you didn't regain full consciousness for far too long.'

The woman's kind, dark eyes seemed to catch her gaze and hold it. Peggy couldn't believe she was being told lies by someone with such an honest face.

'Things have changed for you now, Peggy. There's not only yourself to think about. If you keep refusing food your baby might not survive.'

She mouthed the word 'baby' then said slowly, 'I still can't believe I really am pregnant.'

Sarisha reached out and took Peggy's nearest hand between both hers. 'I'm on your side, my dear. I know the joy of having children because I've had four. But even more importantly, I'm on the baby's side. It can't speak for itself but it deserves to live, don't you think?'

'Yes, of course.'

'Just try one bite. Please.'

She held out the spoon again and it was so small, with just a little food that looked like porridge on it, that Peggy had opened her mouth and swallowed it before she thought what she was doing.

'I don't want to get fat,' she warned.

'I agree absolutely.'

She hadn't expected that and stared at the nurse.

'It wouldn't be good for the baby if you got fat, so I agree absolutely.'

'You do?'

'Of course. A healthy weight is important to you both.

Now, have a good long drink of water for me. You need to rehydrate as well.'

And once again, Peggy found herself obeying. Well, water wasn't fattening, was it?

'Just swallow a few half teaspoons of this and I'll stop pestering you.'

The nurse chatted gently about when her own children were babies as she slowly fed Peggy a few small mouthfuls, then put the spoon down. 'There. That's enough for now.'

Outside the door another nurse shook her head in disbelief and looked at the doctor, who had stayed to check. 'How does she do it?'

'I don't know, but I'm glad she sometimes manages where others fail.' He glanced at his watch. 'I've got other patients waiting. Can you keep an eye on them in case Sarisha asks for help and fetch me at once if I'm needed. This could be a turning point for that young woman.'

After the food, Peggy closed her eyes, and that gentle voice said, 'You should try to get a little sleep now. I'll stay here with you, shall I?'

Sarisha watched the patient's breathing slow down. Peggy looked pale, exhausted and horribly frail. She didn't answer the question but she kept a tight hold of Sarisha's hand.

When she woke again Peggy asked, 'How long have I been asleep?'

Sarisha lied to her without blinking. 'Two hours. Time for a tiny bit more food, don't you think?'

'Only a little.'

'Of course. Your food has to be measured carefully because as I said before we don't want a pregnant woman to get fat. But the baby needs nourishment so you'll have to eat a little more than usual.'

'I didn't dream it, did I? I really am expecting a baby?'

'Yes. I envy you.'

'*You* do?'

'Yes. I loved having children. But my husband said no more after we'd had four daughters, and he was probably right. Does your guy want children?'

'No. And we've split up.'

'Poor thing. He doesn't know what he'll be missing. Still, I gather you've got family to help you? Am I right?'

'I suppose.'

'And you're a modern young woman. You'll manage just fine.' She fed her more of the food, chatting gently, then said, 'That's enough for now. Look, I have to take a break but I'll call my friend Annie in to sit with you for a while. I'll just go and fetch her.'

After a hurried consultation outside the door about making sure the patient didn't try to vomit up the food, she brought another woman in.

'You'll come back?' Peggy asked Sarisha.

'Of course I will. I want to help you give that baby a healthy start. Don't worry. I'll stop them trying to feed you too much.' She winked at her colleague and left.

Peggy lay in bed, closing her eyes but not dozing this time. She had too much to think about. Was it really possible that she was pregnant? She'd been desperately wanting a baby for the past few months; she didn't know why, she just had.

They wouldn't tell her that if it wasn't true, surely? No, of course not, and anyway she trusted Sarisha far more than she trusted doctors.

What would Mike say about it?

It took a few minutes of fighting tears before she could face the truth: he'd say to get rid of the baby. It only took a few seconds longer for her to add mentally that she would never do that.

Another thought crept into her mind: he'd think she'd got pregnant on purpose and would probably claim that he wasn't the father. It could only be his, though.

She pressed both hands to her belly, feeling protective in a way she'd never experienced before. What could Mike actually do about preventing her from having the baby? Nothing.

She'd been hoping against hope that he'd marry her, but he'd been absolutely scathing about 'golden shackles' and had told her he wanted to split up because she was getting too clingy. Give the rat his due. He'd always made it clear that marriage wasn't on the cards. The trouble was, he could say such charming, romantic things when he wanted to make love that she'd started to hope she was his special woman, the one who changed his mind.

It took her a while longer to admit to herself that even if he was forced to take responsibility for the baby, he'd make her life a misery about it because he wasn't a big earner. And she was quite sure he wouldn't want her to move back in with him and bring the baby.

She'd seen him swerve to avoid approaching a baby or small child at one of his family functions. They'd had a big argument once when she stopped to chat to his cousin's two-year-old, who'd only wanted to show them her toy rabbit.

It was as if she was seeing Mike clearly for the first time. Oh, what a fool she'd been to keep on hoping he'd change. He hadn't lied to her; she'd lied to herself.

She rubbed her aching forehead as memories played back at her, and then suddenly she began to sob. What was she going to do? How would she cope?

Then arms went round her and she knew Sarisha had come back. 'I must be – the most stupid woman – on the whole planet to have got together with him.'

Soft laughter surprised her. 'There are a lot of women stupid enough to fall in love with the wrong man. And vice versa. What matters now is whether you're stupid enough to stay fixated on your fellow.' She patted the bedcovers above Peggy's stomach. 'Or are you going to put your little one first?' She waited and leant sideways to get a tissue from the box beside the bed. 'Here. Blow your nose and think about your baby. He or she needs some more food.'

That caught Peggy's attention. Was it a girl or a boy? She'd love it already whichever it was.

Sarisha now had a small pot in her hand. 'Here we

go. Just a few more mouthfuls. For the baby's sake. It's a sort of fancy yoghurt.'

'No sugar in it?'

'Perish the thought.'

'What exactly is in it?'

She lied again. 'A special low-calorie protein.'

When Aaron and Emma got home they saw a police car outside the house next door, its lights flashing.

'What the hell has happened now?' He waited impatiently for the garage door to rise, and could immediately see that the lights weren't on in the living area.

'Where's Mara? Shouldn't she be home by now? It's too early for her to have gone to bed, surely?'

'You'd think so. She wouldn't be sitting in the dark, though. Perhaps she's still with Hal next door.'

'That's where the police are.'

He didn't wait for the garage door to finish going down but rushed out to the patio. When Mara wasn't anywhere to be seen he headed next door, stopping dead with one leg over the wall when he saw the window that someone had tried to smash. 'Look at that!'

Emma joined him as a police officer came across to them. 'And you are, sir?'

'We're the neighbours and – Oh, there you are, Mara. Are you all right?'

'I'm fine.'

'What's happened?'

'We came back to find that someone had tried to break in. Hal is just answering a few questions.'

The officer looked from her to Aaron. 'No need to tell me that you're a relative of this gentleman.'

'He's my father.'

In spite of the seriousness of the situation, Aaron beamed at her.

It was half an hour before the police had finished asking questions and checking for fingerprints.

One of the officers said, 'The intruders didn't get inside so there's no need for us to bring a forensics team to check the interior. We'll put the word out to keep an eye open for canal break-ins and if you hear any suspicious noises or you're bothered again in any way, please call us at once.'

Hal nodded. 'I shan't hesitate. I'll have to find someone to repair that window ASAP. I wonder where to get that glass. It might be among my mother's paperwork.'

The other officer was answering a call and turned to his colleague. 'Traffic accident just south of the bridge. Can we attend?'

'Yes.'

'Sorry, sir, they want us to leave straight away.'

When he'd seen them out, Hal came back and looked at the others. 'Please sit down. I need a drink. Can I get you folk anything?'

'A whisky would be lovely,' Emma said. 'It's been one of those evenings! We had an unexpected visit to the hospital.'

Mara stiffened. 'Are you both all right?'

'It was for Peggy. She fainted.'

'May I interrupt a minute? My mother only had one sort of whisky.' Hal showed her the bottle.

'That'll do fine. I'm not a snob about what I drink.'

'I'd prefer a beer,' Aaron said. 'If you haven't got any, I'll nip next door and fetch some. I've got plenty at home.'

'I do have a couple of bottles.' Hal smiled. 'But that's all. It depends how drunk you want to get. Go on. Tell us about your evening. What was wrong with your daughter?'

When they'd all brought each other up to date, Emma nudged Aaron with her elbow. 'Time we older folk were getting to bed now.'

But to her disappointment, Mara stood up as well. 'I think we could all do with an early night.'

Hal walked to the door with them, hesitated, then grabbed Mara's arm and waited till his neighbours had tactfully led the way into their house. 'Did you mean it about helping me with Mum's clothes?'

'Yes, of course I did.'

'Then I'll see you in the morning perhaps?'

'About ten be all right? I want to find out how Peggy is before I start.'

'That'd be fine.'

He walked slowly back inside and sat for a long time with an untasted refill of his drink in his hand, trying to work out why someone would be targeting him. Or perhaps they were targeting his house?

Yes, that might be it. The person wanting to buy it had sent an agent to approach him as soon as he arrived, so he must be extremely eager. And the would-be buyer's real estate agent had already approached him again. That didn't necessarily mean they were behind this, but he felt they were the most likely. Who else could be causing trouble? He didn't know anyone in Mandurah except for his neighbours and he couldn't imagine his quiet, reclusive mother making enemies.

Did this person really think he'd sell the house out of fear of intruders? He must be crazy.

Hal yawned. He'd not learn anything by sitting here, so he went up to bed, setting the alarm system for the rest of the house after he'd locked the door of his suite. He was really glad to have that protection, would be much more careful to use it from now on. He'd been lulled into a false sense of security by the peaceful surroundings, should have known better.

Unfortunately he didn't have any protection from his thoughts, which stopped him falling asleep easily. He was sorry the incident had spoilt the rest of his evening with Mara. You couldn't mistake it when someone was as attracted to you as you were to them. Early stages, but still, there it was. He didn't intend to let the opportunity to get to know her slip.

He really liked her. As well as being attractive physically, she had an honesty and openness to her that he really appreciated.

His thoughts kept going back to the attempted break-ins. First thing tomorrow he'd go online and see what he could find out about the real estate agency that had sent a rep to approach him, and the rep herself.

And then after that . . . he yawned, snuggled down a little and let the world slip gently away.

Chapter Fifteen

Peggy woke late, for her. Nearly nine o'clock by the numerals on the dial next to her bed. Hold on! That wasn't her clock, and where was that beeping coming from? So annoying.

It took a few minutes for her to remember where she was and why. By that time a nurse had come in and was taking her blood pressure, promising to bring in a light breakfast shortly.

'I'm not hungry,' she said automatically, then hesitated. 'But perhaps I'll just eat a few mouthfuls.'

The nurse wasn't anything like Sarisha and gave her a disapproving look but didn't say anything else.

Peggy forced down a few spoonfuls of the same mush and asked if she could have something more healthy to eat next time, like fruit.

'I can get you a banana now, if you like, but only if you eat all your porridge first.'

She sat staring at it for a while, then managed to choke the rest down. She had to lean back against her pillows for a while afterwards, feeling like throwing up, but then she remembered the baby and the quick rush of joy banished the remaining nausea.

She unpeeled one end of the banana. She wasn't hungry now but Sarisha was right: the baby would need her to eat more. She took a bite and then forced down a couple more mouthfuls until a voice made her jump.

'Hi, Pegs.'

She looked up to see her brother standing in the doorway, and why the sight of him should bring tears to her eyes, she couldn't think. 'Rufus. Come in.'

'I will if you'll finish eating that banana.'

'I can't. I had a whole bowl of mush first.'

He came across and gave her one of his rare hugs. 'You've let that sod brainwash you about food. Just because he's a walking skeleton doesn't mean the rest of the world has to be.'

She could only shrug and took another small bite of banana to hide her inability to respond as sharply as usual. Rufus had said the same thing several times before.

'Does Mike know about the baby?' he asked.

'No. How do you know?'

'Mum phoned me. I got worried about you, so Jenn said I should come and visit you to set my mind at rest.'

'If you had to be forced to come, you needn't have bothered.'

'She didn't force me, you idiot, no one needed to do

that. I thought if I could see you were all right, I might manage not to punch Mike in the face next time I run into him.'

She gaped at him. Rufus had never got into fights, not even when he was younger and less in control of his temper.

He shrugged. 'I know. Fighting is so not me. But you're my sister and my disgust with that fellow is rather strong, so for once it'd give me a great deal of satisfaction to wallop him. I'd be quite safe. He's a real limp lettuce physically. Makes me feel like Tarzan.'

'He's lean and toned.'

'No way. He's scraggy and skeletal. There's nothing toned about that oik. When does he ever do any exercise? And don't you dare let him take you over again. I lost my sister for a while there.'

'You needn't worry. I'm not even going to try to go back to him because he wouldn't want the baby – and I do. Very much.'

'Good. I brought you the traditional hospital present.' He picked up his shoulder bag and pulled out a paper bag containing a small bunch of grapes.

She stared at them. They were full of sugar, but also vitamins, and she need only eat a few at a time. 'Thank you.'

'If you eat one now I can have one too.' He plucked one off the bunch and held it towards her mouth.

She forced herself to eat it and was surprised that she'd forgotten how nice they tasted. How long was it since she'd eaten a grape? 'Only the one. I've just finished a huge breakfast.'

'OK.' He ate one and nodded. 'Mmm. They're good. I might buy another bunch on the way home. Jenn likes grapes, too.'

'You're all settled in with her now?'

'We're still getting used to one another's small ways. I wouldn't call that "settled in". But it's a promising start and I hope we'll end up together.'

His smile at the thought of his partner was so fond that Peggy felt like weeping with jealousy and had to dig her fingernails into the palms of her hands to keep her emotions under control.

'When Mum told me you were going to make me an uncle, I felt very happy. Hopefully it'll be a girl and won't look at all like Mr Scarecrow.' He chuckled. 'Remember how you used to call them "squarecroaks" when you were little.'

She couldn't help chuckling at that, then her smile faded. 'You never did like Mike, did you?'

'No. Are you really not going back to him?'

'He wouldn't have me and anyway, he loathes the idea of having children. I do want them. So very much. What sort of life would this poor thing have even if he did take me back?'

'A very unhappy one. And so would you. Don't do it, Pegs.'

'Don't worry. I won't. I've already worked that out. The baby comes first from now on.'

After he'd been there for a few minutes, Sarisha

bustled into the room. 'You're looking a lot better this morning, Peggy.' She turned to Rufus. 'Time's up, Mr Buchanan. Ten minutes is long enough until your sister has her body functioning properly again.'

When he'd gone, she produced what looked like a jelly baby sweet.

'I shan't be eating any sweets,' Peggy said firmly.

'This isn't a sweet; it's a vitamin pill in disguise. We give them to children this way, but I think you'll digest this type better than the standard pill.'

She didn't want to put anything else into her mouth. 'I've just had a huge breakfast. Can't that thing wait till later?'

'Not if you want to build yourself up a bit and be released into the wild again.'

'What do you mean by that? I can release myself at any time.'

'I don't think you're that stupid. Your mother has arranged for us to keep you here in our special unit for a while.'

'What's special about it?'

'It's for anorexics at risk because of other factors. Until you prove that you can manage your body properly, you really do need to stay here. You said you wanted the baby. Didn't you mean it?'

'Of course I did.'

'Good. The dietician will work with you to make sure you eat super-healthily and that you're eating enough. We'll be monitoring the baby's progress as well as yours.'

'Or I could just walk out and choose my own food.'

'And look where that's brought you. Would you really do that to your baby? It can't grow properly without nourishment. Not to mention how it'd affect your parents, who're outside now, anxiously waiting their turn to see you.'

'Oh, very well. I suppose I'll stay on for a while. I trust you not to let me get fat, though.'

That firm hand came down on hers. 'No one who works here will try to make you fat, I promise. Fat isn't healthy either. Now, swallow that vitamin then let me show in your parents.'

'I feel such a fool winding up here. What shall I say to Mum and Dad?'

Sarisha smiled. 'They'll probably hog the conversation telling you how worried they've been. Just say you're sorry. Ask them to tell you about the excitement at your new neighbour's last night.' On that she whisked out of the room.

Footsteps heralded the arrival of Peggy's parents and somehow she got through the short visit without upsetting them still further.

She couldn't believe there had been an attempted break-in next door, or that Mara, who seemed rather quiet and plump, had been out with Hal Kendrell, the poet's son. What could he see in a podge like her?

By the time they left she was ready for a nap and this quiet place was perfect for it. Her visit from her parents had made her realise that she didn't want to go home until she could cope with other people hovering over her and pestering her to eat.

She drifted into a favourite fantasy, wishing she could find a cave deep in a green, leafy forest and hibernate there for a while, especially now, when she needed to adjust to such important new parameters to her life.

Should she tell Mike about the baby? On the one hand, it seemed only fair; on the other, he might – no, make that *would* create a fuss about it, or even try to cause trouble for her.

How quickly her life was changing and with it, her attitude to Mike.

She not only wanted that baby very much indeed, she didn't want him coming anywhere near it.

Mara woke up the morning after the attempted break-in feeling happy. While the evening had brought trouble, it had also brought her a new friendship. She really liked Hal, with his quiet, unassuming ways and his lovely tall body. She was looking forward to spending the day with him.

The main cloud on the horizon was still there, however. When she phoned her father, she once again got no answer and had to leave another message. Was her mother deleting the messages?

If she didn't catch him in today, she was going to phone the neighbour and ask Sally to check on him. They'd been living next door to one another for many years and Mara was very fond of her, as if she was an honorary aunt.

Why hadn't she thought of Sally before? She'd be ideally situated to judge the situation and find out if Mara needed to go home.

When she got up, she found that once again she was the only one awake. Well, Rufus was living with Jenn now and Peggy was in hospital, so of course the house was going to be quieter. No one now had to rush to get to work.

She had a nectarine as a breakfast starter, murmuring in pleasure as juice dripped down her chin. She was just wondering whether to scramble some eggs for breakfast when Aaron came down. He was looking bleary-eyed, as if he hadn't slept well.

'You need a cup of coffee. Sit down and I'll make it.'

'Would you mind bringing it to me in the office? Something cropped up overnight.'

'Not Peggy?'

'No, no. Emma's just phoning the hospital now to check on her but they'd have contacted us if there were any problems. No, this is to do with my business. Things are getting rather complicated.'

Looking worried, he walked away before she could ask what exactly had happened. It must be something serious, she decided as she waited for the kettle to boil.

As she was making the coffee, Emma came down to join her, looking happier than yesterday.

'Is Peggy all right?'

'Yes. And they've managed to persuade her to eat several small snacks. Isn't that wonderful?'

Fancy having to be persuaded to eat, Mara thought, but didn't say it. She knew she was lucky with her metabolism when so many people were fighting weight gain.

She finished making the coffee. 'Aaron asked me to take this into his office. Do you want to do that or shall I?'

'I'd better do it. He's trying to get out of flying over to Sydney, but I doubt he'll manage it. That's going to upset him, because he wanted to spend as much time as possible with you.'

Oh dear! What would she do with herself if that happened? Mara wondered.

She waited till Emma came back to ask if anyone else would like breakfast.

'Good idea. Would you mind scrambling enough for all three of us? I'm sorry to tell you Aaron has no choice about going over there. One of his key workers had already resigned and now a guy has fallen down some steps yesterday and broken his leg *and* one wrist. Pete's in hospital and there's a possible buyer for the business on the horizon who needs showing round by someone who can give explanations and answer questions.'

'Oh. I see.'

'I hope you'll forgive him. Aaron's really upset at the thought of leaving you.'

'I can entertain myself. I shall be out of your hair today anyway because I've arranged to help Hal with clearing out his mother's clothes.'

'He seems a nice guy. Quiet but not as reclusive as his mother.'

'Yes. He's good company, so don't worry about me.'

'I wouldn't anyway. You're a very easy and considerate guest.' She turned to leave then swung round. 'Have you heard from your father yet? The English one, I mean, of course.'

'No. If I don't catch Dad later today, I'm going to ring our neighbour.'

Mike took his new potential girlfriend out for a meal, guiding her carefully to choose the lowest calorie dishes. Gina was a bit overweight, but he could soon help her to lose the flab.

Unfortunately, she wouldn't be guided as to the choices on the menu, and when a huge plateful of food was placed in front of her, she ate it with relish, clearing the whole plate.

'Peggy wouldn't have eaten that much,' he said disapprovingly. 'Women of your age have to be careful with their weight, you know. It can creep up on people.'

Gina leant back in her chair, looking at him thoughtfully. 'This is bizarre. After inviting me out to dinner, you've spent the whole time trying to persuade me not to eat. And to make sure I don't enjoy it to the full, putting on weight is all you've talked about.'

He stiffened. 'I do know something about nutrition. It's a particular interest of mine.'

'Is that why you're so scrawny?'

He scowled at her. 'I am *not* scrawny. I'm lean and toned.'

'You are extremely scrawny. I didn't realise how bad till I saw you in that outfit. And actually, I didn't know when I accepted your invitation that you were Peggy Buchanan's ex. Someone told me your attitude to food is why she's in hospital at the moment.'

That startled him. 'She's in hospital? Are you sure? Why?'

'She's been eating so little she fainted and didn't regain consciousness properly.'

'Rubbish. Peggy has been eating very healthily for the past few months.'

'Nope. She was badly malnourished. They were afraid she'd lose the baby, she was so thin.'

He stared at her, unable to form a word, so shocked was he at the word 'baby'.

Gina finished off the food on her plate and stood up. 'Thank you for my meal but I'm ending our association now. You talk a good talk when you invite someone out for dinner. But you're very boring, the way you go on and on about food. I'm surprised your ex stayed with you for so long.'

'Wait!' he said, grabbing her arm. 'How did you know Peggy was in hospital?'

'I work there, though I shouldn't have said anything to you. It just slipped out, you being her ex. I hope you don't get her back and then starve the baby as well.' She shook his hand off. 'Do not call me again!'

Mike sat there, shocked to the core, as she walked out.

'Have you finished, sir?'

He looked at the waitress and nodded, even though his plate was still half full, then got up and paid for the meal.

When he got outside he sat in his car for ages before he started it up and drove slowly home.

He spent the rest of the evening in front of a muted

television, though he normally watched the late-night news avidly. Could it be true about Peggy expecting a baby? It must be. Why else would Gina say it?

How could that possibly have happened?

He went up to bed at his usual time, but lay awake for ages. All he could think of was that he'd have to go to the hospital in the morning and see Peggy, persuade her to get rid of it. The last thing he wanted, the very last, was to be stuck for the next twenty years paying maintenance, or even worse living with a child.

Surely she'd see sense? She'd always been very persuadable when they were together.

He slept badly, tossing and turning, and the night seemed interminable.

He should have had a vasectomy years ago, then he'd have been safe. But he didn't like the risks associated with even minor operations. And he'd always been very careful to avoid hospitals. Such sources of infection!

Peggy must have forgotten to take the pill, damn her. That was the only explanation. She must be very fertile.

He could fix it, would fix it. This was not going to happen.

Chapter Sixteen

When Mara went next door at ten a.m. precisely, Hal greeted her with a quick peck on the cheek. He was looking apprehensive and making only a poor attempt at a smile. Clearly, sorting out his mother's clothes was a big worry for him.

She'd not have felt the same if she had to clear out her own mother's things because Kath didn't own much and had everything rigidly organised. She had complained several times about the amount of 'rubbish' Mara insisted on keeping when she came back home, and Mara had wisely kept her suitcase and trunk locked, because she knew her mother searched her bedroom regularly.

She hadn't realised what a relief it would be to come to Australia, not only because she was delighted to meet her birth father but also to escape the non-stop nagging, which had been getting her down since she moved back.

She threaded her arm through Hal's. 'Show me her

room, then if you want to leave me to it, tell me what sort of things you might wish to keep and I'll set them aside for you to check later. You can get on with something else meanwhile.'

'I think I'd better stay with you. As far as I can work out, I may have to decide about something specific at any moment because I know so little of what she might have in there. It's not that I don't trust your judgement but I can't think what sort of things I might like to keep yet. If anything. But getting the clothes and whatever else we find sorted out will give me a good start.'

He gave her a wry look and added, 'Frankly, the thought of sorting through my mother's underwear and other intimate clothes creeps me out big time. I'm being unreasonable, I know, but there you are, that's how I feel. I don't want to touch them, even.'

'That's all right. It won't worry me.'

'When we've finished, I'll leave it to you to tell me what's worth sending to a charity shop and what needs throwing away.'

She looked round with interest as they walked up the broad stairs. 'This is a beautiful house, up here as well as downstairs, even with so little furniture in it. Why is that, do you know?'

'I think she only bought what she would need to live here alone. She never liked to waste money.'

Mara stopped and gestured with one hand. 'I love that stained glass panel in the landing window. It throws jewel colours everywhere.'

'I agree. I thought at first when the lawyer told me

I'd inherited it that I'd sell the house, but even after such a short time, I'm wondering whether to make it my permanent home.'

'Who wouldn't want to do that? It has a lovely atmosphere. And I envy you living close to the water, with dolphins and pelicans calling to visit. Watching the sunsets reflected in the canal would be really hard to take, too. I should think your mother enjoyed her time here greatly.' She was pleased to see him relax a little more at that thought.

'Yes. You're right. She wrote to me every Friday and regularly mentioned that sort of thing.' He stopped and took a deep breath. 'Here we are.' He opened the door and stood aside to let Mara go in first.

'Oh, what a lovely set of colours in those curtains! So subtle and yet they seem to tie in with the sunshine and water outside. Do you think she designed the décor herself?'

'Probably. When I was a boy, she used to earn her living in a department store helping people choose their furnishings. Creating harmonious interiors remained a minor interest of hers. But at the same time as her poetry took off, a few of her investments from the money her parents had left her also hit the jackpot, and she stopped going out to work for others. You don't think of poets being financially savvy, do you, but she was very shrewd.'

'It's going to be such a pity if someone redoes this beautiful room.'

He looked round. 'The someone who makes that decision will probably be me and I wouldn't change a thing. You're right. It is beautiful. Only I'll feel better coming in here once I've cleared her personal stuff out. It always feels as though there's a ghost lingering in the cupboards and drawers.'

'If there is, it'd be a friendly one. No one who wrote poetry as beautiful as hers could possibly be nasty.'

He gave her a slightly surprised look. 'You're very perceptive. I think she'd have liked you. You seem similar to her in that you're not nasty-minded about anything. You have such an open, friendly expression most of the time that I bet people trust you instinctively.'

That was the sort of compliment that pleased her most. Looks could fade but character could remain vibrant till you fell off your perch. She knew one or two older neighbours in their eighties who were wonderfully alive at heart, even though they'd slowed down physically.

'Well, thanks to my birth father's generosity, I'm getting the chance to live in this beautiful place even if it's only temporarily. Having to go back and live with my mother again when I lost my job was . . . well, let's be polite and call it difficult.'

'That's being polite?'

'Yes. She has a personality disorder and sets rigid rules for living for everyone. She thought I'd obey them like Dad does but I wouldn't . . . couldn't. I choose my own path through life, and that includes my own possessions and clothes.'

'Why did you stay with them, then?'

'The usual reason: lack of money. I'd just invested most of my savings in the raw materials for a business

I was going to start up when I was made redundant. I simply couldn't afford the expense of living in London.'

'You *were* going to start up a business? Past tense?'

'Yes. Part-time at first. Only I need to support myself till it starts making money. I was going to ask if I could change to part-time work. I'm not greedy for clothes and all that ephemeral rubbish so I don't need a big income, but I'm rather fond of eating every day, as well as paying my rent and buying the raw materials.'

'May I ask what the business was, or is?'

She usually told people she'd reveal all when her project got going, but somehow she trusted Hal not to ridicule her secret passion, so launched into a halting explanation of the possibilities of creating artistic collectible toys, or ornaments, or whatever you called them, handmade and one-offs. She knew she had a gift for making delightful little toy creatures, had been selling them to acquaintances and online for a while. But she hadn't been able to create and make enough to live off, let alone get ahead of herself and build up stocks.

'Do you have any of them with you?'

'Just one small teddy bear. He was one of the first I made with top quality materials – the very best mohair fur.' She had lost count of the number of people who'd offered to buy him, but she could never part with him.

'May I see it?'

'*Him.*'

'Sorry, him.'

'You can't be interested in luxury collectible toys?'

'I'd like to see your work. And actually, I've always

been rather fond of teddy bears.'

'OK. I'll get Archibald out to show you later.'

He chuckled. '*Archibald?*'

She could feel herself flushing. 'Yes. They all seem to have names already and he became Archibald as soon as I put his face together. He's a lilac-coloured bear wearing full evening dress. I even managed to make a top hat, though I had to leave that behind. It was too fragile to survive being crammed into a suitcase.'

She could see that he was about to ask more questions so said firmly, 'Now, let's get back to these beautiful clothes.'

Not waiting for his agreement, she began to go through the clothes hanging in the wardrobe, checking each one as she slid the hangers to and fro, in order to see them more clearly.

He started to speak as she came to the end of them but she held up one hand to stop him and went back to the beginning, studying some of them more carefully. Some of them were not ordinary chain-store clothes.

After a few moments' thought she began laying the better ones out on the bed and when she'd done that, she cleared her throat to get Hal's attention because he had crossed to the window to stare out at the water.

He turned round. 'Finished?'

'No. Just had a thought I need to run past you. Would you be prepared to put on an online auction of your mother's better clothes in aid of some suitable charity? Trust me, Hal, these are too expensive and beautiful to sell for peanuts in a cheapie charity shop, and most are hardly worn. Would she have minded that idea, do you think?'

He stood with his head on one side, considering that, then walked slowly along the clothes lying on the bed, staring at them, fingering a few. When he'd finished, he looked up and beamed at her. 'I think she'd have absolutely loved it. She always dressed exquisitely. And she had a couple of charities she supported regularly so we could give the proceeds to them. How would we arrange an auction, though?'

'I have connections who could help. They're a start-up company and they're in the UK, but they'd be working online. They'd need a percentage of the takings because obviously they have to eat too. But they'd make far more than you ever could so that wouldn't matter too much. They're not greedy and a good chunk of money would go to the charity or charities you nominate.'

She held her breath and waited for his answer.

'That's a wonderful idea. You seem full of them.'

'Full of ideas?'

'Yes. A lateral thinker.'

She dropped him a mock curtsey. 'I always do my best to please, sir!'

That brought one of those warm smiles to his face.

'You'd better go next door, tell her yourself and say goodbye properly,' Emma told Aaron.

He sighed. 'I feel so guilty at leaving her when she's only been here for a few days.'

'You won't be away for more than a day or two, a

week at most. I can look after her. She's an easy guest.'

'And you're an easy wife to live with. Thanks for that.' He gave her a quick hug. 'Here goes.'

He went next door and called a hello, but got no answer, so hammered on the glass door, staying clear of the smashed section.

He saw Hal hurry into the living area and come across to open the patio door. 'Hi, Aaron. Did you want Mara?'

'Yes, please.'

Hal went back into the hall and called, 'Your father's here to see you.'

Mara joined them downstairs and Hal tactfully moved into the kitchen, leaving them standing together outside.

'I'm sorry, but I can't get out of flying to Sydney now Pete's out of commission for a while. There's too much at stake and my whole retirement plan depends on it, so I want the highest price I can get for the business. I'm so sorry to do this to you, Mara. I'll get back here as quickly as I can, I promise. It'll only be for a few days, if that.'

'Are you taking Emma with you?'

'Not this time. She'll need to keep an eye on Peggy.'

'Oh yes, of course. Well, you really don't need to worry about me. I've been thinking of hiring a car and if I do that I can go out exploring the area. The road rules don't seem to be all that different here from the ones in the UK. I had a look online at the highway code to check it out. And I've found a place that hires out cheapie vehicles.'

'Good idea, but let me hire one for you. Or rather,

Emma will arrange it. My company gets good discounts on that sort of thing.' When she didn't answer, he added, 'Really. I'd like to do that for you.'

'Well, thank you. Just a smallish car.'

'You can discuss the details with Emma.' He glanced at his watch. 'I have to leave for the airport within the hour, I'm afraid.'

She couldn't hold back a little laugh. 'It's all right. Stop looking so anxious, Aaron. I won't take a huff. I hope your business goes well.'

He rolled his eyes. 'I hope it sells once and for all. I'm well over rushing around the world like a madman. Emma and I both want to enjoy some of the money we've made over the years. She's always been part of it.'

After another of his hesitations, he leant forward and kissed her cheek. 'Take care.'

She watched him clamber back over the wall, then went inside to tell Hal what was going on.

He listened with his usual intentness. 'Bad timing with regard to your visit, but if he can sell his business, it'll be a load off his shoulders. I should know. It's what I've just done, sold up completely.'

'Your turn to come clean: what sort of business did you run?'

'I was working in a consultancy for recruiting top-end personnel. Two of us set it up and it did rather well, if I say so myself. When I decided I'd had enough and wanted out, my partner bought me out. He's more ambitious than I ever was.'

'Well done you.' She waited but he didn't offer

any more information so she changed the subject by confessing, 'Um – I'm getting a bit hungry now.'

'Me too.'

They had a quick lunch and continued working through the afternoon, then suddenly, all the drawers were empty, two rubbish bin liners had been filled and the sellable expensive items had been carefully put away again.

She stretched. 'I'm a bit stiff now.'

'You've worked incredibly hard. I just—'

Suddenly Mara's phone rang and she recognised the special ringtone so ran across the room and snatched it out of her handbag.

'Dad! Is that you?'

'Yes, love.'

'Where have you been? I was worried sick when I couldn't get hold of you.'

'I had a fall, wound up in hospital.'

'*What?*'

'It was nothing serious.'

'How did you manage to fall? You're usually quite nimble.'

'Um – well, that's the bad news, I'm afraid.'

'What has Mum done now?'

'She had a really serious incident, worse than ever before. She attacked me and – well, that's how I fell. The doctors at the hospital said I was run down and I certainly felt exhausted.' His voice wobbled. 'I was at the end of my tether with her.'

'Oh, Dad! I should have stayed with you.'

'I'm glad you didn't. You'd only have argued and made matters worse. You're not as good at treading softly as I am. She went downhill very quickly after you'd gone.'

Silence.

'Tell me what else is worrying you, Dad.'

'I can't do it any longer, Mara love – stay with her, I mean. I just – can't.'

'It's a miracle you've done it for so long, Dad.'

He managed a faint, rusty chuckle. 'Sally next door said that too. A miracle achieved with the help of my golf and the fact that Kath preferred having the house to herself during the daytime.'

'Yes. I noticed. So what are you going to do – for yourself and for her?'

'There's nothing I can do at the moment. She lost consciousness suddenly on the way to hospital and she's still unconscious. They've been running tests on her and they think there's a growth in her brain.'

'I'll book a seat on the next plane home.'

'Please don't. If it's what they've hinted at, I'd rather you stayed there for a while longer, then I won't have to worry about you.'

'What are they hinting at?'

'They think this was caused by a slow-growing tumour in a difficult place and well, they say if that's confirmed it'll be inoperable. They've stressed that you can never quite tell, though.'

'Dad, are you trying to let me down slowly?'

He sighed. 'You always could read me. Yes. They're pretty certain she won't recover, actually. All they don't know is how long it'll take for her to die. Weeks rather than days probably. If I've understood correctly, she's still breathing on her own and has some brain function, but her systems are shutting down gradually. They used a lot of long words, but I think I've got the basics right.'

'Oh, dear. But if you've already collapsed with exhaustion, surely I ought to be there helping you. You should have rung me sooner.'

'I had to get things straight in my head. I don't think anyone can really help Kath, love, and when the time comes, well, she always said not to resuscitate her, you've heard her.'

'Yes. She was very determined about that. But I could run the house, cook and wash for you and so on.'

'I can do that for myself. It helps pass the time. It seems a pity to drag you back all that way. No, you stay there and enjoy your holiday, love. I'll let you know when it's time to come home.'

'But Mum—'

'We've been losing her for a while, a couple of years at least. We both knew something was wrong, only she wouldn't seek help. Turns out they couldn't have helped anyway, so I feel better about that. Once she loses all signs of brain function they'll tell me and I'll let them turn off her life support.'

Mara couldn't think what to say. It sounded so heartless not to go back, only he was right. The real Kath had already left them.

He broke the silence. 'Sally's going to help me with the cooking. She's such a kind, generous woman.'

'Oh. All right, then. If you're sure.' Mara had known that he was fond of their next-door neighbour for a while. The two of them looked so comfortable together when they chatted. Though of course she knew he'd never have done anything about it.

'How are things going down under? Is this Aaron chap still being nice to you, Mara?'

'Very nice indeed. You'd get on well with him and his wife. But there's a business crisis. He's in the middle of selling up to retire, so it's really important. He's had to go over to Sydney for a few days. It fits in well because I'm helping out a neighbour whose mother died recently. He has her house to clear and was freaking out at dealing with her clothes.'

'Then you carry on doing that, Mara. Stay there, please. I'm back at home now and it's lovely and peaceful, which is just what I need. I promise to keep you in touch with what happens.'

So she let that drop and tried to end on a lighter note. 'How's Ernest?'

'He's making sure I don't get lonely. How's Archibald?'

'He's enjoying Australia.'

They both chuckled and he said, 'I've got him back again now. I had to leave him with Sally after you left to keep him safe. Kath even tried to break into my little shed. I'd have been really upset if I'd lost him. You know how your mother hated your toys. I never could work out why.'

'Me neither. I'd have made a brother for him if you'd lost him.'

'Eh, us and our teddy bears. We're a pair of daftheads, aren't we?'

Her dad had fallen for the teddy bear she'd made while practising, so she'd given it to him. They'd chosen names and sent imaginary messages from one toy to the other. Her mother had thought that utterly stupid, but for once the two of them had stuck to their guns and continued making jokes about their little pets.

'Now I'm home again, so you can email me or phone any time you like.'

'You're all right again, though? Physically, I mean. Why did they keep you in hospital?'

'To run tests on my heart. But it wasn't as bad as they'd expected. I had a good old rest and it did me a world of good. I'm on some pills which will keep my blood pressure down and I'm sleeping wonderfully well. It's nice to eat what I want when I want.'

'Mum did insist on ruling the roost, didn't she?'

'Yes. When I let Sally know I was coming back, she cooked me a casserole. It was delicious. She's going to show me how to make it myself.'

'She's a good cook.'

'And a good woman. Anyway, I must get off the phone now, Mara love, or this will be costing a fortune. I'll be in touch. In the meantime, you enjoy yourself out there. Bring home a bagful of happy memories.'

'All right. Love you!'

When the call ended, she stood there for a few moments coming to terms with what her father had told her. She was deeply sorry about her mother, but it explained the way she'd changed over the past couple of years. It was better that they hadn't known about the tumour really, if it was inoperable.

In the end Mara went to find Hal and the minute he saw the expression on her face, he held out his arms.

'I can see that it was bad news.'

She walked straight into those strong arms and nestled against him. Sometimes, you could keep a straight face and hide that you were troubled and other times, like now, you were so upset you either needed to be held or to bawl your eyes out.

He'd offered the shelter of his arms without even knowing what was wrong. He was such a lovely man.

Mara let Hal hold her, which he did without asking for an explanation, till she was more in control of herself. 'Thank you. I needed that.' She was then able to tell him what was going on.

He looked at her solemnly when she'd finished. 'And now you're feeling guilty about not feeling more upset.'

She nodded.

'It sounds to me as if it was a merciful release – for all of you.'

As his words sank in, she felt a little of the burden of guilt lift. He'd just lost his mother, would understand better than anyone.

'If you need anything – even if it's only a cuddle – you only have to ask, Mara.'

'I might just do that. Things are in such a tangle in my head at the moment, as well as in my life.'

'It'd be my privilege to help you in any way you need.'

So she hugged him again. 'What do they say in Australia? "Good on yer!" But the hugs are the main thing I need at the moment till I can see my way more clearly. Dad's a good hugger.'

'I have an inexhaustible supply of hugs, but I have to warn you that I don't feel at all fatherly about hugging you.'

She smiled. 'Good. I don't want you to feel fatherly about me.'

Who'd have thought so much could happen to her in such a short time? The trouble with Darren seemed very unimportant now.

Chapter Seventeen

Later on, Hal asked Mara if she'd mind helping him work out what extra furniture he'd need if he wanted to live a more normal social life.

When someone rang the doorbell, he went to peek out through the security spyhole in the front door. Letting out an annoyed grunt, he went back into the kitchen. 'It's that woman, the real estate agent, Mara. How she has the cheek to come here again, I do not know. Well, I'm not answering. I do not wish to speak to her.'

But the doorbell rang again, then there was another ring soon after, then yet another.

'She's not going to go away, Hal. She must have seen us from somewhere on these canals when we were walking about outside studying the patio. Do you want me to answer the door and pretend to be a cleaner who doesn't speak good English?'

He grinned. 'I'd like to see you do that. Thanks, Mara, but she'll have seen you if she's seen me and she doesn't sound to be going away.'

'She or her client must be in a house on this canal to see what we're doing, don't you think?'

'Yes.'

The doorbell rang again. 'I'll answer it but could you stand out of sight nearby and listen to what she says, so that we can compare notes afterwards? She might give us a clue or two as to whether it's her mystery client who's sending her to hassle me or whether it's her own idea of a good way to force my hand and earn a substantial commission.'

The doorbell rang again and he yelled 'Coming!' but waited till Mara was standing just inside the doorway of the small room nearby before he opened the door.

Diana Vincenzo was there, flashily dressed as ever with another low-cut cleavage. The same luxury car was parked behind her on the drive.

'Yes?'

'I need to talk to you, Mr Kendrell. I have some really good news. May I come in?'

'No, you may not. I told you not to bother me again and I meant it.'

Her smile vanished to be replaced by a look of outrage at his bluntness.

He tried to close the door and she had the cheek to stick her foot in the way, so he said it again, loudly and slowly, 'I do *not* wish to sell this house. Please stop pestering me.'

Her scowl turned into a glare and her foot remained in the way. 'If a client asks me to approach you, I shall do my best to follow his instructions, whatever it takes.'

'Well, if he's an honest man he'll give me his name.'

She hesitated, then said. 'He's called Enrico Moretti. But he prefers me to deal with you for him.'

Hal leant against the door frame. 'Let's get it over with, then, and make this the last time you approach me. Tell me this good news.'

'It's not very civilised to discuss business on the doorstep.'

'Maybe I'm not feeling civilised today, and as I've said, *I* have no business to discuss with you. If you can't say what you want, I'm happy to manage without a conversation.' He made as if to close the door again, edging his foot towards hers.

She jabbed out one hand, placing it flat against the door to stop him closing it. 'Very well. If we must. My client has very generously raised his offer to buy this house by $100,000.'

He didn't even have to think about that. 'The answer is still no.'

She stared at him in obvious shock. 'You haven't even taken time to think it over. He'll be paying you top dollar, you know.'

'I don't need to consider it, nor do I need the money. I am *not* selling. How much more plainly can I say it?'

'I'm sure you'll come to regret that once you've had time to think it over. And I must warn you that my client doesn't take well to being thwarted.'

He was about to close the door forcibly but that got his attention. 'Are you threatening me?'

'Of course not. But my client is very determined and he might make things, er, uncomfortable for you in this town. He has some friends in useful places and he's very well thought of, while you're a stranger.'

Hal didn't believe that the man could be well thought of if what had happened recently was down to him. Bully-boy tactics didn't win a man many friends. 'That sounds like a threat to me.' He waited, feeling what he called his 'stone face' slip into place, the one he used to wear when on a job.

'Of course it isn't a threat. As if I'd ever threaten anyone. But I can't control what other people might do. I heard that someone has tried to smash their way into your house already. You might not be safe here but my client can afford to put in much better security.'

Hal decided to let her go on talking. 'The would-be intruders didn't succeed in getting inside, so my security can't be all that bad.'

'Or you were lucky and they got interrupted.'

'How does he know so much about me?'

She hesitated. 'He's renting a house nearby.'

'Well, tell him to buy that one instead. However, in case of more intruders, I'm going to have really top-notch CCTV cameras installed as soon as it can be arranged. Kindly tell your client that I plan to live here permanently, so he'll be able to watch me enjoying my inheritance.'

Her scowl grew deeper, making her features seem suddenly fox-like. 'You might regret that, Mr Kendrell.'

'I don't think so.' He took her by surprise, kicking her foot away and shutting the door, even though she tried to hold it open. Then he turned to Mara. 'Do you think you can remember the gist of that conversation?'

She held out her phone. 'Even better, I recorded every word of it.'

'Brilliant. You are a treasure.'

'We aim to please.'

'Now, on another topic, since your father's left for the eastern states and your stepmother will no doubt be going to see her daughter in hospital, why don't you stay for tea? It'd be silly for us to eat alone when we're only fifty metres apart.'

'That sounds like a good idea. What's on the menu? Or shall we get some takeaway delivered?'

'We already have leftover curry but there's not quite enough for two. I haven't built up much by the way of emergency supplies yet, I must admit, so I'll order in some more food.'

'Why don't I go and get a few vegetables, then I can cook us a satay with noodles to go with the leftovers? Emma has an extremely well-stocked fridge and she'll not have her family around to eat the fresh stuff up before it spoils so I'm sure she won't mind.'

'Done.'

She slipped over the low wall again, was quite used to doing that now, then went to find Emma.

Instead she found a scribbled note stuck to the inside of the patio door:

I SAW YOU'D TAKEN YOUR HANDBAG, SO PLEASE USE YOUR FRONT DOOR KEY TO GET INSIDE. I'M VISITING THE HOSPITAL.
   EMMA

Mara went back to tell Hal what she was doing then went out of his house the front way and let herself into the next house.

The watcher sitting in a car further along the street saw the woman go out and return with a bag of what looked like food. She must be cooking tea for Kendrell. Obviously they were getting on like a house on fire. He sniggered at the thought of what that would probably lead to.

He'd like to get his hands on her, that was sure. She wasn't beautiful exactly, but she was a tall, fine woman with a nicely rounded figure.

When nothing happened for an hour or so, he gave up and went to report back to Mr Moretti. The old guy was sitting in the canal-side garden of his house having a drink with that estate agent female, using binoculars to keep an eye on the comings and goings at the poet's house.

If you asked him, the old guy was acting stupidly, but he paid well.

* * *

Enrico listened to the man's report and dismissed him for the day. When they were alone, he said to Diana, 'I will definitely find a way to get Kendrell out of that house. You've disappointed me, Diana.'

'I can't perform miracles. Is it worth it, Enrico? I can find you other canal houses to look at, bigger and better ones.'

'I've tried renting one you recommended. It's too noisy on the main canals. My wife might have liked that but I didn't. Now she's dead, I'm determined to get that one, with those particular views and situation. I don't enjoy the non-stop drone of boat engines passing. If that fool poet hadn't sneaked in and bought it for cash, I'd have got that house at a good price two years ago.'

'The poor woman had cancer.'

'Why do you think I held back on driving her out? No one can say I'm not generous. I guessed she wasn't well because you could see the transparent look on her face, and when I got someone to check up on her, I found I was right. So I waited. I didn't expect her to last that long, I must admit. Now she's gone, I no longer need to hold back.' His voice grew harsher. 'As I've said to you before, I always get what I want in the end, whatever it costs.'

Diana hoped he hadn't seen her shiver. She concentrated on her drink. He was speaking like a reasonable man today but since he'd lost his wife, he'd done some strange and reckless things, as if he believed himself above the law.

She'd known him for years, because he was a family friend. She'd always been a little afraid of him, even though he'd never turned his anger on her. Now, well, if he told her to go on pestering Kendrell to sell, she wouldn't dare refuse.

What the hell was he planning to do, though? If only his wife were still alive. She would have reined him in. No one else could, certainly not Diana.

Emma went to the hospital that evening to visit her daughter. She could see a difference in Peggy even as she hesitated in the doorway and relief flooded through her. 'You look a bit better today, love.'

'I'm feeling a bit better, Mum. They're not trying to make me eat fattening rubbish here.'

Emma bit back an angry response to that because she considered she provided her family with healthy meals, not rubbish. Whatever it took, she told herself, reining back her annoyance.

She offered Peggy the little gift-wrapped parcel she'd brought. 'This is for you.'

'It's not food, is it? I'm not allowed to eat anything unless they've checked it.'

'They already asked me what was in the parcel and approved its contents. If you unwrap it, you'll find out what it is.'

This time when she held it out, Peggy took it and unwrapped it slowly and carefully, keeping the paper intact as she always tried to do.

'Oh! Oh, they're adorable.' She held up the pair of

fluffy white booties, then rubbed them against her cheek. 'Imagine a creature with feet this small.'

'You had feet that small once.'

'I suppose so, but I don't remember it.' She gave her mother a tearful smile. 'That's a perfect present. I shall enjoy looking at them.'

'And gradually building up a collection of starter clothes. We used to call it a layette. Do people still use that term?'

'I've not noticed it being used much by my friends.'

They chatted for a while, then Sarisha came into the room. 'Peggy needs to sleep now, Mrs Buchanan. I'll walk you out, shall I?'

'Look what Mum brought me.' Peggy held out the bootees.

'Charming. And useful.' The nurse gave Emma a nod of approval.

The two women stopped at the entrance to the special unit.

'She has a good chance of coming through all right,' Sarisha said. 'I get a feel for who is more likely to beat this horrible, senseless obsession, and she's a survivor. I'd guess the thought of the baby will spur her on if she falters.'

'Thanks for telling me that.'

'I shouldn't have done, really, but you've been looking so worried. I will remind you, though, that nothing is ever totally certain.'

'You're right that I'm worried sick about her. I do hope you're right about the whole situation. We shall look forward to having her back home with us.'

'That won't be for a while. The hard thing is to keep patients on track when they go home after the first steps have been taken in hospital. It's never easy. There is a residential hostel that could help Peggy through the next stage but it's not a free service so you'd have to pay for it. She might prefer to go there first.'

'Money doesn't matter. We're not short of it. It's getting her better that counts, even if we have to send her to Timbuctoo riding on a camel.'

Sarisha laughed. 'I don't think you'll need to go to such extremes. Do you have a business card? Thank you. I'll email you a link to the relevant information about the hostel.' She slipped it into her pocket, gave Emma another of those friendly nods and walked away.

Emma continued out of the hospital, feeling weary now. She'd have an early night, would perhaps be able to rest more easily.

An hour later, Sarisha came to the door of Peggy's room again, looking annoyed. 'There's a very bad-mannered man in the foyer demanding to see you. Says his name is Mike Cruikshank.'

'Oh, no! That's my ex.'

'Do you want to see him?'

She didn't have to think about it; she'd already decided. 'Definitely not. Can you send him away?'

'I shall be delighted to do that.'

Peggy heard shouting in the distance and when

Sarisha returned, the older woman's clothing and hair looked a bit untidy, as if she'd been involved in a physical struggle.

'Your ex was very determined to see you. We had to call security to get him out of the hospital.'

'He can be rather pushy when he's angry, but I'd never have expected him to go so far.'

'Well, we can be very determined when it comes to looking after our patients. He's barred from even coming into the hospital now for a full month and his photo is on record.'

'Oh, good.'

Peggy snuggled down but she didn't sleep well that night. She was surprised at how worried she was about what Mike would do next. How had he found out? She'd guessed he'd go mad at the thought of her having his child. Now, she was suddenly afraid he'd come after her and try to force her to get rid of it. As if she would ever do that!

Why had she not taken fully on board what a selfish pig he was before? How had he dazzled her for so long? Her own behaviour seemed totally incomprehensible now. No, not quite. She blushed, all on her own in hospital, at the memory of how good he was in bed.

She wouldn't fall for that again, but how would she keep him away from her once she got out of here? He didn't grow angry often, but could be rather frightening on the rare occasions when he did.

She would, she decided, ask Sarisha's advice about

that tomorrow. And perhaps her father's advice too once he returned from the eastern states.

She fell asleep clutching the bootees and when she half woke up a couple of times, she found their soft fluffiness a great comfort.

Chapter Eighteen

The following day, the car Emma had hired for Mara was delivered and she had her first drive in Australia by going slowly up and down the street and then, feeling rather daring, she went round the nearby streets as well.

The car was easy to drive and comfortable but she couldn't get the satnav to work. Even if she'd had one, she'd have felt a little nervous about driving too far on her own the first time, in case she broke the law without realising it.

She was dying to see more of Western Australia than the town of Mandurah, but with only her phone's satnav to guide her, it would be a bit difficult because she couldn't fiddle with it while driving. What's more she had no knowledge of where might be a good place to head for.

When she went back into the house, she saw Hal

sitting on his patio staring into space, looking sad. Emma had gone out again, leaving another of her apologetic notes, so Mara asked him if he had time to come out with her in the car for an hour or so, just in case she ran into any situations where she didn't know what to do.

To her delight, his face lit up and he accepted at once. 'Mind you, I don't know Western Australia either but I did check out the driving rules while I was on the plane and I can check where we are on my phone.'

With him beside her she felt better and after the first few minutes, she was driving more confidently. They wound up going further than they'd first intended, ending up at a seaside suburb called Cottesloe.

'This place looks nice,' he said when she stopped by the side of the road.

They studied the map. Cottesloe was on the coast north of the port of Fremantle and quite a way from the centre of Perth, which was inland from its port.

'If we go a little further along this road and turn left, there appears to be a car park overlooking the beach,' he said. 'It's past noon and I don't know about you, but I'm hungry. I didn't bother with much breakfast.'

'I'm hungry too and I did have a good breakfast.'

When they reached the car park and got out, she pointed to one side. 'That café is in a prime position with sea views. Let's grab a coffee and a scone.'

'No, let's have a proper lunch. My treat. And let's switch our phones off. I don't feel like being interrupted when I'm enjoying your company.'

'Good idea. I don't like the way a lot of people interrupt conversations to answer their phones. It's just plain rude, if you ask me.' She glanced at her watch. 'It's still night in the UK so Dad won't be calling me and he's the only one who matters to me.'

'It must feel strange to have another father turn up.'

'Very strange indeed. Aaron seems nice, though.'

'I get that impression too. Does he feel like a father, though?'

She shook her head. 'No. More like an uncle or a family friend. No one can replace my dad.'

As they sat and chatted over their meal, they watched families playing on the beach and Mara felt glad she'd taken her father's advice and not rushed off back to England again. She'd only be sitting inside the house because winter was coming on fast over there.

This was everyone's dream of a glorious holiday down under: a sunny day sitting near pale golden sands with a sparkling blue sea in the background where surfers were frolicking. Aaron and Emma had been afraid to let her go for walks at first in case she got sunburnt but she was getting a nice light tan now and knew to put block-out on and wear one of Emma's sun hats.

Once again she and Hal were getting on like a house on fire. She wished she wasn't only here temporarily or that he was still living in England. She wished . . . *No, leave it, Mara*, she told herself. *Just accept what is and enjoy the moment.*

After a leisurely lunch they set off home. She was sorry when they arrived and Hal left her, even more so when she found another note propped up on the kitchen bench, saying that Emma had gone out again to visit Peggy at the hospital and would be calling on an old friend afterwards for a chat and catch-up, as previously arranged, so not to wait for tea with her.

The fridge still contained lots of fresh food that wouldn't keep much longer, so on impulse Mara went next door to invite Hal round for a meal. Since he wasn't outside or visible inside, and there was no response when she knocked, she went back into her own house, feeling disappointed.

There she hesitated. Perhaps he didn't want to spend any more time with her so hadn't answered. Or perhaps he had simply not heard her knocking. In a fit of what-the-hells she decided to go round and invite him. He could only say no after all. She went the front way this time and used the doorbell, which had a nice loud peal.

He answered almost immediately, looking surprised to see her.

She could tell what he was thinking. 'I tried the patio entrance but there was no answer.'

'Sorry about that. I was upstairs in my bedroom and I'm afraid I didn't hear you knocking.'

He waited for her to say what she wanted, head on one side and a lovely smile on his face now. That smile gave her the confidence to ask, 'Would you like to come round for tea?' When he hesitated, she added quickly,

'We've still got plenty of leftovers, you see, but if you're tired, it doesn't matter.'

'It's you I was thinking of, actually. You're sure you're not too tired to cook after your great Australian driving adventure today?'

She couldn't help chuckling. 'I didn't promise you a fancy gourmet meal. I don't think I could even make one.'

'A simple meal will be fine. I don't need bribing to enjoy your company, as you may have noticed.'

He paused and the air seemed suddenly charged with emotional electricity, or whatever you liked to call an attraction of two people for one another. There was no mistaking it, even in the early stages like now.

For a moment or two all they did was stare, then he shook his head, looking like a dog shaking off water. 'You're sure Emma won't mind me coming round?'

'Certain. Some of the food can't be frozen.'

Hal swept her a mock bow. 'Then I accept your kind invitation with great pleasure. What time?'

'As soon as you like. Since we'll only be having something simple, it might be fun to prepare it together.'

'It might indeed. Just let me get online and go through my messages, then I'll come across via the patio and bring a bottle of wine.'

As Mara was walking back to her front door, she noticed that the large black car with darkened windows was there again, the one that had been parked down the street yesterday when they were watching the real estate agent leave. It wasn't on the driveway of a house and there were few cars parked on the street itself because, unlike the cluttered streets in England, there was plenty of space for visitors to park on people's drives.

It seemed strange to see it there two days running and she could tell that there was once again a bald man sitting inside it.

When she got inside, she forgot about it as she investigated the contents of the fridge and freezer for a few more bits and pieces.

She would make something that could be eaten cold as a way of repaying Emma: a prawn salad for starters with a simple chicken and vegetable risotto perhaps as the main course. Her stepmother might be relieved to find a meal ready when she got back, unless she'd already eaten with her friend. The risotto could always be eaten with a salad the next day.

On her way into the hospital, Emma wondered what she could take as a little cheer-you-up present for her daughter today. Nothing edible, of course.

She veered across to the kiosk and in the end chose a book by one of Peggy's favourite authors from the display in the foyer. Even if her daughter had read this one, she might like to read it again out of sheer boredom.

Emma couldn't help staring at a man sitting by himself in one corner because he was wearing a highly unflattering grey wig that looked well past its use-by date. What an idiot! He'd look far better bald. He seemed to be trying to hide behind a newspaper, but didn't realise that his profile was reflected clearly in a window to one side of that row of seats. Something about him seemed familiar so she studied him more closely.

It wasn't – it couldn't be – yes, it was! Her daughter's ex. But hadn't Sarisha phoned to tell them Mike been banned from entering the hospital after his behaviour yesterday? How had he found out about the baby anyway? What was he doing here today, and in that pitiful disguise?

Her heart sank. There could only be one reason: he was determined to see Peggy. Well, if he thought he could sneak into her daughter's room and bully her into getting rid of his baby, he was in for a shock. She wasn't surprised that her daughter had gone over the top about the baby, however, because that was how Peggy usually tackled life.

Emma tried not to let her eyes linger on him and pretended to concentrate on the revolving stand of books, taking out the one she'd been thinking of buying and holding it up to conceal her face as if she was reading the blurb on the back cover.

But she remained very much aware of what he was doing and when the security guard turned to speak to someone, Mike got up and walked quickly towards the back of the foyer. She knew that led only to the lifts so she barely hesitated but dumped the book back on the stand and followed him.

He stopped in front of the row of lifts, so she waited out of sight behind a water cooler. When he got into a lift she watched the indicator to see which floor he got out at.

The lift went straight to the top. Oh dear! That was the floor where the special unit was situated.

She turned round and ran back into the foyer, relieved to see the security officer still standing at his post near the entrance. She gasped out her tale, ending, 'You have to stop him harassing my daughter. She's pregnant as well as having some problems due to anorexia.'

He fiddled with his phone and showed it to her. 'Is this him?'

'Yes.'

'Perhaps you'd come up to that floor with me, Mrs Buchanan? We must hope the nurses on duty will stop the man getting into the unit.'

He pulled out a small control device and they walked briskly across to the lifts. He used the device to commandeer the end lift. The people who were waiting automatically started moving towards it, but he had only to say, 'There's a security problem, I'm afraid,' for them to jerk hurriedly away.

Emma got into the lift with him, feeling tense and desperately hoping the nurses had managed to stop Mike from getting to her daughter.

When Mike got out of the lift he saw a nurse standing nearby so looked up at the signs and then moved past her towards the other wards.

He waited till she'd turned away to answer a question from some other visitor and edged past a trolley full of cleaning materials so that he could sneak into the special unit unseen.

Peggy looked up as he burst into her room, gaping at him. 'Get out of here! I don't want to see you ever again.'

'Well, I want to see you.' Mike took a deep breath and said coaxingly, 'Darling, we have to talk.'

'Don't you "darling" me!'

As she reached out to press the button to summon a nurse, he moved to stop her. When she scooted back away from him, he grabbed her arm, dragging her into a sitting position at the other edge of the bed. 'Get your dressing gown on quickly. You're coming with me. You and I need to have a very important talk without any stupid do-gooders interfering.' He gave her a slight shake. 'Hurry up!'

She sagged limply as if about to obey him, then suddenly began screaming for help. When he tried to put his hand across her mouth, she struggled fiercely to get away from him but he was much bigger and stronger than her.

A nurse looked into the room, damn her. Mike dug his fingers into Peggy's arm, yelling, 'Don't you dare come any nearer! You can't keep her here against her will and she wants to come with me, don't you, Peggy?'

'No, I don't.'

His grip on her arm tightened till it was painful and he gave her a little shake.

Peggy pretended to sag, but shook her head slightly.

The nurse stood still but stayed in the doorway, saying in a soothing voice, 'Please move away from the patient, sir.'

Instead Mike quickly hauled Peggy upright, keeping

her between the nurse and himself. 'I told you, she wants to come with me. Tell her, Peggy.'

'I don't want to go with him. He's trying to force me.'

He shook Peggy hard and she squeaked in shock and pain as he banged her head against the metal bed head.

'Don't come any closer,' he warned the nurse.

Mike had such a wild look and had already hurt her so Peggy didn't dare do anything else to upset him till a burly security guard suddenly appeared behind the nurse. When Mike's grip on her arm slackened, she remembered a self-defence class she'd once taken, so groaned faintly and sagged as if she'd fainted.

As Mike struggled to hold her limp body upright, she managed to turn sideways without him realising and punched him a couple of times. By sheer good luck her third punch landed in a man's most vulnerable spot.

It was his turn to yell and he let go of her as he doubled up in pain, clutching himself.

By that time the security guard had run across. As he grabbed Mike, the nurse tugged Peggy away from him. 'Let's get you out of the room. Quick.' Once outside the door she pressed an alarm button on the wall then paused to watch what was going on.

Mike proved what he'd always claimed, that he wasn't any good at fighting. Well, unless it was with women who were smaller than himself, Peggy added mentally, watching his ineffectual attempts to escape. She must have been crazy to think herself in love with him.

The security guard was soon holding Mike helpless by twisting one of his arms behind his back.

Another security officer appeared beside them in the doorway. 'What the hell's going on?'

'That man attacked this patient,' the nurse told him.

'Oh, did he.' He went across to lend a hand but Mike was now begging to be released.

'Let's find somewhere for you to sit down,' the nurse told Peggy.

Her mother ran across from near the lift. 'Thank goodness you're all right!'

She flung herself into her mother's arms. 'Mike's gone crazy, Mum. He just tried to drag me out of the hospital by force. What did I ever see in him?'

'Who knows? He could switch on the charm at times, though he never fooled me.'

The nurse grinned. 'He didn't look charming clutching himself like that, though, did he?'

Peggy suddenly saw the funny side of it and let out a crow of laughter. 'I actually managed to hit him where it hurts most, Mum. You read about people doing that.'

'Well done, you.'

'I'm not getting rid of the baby, Mum, even if it is his.'

'That's your own choice. We'll back whatever you decide.'

Sarisha ran round a corner to join them just then, studying Peggy carefully. 'I got called up from my break to help. Come with me till they've got that idiot out of the unit.'

Emma had expected Peggy to collapse once the crisis was over, but instead, her daughter was looking more alive than she had for ages, eyes sparkling with triumph and excitement.

When Sarisha suggested something to drink, Peggy didn't even ask what was in the milky liquid but swallowed it in big gulps, looking at the empty container in surprise when she'd finished. 'That tasted good.'

'It was sweetly flavoured by defeating your ex.' Emma gestured to her own lower abdomen. 'She hit the bullseye, Sarisha. I never heard a man shriek so loudly and shrilly before.'

Sarisha laughed and patted Peggy's shoulder. 'Well done.'

'I hope he's in agony. What will they do with him now?'

'Call in the police and hand him over. He'll probably be warned and slapped with a restraining order to stay away from you.'

'They won't lock him away?'

'I doubt it. Unless he has a record for violence towards women, and perhaps not even then. It's an unfair world sometimes.'

Peggy didn't say anything but she frowned.

'What's the matter?' Emma asked.

'I think he'll only pretend to obey a restraining order. He can be very stubborn when he wants something. And cunning. He'll come after me again, I know he will.'

'If we could get you to a special hostel for cases like yours, he won't know where you are.'

'He'll find out. He boasts about his Internet skills.'

'Why are you so sure he won't obey?'

'He loathes the thought of having a child, particularly the idea of being charged for its maintenance for years till it grows up. He's utterly selfish about what he does with his money. I paid most of the bills while I was living there. How could I have been so stupid?'

'The more I find out about him, the more I wonder why you stayed with him.'

Peggy shook her head. 'I thought he was the love of my life and you had to love someone faults and all.'

'Blinded by your hormones,' Sarisha said. 'You must be going through a very maternal phase and you wanted a mate.'

Peggy's hand went instinctively to her stomach and she gave a faint smile as she looked down at it. 'I suppose. I won't be blinded again. I hope it's a girl, though.'

Mara and Hal enjoyed their meal together, then sat outside on the patio chatting about anything and everything.

When they heard the garage door start to slide up she was surprised. 'Look at the time! Emma's back.'

'I'll just wait to say hello then leave you in peace. I've enjoyed our evening very much.'

'Me, too.' She plucked up her courage and looked him straight in the eyes. 'Pity I'm only here temporarily.'

'Great pity. You could change the date of your return flight, move in with me and see where our attraction leads.'

'It's too soon to do that, Hal. We've only known each

other for a few days. I'd need to know you a lot better before I moved in. I made a bad mistake about that sort of thing last year, you see. Besides, I don't have a job here and I'd run out of money.'

Emma came in from the garage just as Hal was opening his mouth to reply and perhaps it was just as well.

Once she'd given them a brief outline of the excitement at the hospital, she accepted Mara's offer of a meal with alacrity. 'It's improved my appetite enormously to hear how Peggy's opinion of Mike has changed.' She accepted a plate and sat down at the breakfast bar. 'Ooh, thank you. That'll be lovely.'

Hal judged it time to leave so Mara walked with him to the wall. 'I'll get back to you tomorrow with details of the online auction company I mentioned,' she promised.

'Thank you. And maybe we'll have another drive out.'

'If Emma doesn't need my help.'

'I wish—' He broke off.

'What do you wish?'

'That there were just the two of us, not all these other people and their needs. You're right about the most important thing: we ought to invest some time in getting to know one another better because we'd be fools to deny such a strong initial attraction.'

'I'd still have to go back to the UK at the end of the six weeks.'

'You could take a few more weeks at least.'

'No. And not just because of the money side of things. There's my mother to think of.'

'Ah. Yes.'

'She's not expected to recover from the coma and my dad is facing a difficult time. He shouldn't be doing that on his own.'

'No. Of course not. You sound to love him dearly.'

Her voice grew softer. 'Oh, I do. He's been both father and mother to me. If I seem unfeeling about my mother it's because she's been growing increasingly strange and – and unpleasant to be with for the past few years. We were never close but lately she's been like a stranger.'

'Has she been that bad?'

'Yes.' Mara decided to tell him the rest. 'It's not her fault exactly. She has a personality disorder and has always been difficult but she's got worse as she's grown older. A lot worse. Never as bad as during the last couple of years, though. We didn't realise she had a brain tumour and Dad was at his wits' end as to what to do because she's refused point-blank to see a doctor about anything since her last big incident.'

'I'm sure you'll be a great comfort to him. I really envy him having you to love. When I was younger, I thought I didn't want a wife and family, but as I've grown older and got to know people who are very happy together and have great kids, I've envied them.'

Mara couldn't think what to say to that, so just squeezed his arm.

He turned his hand to grasp hers. 'I'm not sure whether I'm too late for love, family and the whole shebang. I am nearing forty, after all, nearly ten years older than you.'

'Forty's not old these days. I'm thirty but mostly I feel young and I have plenty of things I want to achieve. Have you any idea what you want to do with your life now?'

'Not really. I wound up my business interests just before my mother died, and here I am with my own future on hold, clearing out her past, not sure of anything.'

'*Alone and palely loitering*,' she quoted.

He added the next line of the poem. '*The sedge is wither'd from the lake.*'

They chanted the last line of that verse together in mock doleful tones, '*And no birds sing.*'

He smiled at her. 'I've not met many women who can quote Keats at me. And accurately too.'

'Nor have I met many men who can continue the verse. I've always loved that poem.'

'"La Belle Dame Sans Merci". I hope you're kinder to your swains than the lady of the title was, though.' He took hold of both her hands. 'We've made a good start on our friendship, don't you think?'

'Yes. Very good.'

'So we definitely ought to see where it leads.'

When he placed a gentle kiss on each of her hands in a kind of promise, she shivered in reaction. 'I agree, but that won't change the fact that I still have to go back to Dad.'

He gave her another quick hug. She was growing addicted to those hugs.

'Well, while you're here we'll give our friendship a chance to ripen a little, shall we, Mara? That at least we can do.' He dropped a quick kiss on her nose, and swung his legs over the wall, then turned to say, 'To be continued,' before vanishing into his house.

She stayed where she was, smiling, and as a small boat chugged quietly past, she turned automatically to watch it, then frowned. The man at the wheel was completely bald like the driver of the car had been. Sheer coincidence, she told herself. Lots of men lost their hair when they grew older and some shaved their heads completely. He couldn't be the one from the car.

Then she looked round their end of the canal and frowned. Where had the boat been while she and Hal had been chatting? It hadn't gone past, so must already have been at this dead end, waiting quietly without its lights. Only, the other houses nearby seemed to be unoccupied at the moment. She'd not seen any lights or people inside them, not once.

A shiver ran down her spine. What was going on? She nearly followed Hal to tell him about the boat and ask what he thought. No, she mustn't be a pest. She could mention it tomorrow.

When she went to bed, she lay hugging Archibald as she sometimes did, not finding the teddy bear as comforting as usual, however. 'Fine lover you make,' she muttered, giving him a little shake. Hal's hugs were much more satisfying.

She set the little bear down by the side of the bed and lay thinking about Hal and wondering if she dared hope for something permanent to develop between them.

Her mother had now gone beyond human help, had

never seemed to want anyone's love, but Mara wasn't deserting her father whatever happened in her own life. He had never deserted her or her mother.

Only, she wasn't letting go of her hopes, either. Not yet anyway.

In the meantime she needed a good night's sleep. She closed her eyes and began her usual get-to-sleep trick of counting back from one hundred, this time in threes . . .

Chapter Nineteen

Phil walked restlessly round the house. It was all immaculately tidy and there were no small DIY jobs needed. He wasn't used to having nothing to do and that was fretting him. To make matters worse, he'd been forbidden by the doctor to play golf or do anything physically energetic or stressful for a few days.

He'd had someone to look after for many years and had derived satisfaction from feeling not just useful but absolutely necessary to her, even though Kath hadn't thanked him for his care for a long time now, poor lass.

He could go to the golf club and sit in the members' lounge but it looked out over the golf course and it'd make him feel envious to see others playing. He smiled ruefully. He'd never become a really good player but he got a lot of pleasure out of being a mediocre one and walking round the course in the open air chatting to his friends. In fact, it had been a life-saver to him over the years.

He looked across at the teddy bear Mara had made him, which sat openly on the table now that Kath wasn't there to hurl it at him. Pale gold fur and wearing an old-fashioned seaside outfit: striped blazer, white shirt and trousers, topped by a straw boater hat. It was a delightful little creature. He was so proud of his daughter's talent.

'Ernest, my old lad, we just have to make the best of it,' he told it and smiled at his own foolishness even as he made it nod in reply.

He'd go out for a walk round the nearby streets, he decided. A quarter of an hour or so of gentle strolling was not only allowed but recommended, up to two or three times a day at first.

On the way back he bumped into Sally coming home from the library and she invited him in for a cup of coffee. That made a bright spot in the day. He always felt comfortable with her, had sought her advice many times over the years, as had Mara about teenage worries.

Pity her husband had died a few years ago. Donny had been a nice chap and they'd enjoyed pottering about together in Donny's shed. Phil had never felt as relaxed in his own shed because Kath hadn't been able to stand the untidiness that seemed inevitable in such a place and had gone in regularly then complained about how he kept it.

Sally admitted she got a bit lonely since her husband died. Friends weren't the same as a live-in companion.

Phil had had someone to live with and still been lonely once Mara left home.

He wasn't a reader but when Sally offered to lend him a book by her favourite author, he took it out of desperation to fill the long hours sitting alone 'resting'. To his surprise, he found the story quite entertaining, some parts making him chuckle aloud. Who'd have thought books written in the 1940s by a long dead author called Angela Thirkell could be so amusing decades later? Gently amusing was what he liked best. He didn't enjoy humour that seemed to gloat over people's painful experiences.

He looked up from the book and nodded to the teddy bear. 'There you are, Ernest my lad, life's full of little surprises. Sally says she has plenty of feel-good books to lend me when I've finished this one.' But still he sighed. The truth was, he liked people and activities better than reading books, even good books like this one, always had done. A little light reading wasn't too bad, but reading for hours on end wasn't his thing at all. Mara always teased him about being a do-er, not a spectator.

He opened his mouth to say something else then snapped it shut. He'd better not make a habit of talking aloud to Ernest or he might do it when someone was here. He didn't want people thinking he was going crazy.

He'd ring Mara tonight and see how she was getting on. That'd cheer him up. Sort of. The trouble was, her being in Australia kept reminding him that she wasn't his daughter by birth.

She felt to be his own beloved daughter, though, blood

link or not. She always had done, right from the first time he'd met her as a small child and she'd climbed on his knee to show him her toy rabbit. But would the Australian chap win her over to putting him first?

Phil's worst fear was that Aaron would persuade her to emigrate to Australia. So many people wanted to go and live there. Well, he wouldn't mind living in a warmer climate, either. The winters in England seemed to become longer each year as he grew older.

And that chap certainly had a lot more to offer her than Phil ever could. Maybe he'd even help her make her dreams come true by funding the small business she was hoping to start. Phil's friend George had told him that Buchanan was in the process of selling up a whole chain of businesses and retiring early after a very successful career, so the money would be nothing to him.

Phil had retired early too, but not by choice. It had been a form of redundancy. Consequently there wasn't as good a superannuation package as he'd hoped to earn by a few more years' work, even though the company had stuck to the letter of the law about what they paid him.

It was hard to be successful at work with a wife like Phil's. Kath had never gone with him to social events and her health crises had forced him to need time off every now and then. It was a triumph really that he'd managed to stay employed and climb up the lower echelons of the promotional ladders.

He stared blindly at the phone for a few moments till the sight of it reminded him that he hadn't even rung the hospital today to see how Kath was. Not that she'd know whether he did that or not. But he'd know and feel bad about it if he didn't do it every day.

He picked up the phone. It was all he could do for her now, keep in touch till what the doctors had predicted happened. They'd told him gently that it would be a complete waste of time him going into the hospital, because she'd not be aware of his presence. And he'd seen the sense of that because he was definitely run down and the hospital was an unpleasant drive through heavy town traffic.

He'd been hoping for a few years that Mara would marry and give him grandchildren. He was surprised she hadn't done so already because she was such a lovely lass. But then young people all seemed to marry later these days than they used to in his day.

He wished suddenly that he'd said yes when Mara offered to come straight home. No. That'd have been selfish. She couldn't do anything to help even if she were here. Let her enjoy as much of her unexpected holiday in the sun as possible. She deserved it after the way that Darren creep had treated her.

He'd be able to play golf again soon, which would cheer him up no end. It would only be a week or so at most before that was allowed, surely? He could stick to nine holes at first. His friends had phoned once or twice to ask how he was, which was nice, and they'd tentatively fixed on a day next week for a game together.

But none of them had tried to call round to see him, because that had been one of the things Kath refused point-blank to allow. 'They're just coming to gawp and I'm not having it.'

Gawp at what? A house bare of ornaments and so rigidly tidy it felt unwelcoming, even to him.

He opened the book again but fell asleep reading and didn't wake up again till teatime. The first thing he saw was the book lying on the floor near his feet. Eh, Kath would have gone mad at that. He laughed at himself when he picked it up because he couldn't remember a word he'd read and didn't know which page to put the bookmark in.

Thank goodness there was one of his favourite programmes on TV tonight. And there was still some of Sally's latest casserole left. He'd just walk round the nearby streets first. He was determined to get better.

The fresh air tasted lovely and he stopped to chat to another neighbour.

See. He was coping.

Well, what else could you do when your life changed abruptly?

The next day, Emma suggested that Mara accompany her to the hospital for the second brief visit allowed each day. The staff were still watching Peggy carefully, but she wasn't giving them nearly as much trouble. Emma felt her daughter had turned a corner, thanks to Mike's stupidity.

'After we've seen Peggy, we can go out for dinner. There's a really nice café nearby. I've been neglecting you, I'm afraid.'

Mara didn't like to refuse, so when Hal once again suggested they go out for a meal, she had to turn him down. 'Sorry.'

'That's all right. Tomorrow, perhaps?'

'Yes, tomorrow would be lovely.'

Aaron had texted to say he was probably coming back in a couple of days, so she would be spending more time with him then. She was going to be torn between him and Hal.

She wondered if she would ever get to the stage of feeling utterly comfortable with Aaron as she did with her dad in England.

She felt comfortable with Hal already, though, had done almost from the beginning. Strange, that.

Hal didn't feel like going out to a café on his own, so got a packaged dinner out of the freezer, something his mother must have bought.

He followed the heating instructions carefully but the finished result bore no resemblance whatsoever to the photo on the outside, or to what he thought of as real food. It was so tasteless he couldn't be bothered to finish eating it. There was more gravy than meat, accompanied by a few teaspoonfuls of overcooked vegetables and a splodge of nearly liquid mashed potato. He felt cheated.

After a few forkfuls, he looked at the rest in disgust and scraped it into the kitchen bin, vowing never again to buy another so-called 'ready dinner' of that brand, or any other brand either. He'd buy a cookery book instead. He was still hungry, so made himself a cheese and chutney sandwich, which had far more flavour. He finished off with a fresh nectarine.

Feeling at a bit of a loose end, he went outside and strolled up and down the patio, watching the occasional boat circle slowly past his garden and away back to the main canal, their lights twinkling in the early dusk. It might be summer but there was no daylight saving here in Western Australia. And on a hot day, who'd want it when darkness brought lower temperatures and relief from the sometimes searing heat his mother had described very graphically in her emails?

It hadn't officially been what locals would consider a scorcher today but it had felt hot to him after he'd come so recently from a wintry climate. Thank goodness for air conditioning! He'd set it at his favourite temperature of 25 degrees centigrade, the one he used when he could in hotel rooms in hot countries. He didn't need it icy cold.

One small boat caught his eye suddenly. It had no lights at all, which was dangerous as well as against the law. And what was it doing lingering near a jetty just a little way along the other side of the canal to him?

It looked like the same boat that had been around yesterday. Why? There didn't seem to be anyone resident in the nearby houses at the moment, so there weren't any lit-up gardens and homes for tourists to gape at, only a slightly wider circle of dark water to turn round in, with his house and the Buchanans' occupied.

Perhaps the boat's lights had failed and that was why it had stopped? Only that still didn't explain why no one was tinkering with them. Two men were simply sitting there. Had the would-be buyer sent someone to spy on him? Or was he getting paranoid about that?

He shook his head at how boring the evening was. He was missing Mara's lively company, loved trading ideas and opinions with her. He would need to make friends if he was going to live here permanently but he doubted he'd find anyone as easy to get on with as her. Or as attractive.

He wasn't madly sociable and loathed big parties but he certainly didn't share his mother's reclusive nature either.

He didn't feel like drinking wine on his own, so went into the house to make himself a cup of coffee. Then he went outside again with his book. The trouble was, he'd already guessed 'who done it' and the story wasn't very well written.

When he heard a car driving along the street, he assumed it was Mara and her stepmother coming back. He heard the vehicle stop nearby but it didn't sound to be outside their house and there was no sound of a garage door rising. Pity.

Then he stiffened. Was that the front door opening and shutting in the Buchanans' house? It had a latch that made a particularly sharp sound. He'd not have noticed it if he hadn't been outside, listening intently.

Could it be Aaron returning from the eastern states in a taxi? No, his neighbour would have switched the lights on straight away.

Then he realised that someone had definitely gone

into the house next door, because though it was still dark he could now see a faint light moving about inside. No, two faint glows. Torches?

That could only be intruders! What the hell next?

He moved across the patio to stand close to the dividing wall, hoping he'd be able to keep an eye on the house next door without being visible to the intruders. He wasn't taking any risks and would be able to get back inside his own house quickly if they spotted him. Why hadn't the alarm system next door sounded?

He turned to and fro, trying to locate what or who had made a faint sound, but couldn't see anything untoward. Then pain and light exploded in his head and he felt himself spiralling helplessly down into darkness.

As Kendrell tumbled down some steps and lay there without moving, the older man from the boat turned on his companion, who had come out of the next house to join him. 'You didn't have to hit him so hard. You'd better not have killed him.' He bent over to feel for a pulse. 'Thank goodness. It's beating strongly.'

'So it should be. I only tapped him to keep him quiet. You surely didn't want him to see us? He must have a thin skull, that's all I can say.'

'Well, you're lucky this time. He's still breathing steadily. You don't know your own strength sometimes, you don't. But you're good at dealing with security systems, I must say.'

The other man grinned. 'I sat outside and let my special equipment listen as they entered their code yesterday.

The owners here have a rather old-fashioned system.'

There was the sound of a car from the street and both men jerked to attention as they heard the garage door of the house they'd broken into begin to rise.

'Oh, hell! They must have come back early. We'd better get away quickly.'

His companion didn't need telling twice. He led the way through the house, reaching the front door as the car stopped inside the garage and someone switched off the engine. The garage door began to roll down again and the first man rushed across to the car. The second one cursed under his breath as the door didn't shut properly behind him but he didn't go back to close it.

He raced across the street to where his companion was already starting their car. He had to fling himself into the front passenger seat and it set off immediately he got there. He had trouble closing his door, then had to fumble around before he could find the end of his seat belt and fasten it.

'You could have waited till I got in properly.'

'You were in and that's all that mattered. If you lost a bit of weight you'd not be so slow at buckling up. I'm not risking getting caught. How come those two women returned so soon? You told me you saw them leave the hospital and go into the nearby café at half past seven, which was why we came straight here.'

'I did see them go into the café. I even watched them sit down at a table.'

'Well, they can't have stayed there. I wonder what

brought them back so soon? They haven't had time to get a meal or even a takeaway.'

'Who cares? *He* isn't going to be pleased about this. When they see they've been broken into, they may upgrade their alarm system. A child could break into this place.'

Chapter Twenty

As soon as she'd switched off the car engine, Emma unfastened her seat belt, clapped one hand to her mouth and rushed towards the downstairs cloakroom, leaving her car door open.

Mara could hear the sound of retching and vomiting as she too got out of the car. She didn't go into the kitchen, stopping dead to stare sideways through the door Emma had left open into the hall. She was certain Emma hadn't left the front door of the house open. In fact, she'd seen her switch on the security system.

When she heard a car drive away along the street, she felt suspicious, so rushed outside to find out who it was. Unfortunately all she could see were the tail lights of a large, dark vehicle, which was accelerating away dangerously fast. Was that someone who'd broken into the house?

There was the sound of a toilet flushing and Emma came out of the cloakroom, patting her mouth with some tissues. 'I don't know what did this to me. I must have eaten something bad without realising it. I'm sorry to spoil your—' She too stopped to stare at the front door. 'Did you switch the security system off and open the front door?'

'No. The security system was already off and the door open.'

'That's strange. I definitely didn't forget to turn on the security system and I'd never have left the front door open, never in a million years. We hardly use that door anyway because we mostly come and go by car.'

'You should have told me you weren't feeling well. I'd not have minded staying at home. I'll lock the door again now. You go and sit down.'

'Not yet. Someone must have broken in so I'd better check the rest of the house. Let me go first. I know what it should all look like better than you do.'

Emma closed and locked the front door and hurried into the kitchen, switching on all the lights as she went. 'Oh, hell! Someone's definitely been in here. The chairs have been disturbed. They must have bumped into them in the darkness.'

She ran across the living area into the office. 'I don't think they came in here, but look, this side patio door is open. Why do you think they went outside?'

'If there's no damage, we must have disturbed them before they could take anything. There's something on the ground outside. Could you switch the rest of the patio lights on, please?'

Whatever was on the ground was half-hidden by a table and chairs, so Mara moved sideways. It looked like – it was a figure. 'Oh, no! It's Hal and he's just lying there. I'm going outside to check him. He must have disturbed them.'

Emma rushed across to stop her opening the door. 'Wait a minute. Take something to defend yourself with, just in case anyone is still lingering nearby. I'm going to call the police. Here.' She grabbed the knife-sharpening steel from the magnetic knife panel in the kitchen and held it out to Mara.

After grabbing her meat tenderising mallet, just in case, Emma snatched up a phone and dialled triple zero, keeping the mallet lying on the counter nearby and her back against the wall. 'Hello. I need the police and an ambulance. We've just had a break-in. We disturbed the intruders and our neighbour is lying outside unconscious.'

She picked up the mallet and moved across to the half-open door, worried about Mara, as she answered a couple more questions from the emergency services phone responder.

It was quiet on the patio, with no sign of anyone else lingering. Mara edged round to the side of Hal so that she could keep her back turned to the house and watch the garden and canal for anyone approaching her from that direction.

As she bent over him to feel for a pulse, he groaned and stirred.

'Thank goodness,' she muttered. She could see blood on the side of his head, though, where they must have hit him.

His eyes flickered open and shut, then opened again but he didn't seem to be seeing clearly.

'You've been injured, Hal. Lie still. We've called an ambulance.'

He blinked at her. 'Mara? You back already?'

'Yes. Emma was feeling ill, so we didn't stay out for a meal after all.'

'I can't remember – falling. And my head hurts.'

From the kitchen came an exclamation and the sound of someone vomiting then a tap running.

'Emma seems to have a stomach bug.' Mara kept her eyes on Hal, really worried about him.

He blinked and tried to shake his head, letting out a soft 'Ouch' as if this hurt him.

'Lie still. You shouldn't move till the paramedics have checked you. Do you hurt anywhere else or is it just your head? Wiggle your arms and legs one at a time.'

He started doing this and winced suddenly, his words still a bit slurred. 'Left ankle hurts.'

'I can't do anything to help you till the police come except watch out in case the intruders return.' She couldn't resist touching him as she repeated, 'Please lie still, Hal.'

'You go inside. I'll wait here. Too dizzy to stand up yet.'

'No way am I leaving you. I'll whack them if they come back.' She brandished the knife sharpener and saw his lips curl into a near smile. But he didn't try to get up, thank goodness.

A few moments later there was the sound of a siren coming closer.

'I'll let them in,' Emma called from the doorway. 'Scream if you need help.'

When Hal stretched out his hand, Mara took hold of it, but still kept her eyes open.

It was one of the police officers who found the piece of paper that had fallen off the kitchen surface. 'What's this?' He held it up and Emma stared at the big black letters, which must have been printed on a computer.

TELL YOUR NEIGHBOUR HE'S NOT WELCOME HERE. YOU'RE NOT WELCOME EITHER IF YOU ASSOCIATE WITH HIM.

She was shocked. 'Who could have sent such a message? I'll make friends with whoever I want.'

'Has anyone tried to buy your house lately?' the older officer asked. 'In my last posting we had trouble about attempts to drive people out because a builder wanted to redevelop the area.'

'No, but—' She looked up as one of the paramedics helped Hal limp into the house and sit on a chair. He was so pale, she was worried he might faint.

She realised the officer was waiting for her answer. 'Actually, someone's made an offer for the house next

door, which Hal Kendrell, the new owner, turned down.'
She broke off to listen as Hal insisted that he wasn't going
to hospital. Hopefully that meant he wasn't badly hurt.

'I'm sure my ankle is only sprained.'

'We'd prefer to make certain it's not broken, sir.'

'Well, I sprained the other ankle a couple of years ago
and it felt very similar, so I'm not going to waste hours
in an emergency department. I couldn't walk on it if it
was broken.'

'But, sir—'

'I am *not* leaving my mother's house unoccupied.'

'Can't you lock it up?'

'No. I'm staying.' Hal's mouth had a stubborn set
to it that reminded Emma of his mother during a TV
interview she'd seen with a tactless fellow asking stupid
questions.

The paramedic sighed. 'Will you at least let me put a
supportive bandage on it, then, sir.'

'Thanks. That'll help.'

The female paramedic joined in. 'Do you live here on
your own?'

'Yes.' Hal winced as he moved his foot incautiously.

'Could you get a friend to come and stay with you?
You've probably got mild concussion and someone
should keep an eye on you.'

'You could stay here with us and leave your security
system switched on next door,' Emma suggested.

She too was looking pale, Mara thought.

Hal shook his head again. 'Thank you but I'd rather
stay in my own home.'

'Mara could stay with you. I can lock myself in the master suite, which has an extra layer of security. Besides, unlike Hal, I'm not incapacitated. And actually, I'd prefer to deal with my nausea in private, to be frank.'

Mara opened her mouth, shut it again, then took a chance. 'If it's all right to leave you on your own, Emma, I will stay with Hal.'

'Mmm.' She was looking chalk white again and pressing one hand against her mouth.

'There's really no need for anyone to stay with me,' Hal insisted. 'I have a good security system too.'

'And how quickly could you move about to check whether someone has come back and broken into your house this time, sir?' one of the police officers asked.

Hal sighed and scowled at his ankle. 'Not quickly enough, I suppose.'

'Go and keep an eye on him,' Emma told Mara.

'You're sure? All right. No more arguing, Hal. I can rest on the sofa downstairs.'

Emma frowned. 'They must have known we were out to come in here so openly. With all due respect, we hardly know you, Hal. Why should we be able to influence what you do with your mother's house?'

'They, um, may have seen me kissing Mara if they were watching from the canal.'

'That's still not enough to justify breaking into our house.'

Hal grimaced. 'Perhaps they were thinking I'd feel guilty and give in.'

She shook her head, still not buying it as a valid

reason. 'And perhaps the moon really is made of cheese.'

The two paramedics had been murmuring to one another and one said, 'Let us take you next door in our wheelchair, at least, Mr Kendrell. And how about you take these painkillers? No allergies or anything like that?'

'No, none. What are they?' He looked at them, nodded and took the glass of water Mara had quickly got for him to help swallow the pills.

'It will help to ice that ankle regularly, sir.'

'I've got plenty of ice cubes,' Emma said. 'I'll give you a bag of them.' She went to do this and handed an insulated bag to Mara.

One police officer moved away from them to answer a phone call, then came back and nudged his colleague. 'There's another emergency.' He turned to Hal. 'We'll come back later this evening, sir, because we need to ask you a few more questions. Or we'll send someone else if this call-out takes too much time.'

'All right.'

'There is a wheelchair in the downstairs storeroom in my house which I can use for a few hours,' Hal said. 'I think my mother might have needed it towards the end.' He fumbled in his pocket and produced a front door key. 'It's on the left as you go in.'

While the paramedics were getting his wheelchair, Emma made a shooing motion to Mara with one hand. 'Nip upstairs and get a change of clothes and anything else you may need tonight, dear.'

'You'll be careful if I go with Hal, won't you? I still don't like leaving you on your own.'

'Actually, I'd rather throw up in peace and privacy, if you don't mind. Just hurry up and leave me to it.' She pressed one hand to her mouth.

Emma was looking chalk white again, so Mara ran upstairs and grabbed what she needed then left poor Emma to recover in peace. She didn't think the intruders would be stupid enough to risk coming back again or she'd never have left the other woman alone.

'You'll leave the outside lights on, won't you?' she asked, hesitating near the door. 'And you'll phone me if you get worse or anything else happens?'

'Yes to both. Now go on.' Emma clapped her hand to her mouth again, slammed the front door on them and dived into the downstairs cloakroom.

Chapter Twenty-One

Hal let the paramedics wheel him next door. He was about to stand up to get inside but Mara backed up their insistence that he stay in the wheelchair and let them deal with the step.

He pulled a face. 'Oh, very well. It is throbbing a bit.'

The paramedics bumped him backwards over the doorstep and followed his directions into the living area.

They stared first at their patient then at Mara doubtfully.

'Look, I've done a first aid course, so I'm not clueless about when to seek further help. It'll be all right to leave him with me.'

'Well, if you're sure you can cope.'

'Yes, I am.' She fixed Hal with a stern look. 'I shan't hesitate to stop him doing anything stupid.'

'All right, then.'

'Thank you for your help, guys,' Hal called, sighing

in relief as the two of them exchanged long-suffering glances and left.

When he and Mara were alone, Hal scowled down at his bandaged foot. 'The upside of this is that you and I are going to have the rest of the night together. The downside is that I can't do much about my feelings for you because my damned ankle is throbbing and I have to be careful how I move.'

She'd been putting most of the ice into his freezer and now came across with what was left, safely zipped in the plastic bag. 'The main thing is to look after your ankle. Here, let me arrange the ice around your foot. That'll help reduce the swelling and the painkillers should kick in soon.'

'Thank you.' He grasped her hand. 'This is another case of *To be continued*.'

Mara hoped so. She couldn't help smiling sympathetically at the way he kept moving incautiously then wincing and glaring at his ankle so she tried to distract him. 'Do you have any hot chocolate?'

'Yes. It was my mother's so it might be a bit stale, but come to think of it, I wouldn't mind a mug if you don't mind making some. It's a comforting sort of drink.'

'I agree. OK if I get myself a sandwich while I'm at it? I missed my tea because of Emma feeling ill.'

'Get whatever you like, but I don't recommend the frozen ready meals left in Mum's freezer. Tasteless sludge.' He grimaced at the memory.

She investigated the fridge. 'I'll make a cheese and chutney sandwich. It's one of my favourite fillings. I used to make my own chutney till I moved back into my parents' house. Mum wouldn't let me mess her kitchen up or serve her anything but very plain food, either.'

'Difficult to live with.'

'Very. Her disability might not have been visible to the naked eye, but it spoilt her life.'

'It didn't do much good for yours and your father's, either.'

She shrugged. 'These things happen. You just have to accept them and carry on.' She made the sandwich while she was waiting for the milk to boil, then carried his drink over to him before she started eating.

He took a couple of sips, sighing with pleasure. 'It tastes fine to me.' A couple more mouthfuls, then he said thoughtfully, 'I wonder who thought bullying tactics would force me sell the house? It upsets me that the note threatened you as well as me. I don't want you putting at risk.'

'Just let them try.' She took another big bite of her cheese sandwich, sighing with pleasure.

'Does anything faze you?'

'You.'

'Good.' Hal enjoyed watching her demolish the sandwich. So many women pecked at their food. Why was weight such a problem these days? He knew quite a few overweight guys too. Was there something in modern food that hadn't been present a few decades ago? It made you wonder. 'Get yourself another sandwich.'

'I will, if you don't mind.' She made a second one. 'Mmm. You can't beat a nice, sharp Cheddar cheese.'

He smiled at her. 'I can't wait for whoever it is to see me kissing you out on the patio again. We're not going to stop kissing one another, are we?'

'Definitely not.'

'Right answer.'

He leant forward to remove the impromptu ice pack off his ankle, wincing. 'I can only stand so much icing. I'd much rather kiss you again but it hurts to move.'

She finished off her second sandwich and went to put her plate in the dishwasher. As she came back she looked round appreciatively. 'No wonder you want to live in this house permanently. It's lovely.'

'I definitely want to *try* living here. But not on my own. I really like it – when I'm not getting bashed – and I'm ready to put down roots. Could you live here permanently?'

'Let's not go there. We're not nearly at that stage in our relationship.'

'Indulge me. Just hypothetically, could you live here?'

'If there were only us two involved, yes, I probably could. This is a beautiful location. But I have Dad to think about. The father in the UK, I mean, not Aaron. I love Phil to pieces and I'm not leaving him there to spend his final years on his own. I worry that I should have gone back when I spoke to him.'

His voice was soft. 'I'm so sorry about your mother.'

'Yes. I am too. But the mother I had as a small child hasn't been there for a while. I've been feeling guilty about how detached from her I was getting. In one way it's a relief to know these latest changes could mostly have been caused by the tumour.'

'We think we're medically advanced these days, but there's still a lot of guesswork involved, isn't there?'

'Tell me about it. Dad's going to be lost without some focus to his life, though. He's such a caring, loving man. I doubt anyone else could have put up with her for so long. You'd like him, I'm sure.'

'Let's put my question another way, then. If it weren't for your dad, what would you do?'

She shook her head, looking at him sadly. 'In that case, I might hang around and give us a try at being together. But as soon as the doctors say Mum is close to the end, I'm going back to be with him.'

'Then I might have to move to the UK so that we can continue getting to know one another.'

For a moment she couldn't speak, then her voice came out as a whisper. 'You'd do that? Already?'

'Yes. Would you give me a chance if I did it? Continue to see me?'

'Definitely.'

'Good. I'm a great believer in carpe diem, and I reckon this relationship with you is worth seizing.' He moved incautiously and winced. 'You might come across and hold my hand when I'm trying to chat you up romantically, since I can't come to you.'

She did just that, sitting on the floor next to his couch holding his nearest hand.

After a while, he said, 'If I have to move to England for a while to continue our romance, I'll make sure the house is protected. I'd still not sell it to these people, because I can't bear giving in to bullies. Besides, I really would like to try living here.'

She stared. 'Romance? You sound sure we're going to have one.'

'We've agreed to give our relationship a chance, so let's aim high.' He scowled down at his ankle. 'It's exactly the wrong time to be incapacitated, dammit. I'm aching to kiss you properly. Do you think you could squeeze onto the couch beside me?'

So she did that, smiling at him, feeling . . . hopeful.

'Much better!' he murmured as the first kiss ended.

They sat quietly for a few moments, with his arm round her shoulders and her nestled against him, then his phone rang. 'Sorry. Only close friends have this number. I'd better answer it.'

She got up to fetch the phone and handed it to him.

'Charles! Great to hear from you.' He listened to his friend, nodding and smiling. 'Perfect timing. I've got a problem here and unfortunately, I've sprained my ankle and am having trouble sorting it. It'll be a week or more before I'm fully mobile again.'

He explained what was going on, then listened, nodding. 'I'll email you the names and details. Get back to me if you can find a flight.'

When he put the phone down, he beamed at Mara. 'If anyone can find out who is targeting us, it's Charles. He works in security and he's good at it.'

'What if he can't find out who is behind the attacks on you?'

'If anyone can, it's him. He has a magic touch, seems to sense cheating and chicanery where others can't find any leads. Charles says he'll stay in a hotel and only contact me by phone or digitally. I've to email him all the information I have about this Diana Vincenzo. Once we've sorted this mess out, he can come and stay with me. Heaven knows, there's plenty of room.'

He sat thinking, head on one side. 'How about you get us both a piece of fruit cake out of the fridge and I'll email him the details now? Oh, and we'll open a bottle of wine to go with them.'

'You're like a steam roller when you want to do something, even when you have trouble moving about.'

He looked mischievous suddenly. 'I've been told that before, but where you're concerned, I promise you I'll be a very friendly steam roller.'

Unfortunately, the doorbell rang just as he was finishing his email. Mara wished it hadn't but stood up and moved towards the hall.

'Use the peephole first to see who it is!' Hal called after her.

'Duh! I'm not stupid. I've already done that and it's the police.' She opened the door and the same two officers came inside.

They were taking the attempted break-in and injury to Hal seriously, though they still doubted that someone would go to such lengths simply to persuade Hal to sell the house.

'That sort of stuff usually only happens in films or TV dramas,' one added gloomily. 'They put anything and everything in those. Real life for a police officer is a lot less interesting. There's too much paperwork, for a start. Anyway, we'll file this information and tell our patrols to keep an eye on things here.'

When they'd left she looked at Hal. 'You didn't tell them about your friend Charles.'

'He likes to work alone, off the police radar so to speak.' Hal yawned suddenly.

'How about you go to bed now?'

'How about you bring some bedding down here for us both, Mara, and I'll stay nearby? I'm not leaving you to face trouble on your own and I can hardly run downstairs to your aid.'

'I doubt there will be any need for that.'

'I doubt it too, but I'm still staying with you. The external peripheral security is armed so we can both try to grab some sleep. It'll warn us if anyone approaches the house.'

'No way will I be sleeping. I intend to stay awake and keep an eye on the situation. And on you.' She poked him in the chest for emphasis before running up to fetch pillows and blankets.

After sorting out his bedding, she sat down on one of the recliner armchairs.

'At least put your footrest up. You'll be much more comfortable like that.'

She did as he suggested and ten minutes later he watched her as she fell asleep, thinking how adorable she looked with her hair all tousled and wild. She was proving she could be a good friend and he was quite sure, somehow, that she'd be a good lover and even life partner.

Happily married friends had told him that you just 'knew' when you met 'the one'. He hadn't been optimistic that he would meet anyone – till she'd come into his life. How amazing was that, to consider such things so early in a relationship, and with all the other troubles going on?

He yawned and blinked a few times, trying to sit in a more upright position to help keep himself awake.

In the morning he woke first and chuckled as he realised it was nearly eight o'clock and they'd both slept soundly right through the night. Well, no alarms had sounded, so there couldn't have been any intruders.

She was still sleeping peacefully, so he was able to enjoy watching her all over again.

Next thing he knew, it was after nine o'clock and she was waking him up with a cup of tea because he'd fallen asleep again.

He stretched and beamed at seeing her still there. 'Fat lot of use we are as guard dogs.'

'I know. And by the way, *I* love the way your hair sticks up at one side when you've slept on it but others may find it rather comical.' She came across and smoothed it down. 'There you are. All handsome again.'

He grabbed her hand for a moment and kissed it lingeringly, amused at how she reacted, gasping and breathing deeply. He wished they'd been sleeping together in a bed. Oh boy, he definitely did.

If they had, he'd not be drinking tea now and she'd not be fiddling about with that stupid bag of ice.

The morning after the attempt to frighten Hal, Enrico summoned Diana to join him for breakfast in that imperious way he had developed recently of ordering folk around with no concern for what they wanted or needed to do.

She listened to his tirade of abuse about the incompetence of the men he'd hired, trying not to show how nervous it made her that he should even think of hiring men to do such things. Using a financial advantage she could understand, but trying to *hurt* people physically made her feel very nervous.

He'd changed a lot since his wife died and she didn't like the new Enrico. Whoever the men he'd hired were, they hadn't had much success in dislodging Hal Kendrell and she didn't think they would. That Kendrell guy had a very stubborn expression. She found him rather attractive but unfortunately that wasn't reciprocated. You could always tell. Pity.

'Are you listening, woman?' Enrico demanded.

'What? Oh, yes, of course I am.' Only she was a real estate agent not a gangster, and though she owed Enrico a lot, she was terrified of getting dragged into something illegal and losing her licence.

Diana looked across the canal to the poet's house, shaking her head in bafflement. It might have excellent views and be away from the main water traffic, but she could see nothing special about it. She'd tried several times to persuade Enrico to look at other canal properties, houses which were, in her professional opinion, far superior. She'd found him one to try out as a rental, and he'd complained about anything and everything, so she'd found him this house to rent in the same street, because she was sure the owner would have sold it to him.

But nothing she said, none of her careful reasoning seemed to get through to him. All he did was wave one hand in a dismissive gesture and repeat his latest orders to her. He wanted that house and no other.

Today he was looking tired and suddenly seemed to run out of steam, telling her abruptly that he'd see her later. She was glad to get away, but worried that on top of everything else, he wasn't looking well.

On the way home she detoured to drive past the poet's house, but it looked no more appealing than it had last time. She didn't intend to try to speak to the poet's son again as Enrico was urging her to do. Kendrell had been very definite about his refusal to sell, especially to her.

The trouble was Enrico had recently bought a share in the business where she worked. He was now treating her like his personal servant there, which the manager said she'd just have to put up with.

Enrico had made his money from imports and exports. What did he know about the nitty-gritty of selling property? Nothing, that's what.

If it went on like this, she might have to look round for a job in Perth and move away from Mandurah and Enrico. The trouble was, she'd become an expert on luxury canal residences in this particular town and was making a lot of money from selling them. She'd hate to waste all that effort.

No, the best thing to do would be to contact one of his sons. Did she dare?

She nodded and picked up the phone. No choice about it. Maybe they could persuade him to see sense. The elder of the two was rather like his mother. Perhaps that would soften Enrico's heart?

Chapter Twenty-Two

Mike was furious that he hadn't been able to get Peggy away from those idiots at the hospital. Why had she not done as he'd told her this time when she'd been so easily tamed previously? Women were usually susceptible to romantic words and gestures, the idiots, and some even liked you to order them around.

He'd have to tread more carefully next time he broke up with someone, though. Apart from other considerations, it irked him that those fools at the hospital were undoing all his good work and would make Peggy fat again.

Worst of all, they'd encourage her to keep the baby and he was still determined to prevent her from having it. There were far too many people in the world already. No one needed to create more hungry mouths. And on a personal level, he didn't need to be slapped with a compulsory child support order that would drain his finances for years to come.

He had to find a way to get her on her own for a while. He'd pretend to be still in love with her so that she would become malleable again. That was the other key to women: they were hungry for love.

She hadn't answered his pleas to get in touch and might have changed her phone number and email address, so he decided to hack into her parents' email accounts. He was both disgusted and delighted by how careless they were with their online security.

He got Peggy's new email address almost immediately, then found out that her father was over east in Melbourne because her mother was emailing her husband a couple of times a day with updates on their daughter's progress. Their exchanges might provide some helpful information. He'd keep an eye on them.

He was just about to sign off for the time being when another email clicked into place from her mother to her father, telling him that the hospital had arranged for Peggy to go and stay in a special unit for people who'd had eating disorders but were on the mend. Well-Away, it was called, of all the naff names.

And she was not anorexic; she was now a slender, attractive and *healthy* young woman, thanks to him.

That sent him searching for information about the unit. It took all his skills to find out anything at all and it was impossible to hack into its managerial systems. It was located in the south-west, near Margaret River. Hmm. Might be a better chance of getting at her there. He could hire a holiday cottage for a 'romantic getaway'. She'd really fall for that. He sniggered at the thought.

He'd have to be careful how he set about this. He couldn't even study the facilities and layout at this unit, they were all so carefully protected. Visitors were asked to telephone directly to a number that gave no information about who would be dealing with the calls.

Hmm. He doubted he'd be able to catch Peggy before she went down to Margaret River, because she was leaving Mandurah the next day, her mother said, so he needed to hire a cottage ASAP.

Once there, he reckoned his best hope would be to reconnoitre the grounds at this place and see how closely the buildings were guarded. He'd have to find some way of getting in, but one that he could exit by quickly if she caused a fuss – no, surely he'd be able to coax her into talking to him and reconsidering her options?

Of course, it'd mean taking her back to live with him for a while but she was good in bed so there would be advantages to that. There was still time for her to agree to an abortion and her body wouldn't be getting fat yet, surely? How slim could someone remain as they got into a pregnancy anyway? That was an interesting thought.

No, it'd be too risky to let things drag on for long. If anything went wrong, she might run away and carry the child to term. He definitely wasn't going to put on the shackles of fatherhood, not for anyone.

He was going to find such a challenge stimulating. He always did enjoy the intricacies of coaxing a woman into working on her body. He considered that his mission in life and one of his major skills.

He went to study himself in the mirror, admiring

what he saw. *Lean* and *toned* were magic words these days. He'd achieved that in spades, both for himself and for others. He was providing a health service to society, really.

Yes, he'd get Peggy back and cope with the challenge of persuading her to get rid of the little invader once he had her on her own. He always found ways to get what he wanted from women.

The head of Well-Away's IT section noticed that someone was trying to hack into their system and watched carefully. They had to be particularly wary of such invasions because some of their clients' former acquaintances tried to persuade them to leave and go back to their old ways of eating – or not eating.

This hacker seemed to be focusing on a patient who was coming to join them the following day. Why was he trying to find out about the unit before she even got here? Surely he could have contacted Peggy Buchanan directly if he was a genuine friend?

That looked distinctly suspicious and after further observation, he contacted the director. 'You might want to alert the patient to this when she arrives.'

Janice frowned. 'I will. You know what? The man's name looks familiar.' She mouthed it a couple of times then snapped her fingers as she realised who he was. 'That's the man whose influence caused Tessa to stop eating properly over a year ago. Just a sec. Let me check her records. We have to be sure of it before we do anything.'

She brought up the information. 'Aha! He is the one. Look, we've even got a photo of them together. Does he make a habit of stopping young women eating? I bet he doesn't know we'll have two of his victims here at the same time.'

'Are you going to make them aware that he's taking an interest?'

'Definitely. They have to learn to cope with the outside world again. Pity it's so soon for Peggy.'

'Sarisha said the baby has given Peggy something to eat for.'

'And she's usually right. It took Tessa a lot longer to get to this stage, but she's nearly ready to live normally now.'

'I've heard Tessa say she'd like to get her own back on him, so perhaps you'd better not tell her.'

'I didn't hear you say that.' Janice winked at him and walked away.

Hal and Mara enjoyed a leisurely breakfast then took it in turns to shower while the other kept watch. Not that they really believed anyone would be prowling around in daylight.

'Cloak and dagger stuff,' he said cheerfully when she came down to join him smelling of soap and newly washed skin. He plonked a kiss on her cheek, glad she didn't wear make-up, glad she was here with him.

'Better safe than sorry, eh?'

'Better together than apart as well. I'm still enjoying your company.'

'I'm still enjoying yours, too, Hal.'

'Can you spend the whole day with me?'

'I hope so. You're going to need help for a day or two. But I'll have to nip back and check that Emma's OK with that.'

'Do it now.'

'OK. I think I caught a glimpse of her a few minutes ago.'

But before she could do anything, Emma came out of the next house and waved cheerfully to them before clambering over the wall to join them.

Mara opened the sliding door and pulled the flyscreen across it after Emma had come inside, smiling as she realised that she was now doing that automatically. Very Australian. 'Cup of coffee?'

'Love one. I've just had a phone call from Aaron. He sends his love and he'll be flying home tomorrow.' She beamed at them as she added, 'We're going to have a big celebration in a few days' time, because the sale of his business has gone through. We shall soon be free to travel or do anything else we please *when* we please.'

Once they were seated with their coffee, Emma got to the point of her visit. 'I also came to tell you that I'll not be visiting the hospital today, or asking you to, because Peggy is travelling down to the recovery unit near Margaret River.'

'She seemed a lot more cheerful when we last saw her.'

'Yes. Isn't that wonderful? And she's even put on

a little weight. Not much, but it's a start. She's so concerned for her baby's health, you see.'

'That's wonderful. You must be so pleased.'

'Yes. Who'd have thought an unborn baby would be our biggest ally in helping her?' Her excitement faded for a moment. 'I could see that she was forcing food down, though. She didn't *want* to eat anything.'

'Then thank goodness for the baby. She was absolutely glowing with happiness when she talked to me about becoming a mother.' Mara had felt rather envious of that.

Emma brightened up again. 'Wasn't she? I had a call from Rufus yesterday evening as well. He's been asked to stay on here in the west for an extra month to help with a special project, and he'll be staying at Jenn's flat. So they must be getting on well, don't you think?'

'He seems very taken with her.' Mara couldn't help glancing at Hal as she said that. She was rather taken with this man, too.

She tensed when Emma asked straight out, 'Are you two a couple now?'

Hal reached out and grabbed Mara's hand while she was still trying to think what to say. 'Yes. We've got our L plates on, but we're ticking along nicely.'

'I can't do anything until I've seen that Dad is OK.' Sadness washed through Mara as it did every now and then. 'And there's Mum. We don't know how long it'll be but her brain scans show she's declining by the day. She's definitely not going to recover.'

Emma looked at her in dismay. 'Are they sure of that?'

Mara could only nod and blink the tears from her eyes, then before she knew it, Hal had managed to stand up, using the sofa to help him balance. He pulled her into a hug and she let him, resting her head against his shoulder, drawing on his strength.

When she looked up, Emma had gone.

'She understands,' he said softly. 'She blew me a kiss as she left.'

'She's nice, isn't she?'

'Very nice. But not nearly as nice as you.'

Peggy was delighted when she found out she wouldn't be making the journey to Margaret River in an ambulance. She hoped she'd never have to get into one of those horrible vehicles again. She'd felt so helpless and at risk shut into a big tin box.

It had been a bit of an effort to finish her breakfast today, but Sarisha said that was only to be expected, because it took time to change habits. But the baby had to have a share now, so she had to do it.

Sarisha had also talked about what to expect during the next stage of recovery and she'd had some very practical hints to share. Finally she gave Peggy a present, a book of names and their meanings.

'Since you're not with Mike any longer, it'll be up to you to choose a suitable name. When you've nothing better to do and you need to distract yourself from your worries, you can go through the names and see if any take your fancy. Make a shortlist, then see which stays with you.'

Peggy flicked the book open at random and read a few names. Sarisha was right. It was fascinating to find out their meanings and histories. She slipped it into her shoulder bag, smiling. 'What a delightful present! Thank you.'

The journey down to Margaret River was a pleasure because the scenery was so much prettier further south of Perth. She was alone with the fatherly, white-haired driver, so sat in the front.

When he found out she was expecting, he chatted about his grandchildren and also his children, telling her what they'd been like as babies and how their offspring resembled them. 'Little rascals they are!' he kept saying fondly.

It was lovely to hear him talk about them. He sounded to be very much a hands-on father and grandfather. She couldn't imagine Mike doing any of this sort of thing. In fact, he'd make a terrible father. He didn't even like to touch small children or for them to touch him – not that they willingly went near him. They seemed to sense the way he felt.

How had she let herself be taken in by him? That absolutely baffled her now. And it puzzled her too how abruptly the disenchantment with him had happened.

When they were getting closer to the unit, they passed several vineyards. It had been ages since she'd been down in the south-west wine-growing area, ages since she'd enjoyed a glass of wine as well. Mike had said it was sheer poison, but if so, some of it had been very nice-tasting poison. The sign outside one big vineyard reminded her of how good the wines were from their label. One of the best reds she'd ever tasted had come from those very vines.

Not that she'd be drinking alcohol now, but she could look forward to having it again after the baby had been born and weaned.

Mike might decree it to be a major poison, but she enjoyed the odd glass, as did many people.

As she pulled a tissue out of her bag to blow her nose, one of the bootees her mother had given her fell out with it. She'd slept with the soft little things under her pillow. They seemed to give her such comfort, as well as making her wonder about the little person who would be wearing them one day. She'd tell her mother how meaningful they had become and thank her properly the next time she saw her. She felt guilty now at how unkind she'd been to her mother.

The driver slowed down and took a left turn. 'We're almost there. Lovely place they've got here and lovely people who run it. I've brought a few lasses down to stay and taken them back to Perth looking so much better. You're too thin, my lass.'

'Yes. I know that now.' She knew it in her mind, but it still didn't mean it was easy to eat more generously.

The leaflet Peggy had been given said that the unit was based at an old colonial farmhouse that had been remodelled and extended. The brochure gave no details about where it was exactly, let alone providing a site map. The unit wasn't available online either – well, not that she'd been able to find.

As she got out of the car, she was surprised at how tired she felt, tired but also positive about what she was doing. Sarisha had explained that there would be a registration process and orientation to be got through on arrival, then the people running the unit would trust the patients to behave sensibly.

Sensible? Was it sensible to long for a baby like she did? Who knew.

But she'd come here to change her way of eating and give her baby its best chance of a healthy start in life, and she'd put all her efforts into that from now on. That's what a good mother did.

Chapter Twenty-Three

Peggy was surprised at how impressed she was by the head of the unit. The woman was about her mother's age and had a lovely smile. Best of all, she treated Peggy like an intelligent younger woman, not a juvenile idiot.

Janice Meyman didn't look like any doctor Peggy had met before. She was downright glamorous, with curves in all the right places, curves which somehow made Peggy stare down at her scrawny arms and legs, and wish her own body wasn't quite so angular. Even her boobs had shrunk in size. She also wished the skin on her face was slightly rosy with health, like the doctor's, and not so pale.

Once the entry forms were filled in, Dr Meyman stood up. 'Well, that's all the red tape for now. Let's go and find Tessa, who's going to be your buddy, well, she will be if you get on OK with her. If not, we'll find you someone else. No one should go through what you're going through alone. You need a support team and that's what we'll provide.'

'Thank you.'

'Tessa has the next room to yours and she'll answer all the questions you don't quite like to ask me.'

'I didn't – there aren't—'

There was a positive grin on the doctor's face. 'If there aren't any now, you'll find them cropping up from now on. Your peers can sometimes give more meaningful answers to such questions than the staff. Oh, and by the way, I prefer people to call me Janice. It's more friendly, don't you think?'

'Oh. Well yes, it is. Thank you, um, Janice.'

Peggy hoped she'd like this 'buddy' person. It was a stupid, old-fashioned term for an old-fashioned concept if you asked her. But never mind. Someone who had the same problems as her would make a nice change from medical staff and parents, especially parents, even the most well-meaning ones.

How could they understand why she'd got into this mess, when she didn't understand it herself? The only good thing to come from it was the baby.

She realised Janice was waiting for her so forced herself to concentrate. The doctor walked with her to her room, pointing out a couple of common areas for people staying here on the way.

Her room was quite large with both a sleeping and sitting area, not at all cell-like, thank goodness. The cramped hospital room had made Peggy feel worse, not better. This one looked out onto a huge garden full of beautiful flowers and plants, which was another good thing. You didn't get lush flowerbeds like these on the edge of a canal. Too many salty sea breezes.

'Just a minute.' Janice went outside again and knocked on the next door. 'She's here.'

She came back with another young woman. 'Peggy, Tessa.' The two of them eyed one another speculatively and nodded a hello.

Her 'buddy' looked to be in blooming health with rather a mischievous smile, but she was rather thin. Peggy caught sight of herself in a mirror and added mentally, not as thin as she was herself, though.

'You two have more in common than most of the people here,' the doctor said, 'but I'll leave your new buddy to tell you about that, Peggy.'

Tessa's expression changed to what looked like anger and her voice grew sharper. 'I'll certainly do that, Janice.'

Dr Meyman walked to the door. 'I'll leave you to get settled in, then. Remember, Peggy, there is someone available twenty-four seven should you need help or support. You have the list of numbers to call. If you're feeling depressed or worried, please reach out to us. It's what we're here for.'

When the doctor had left, Peggy looked at her new buddy, not sure what to say.

'The staff here are all right, especially Janice,' Tessa said quietly. 'You can trust them with anything, I promise. Let's go and sit in the garden and then I'll tell you about this weird coincidence.'

She led the way right to the far end of the rear gardens to a seat in front of a graceful summer house of white painted wood. It was surrounded by low, flowering bushes and almost invited you inside to tell secrets.

'Do sit down, Peggy. They have CCTV cameras scanning the grounds near the house, and we're not sure whether they pick up sounds as well. We've checked this place and we're pretty sure it's not bugged, so we do our chatting here or else when we go outside the grounds for walks.'

'Who's "we"?'

'There are three of us here at the moment who get on rather well. I'll tell you more in a minute. First, I want to know if it's true that Mike Cruikshank got you in this state?'

'Pregnant, you mean?'

Tessa's mouth dropped open in shock. 'No, I didn't mean that. I didn't even know about that aspect. Janice didn't say a word. No, Mike's the one who got me to stop eating – then after a few months he chucked me out of his flat. And I gather he did the same to you. Am I right?'

'Yes. I was utterly stupid about him.'

Tessa took a deep breath. 'I must be even more stupid, then, because I walked out and left him, then got depressed and tried to kill myself. Thank goodness a friend stopped me.'

Peggy gave her a hug, not something she normally

did to strangers, but her companion was looking so sad. 'Mike isn't worth it.'

'Oh, I agree and I'm well over him now, but I'm still angry at myself for being taken in by him and I still have trouble eating enough to stay healthy. He makes it his mission in life to turn normal women into scrawny anorexics and the authorities don't seem to have found any way of prosecuting him for it.'

'I didn't realise he made a habit of it. I thought it was just – you know, me.'

'No. He's got an absolute fixation about it. I found a diary once in which he wrote down all the details and congratulated himself on his success rate. He's never stayed with anyone longer than a year.' She frowned at Peggy. 'But he hated babies and was usually careful not to get anyone pregnant. What on earth happened?'

'I think he was too eager that night it happened. You know how he enjoys sex. And he thought I was on the pill, only I'd gone off it without telling him because I wanted so desperately to have a baby.' She patted her stomach. 'This has to be his child because I've only been with him during the past few months.'

Tessa let out a long, low whistle. 'Wow! I'd like to have been a fly on the wall when you told him.'

'I didn't tell him because he'd chucked me out by the time I realised I was expecting and anyway I knew his views on babies. I was planning to have the child then bring it up on my own. Unfortunately, he found out somehow and now he's pestering me to talk and I know he'll want to get rid of it. I told him I'm not going to do that, not for anything. I've been longing to have a child for over a year now, even before I met him. Don't you just love babies and little children?'

'Not as much as you do, clearly. I had a friend who got all mumsy like that a couple of years ago, so I know it happens to some women. She's living in Tasmania now, loves being a mother. Good for you, standing up to Mike about it. That man is too fond of manipulating women.'

'Tell me about it. Look, could you just give me a summary of what's going on here because I'm exhausted. It's been a long day.'

'OK. But promise you won't tell anyone about it if you'd rather not join in.'

'Join in what?'

'The Revenge Club. I suspect Janice knows – she seems to know everything, but we haven't talked about it to her and she's never brought it up.'

'Go on.'

'Most people who end up here did this anorexia thing to themselves, but some of us were nagged into it by people like Mike, who think women ought to be scraggy stick insects.' She indicated her body with a scowl and blinked her eyes furiously.

So Peggy gave her another hug. 'Go on. Who else is in your club?'

'There's a former fashion model who's furious about her agent. He kept nagging her not to eat so much and to lose "just a bit more" if she wanted the top jobs. Jordan collapsed one day and was quite ill. Her mother nursed her back to health and sent her here to finish off the process of rehabilitation under professional guidance. She's wondering whether she could sue her agent.'

Peggy let out a long, low whistle.

'And Loreen was quite fat back in the day. Her aunt mocked her and bet she couldn't lose weight if she tried. But when she did lose some weight, the aunt kept saying she didn't look good yet, needed to lose more. Loreen got so mad at her, so eager to show her she could get slim that she went overboard on the dieting till she couldn't stop.'

'Poor thing. I'm glad to be well away from Mike now, that's for sure, because he kept telling me I was fat.'

'Don't bank on it. He'll come after you like he did me. He won't want you to have this baby.'

'You weren't pregnant so why did he come after you?'

'It's all right for him to end a relationship, as he did with you, but not right for one of his victims to end it, as I did.'

'What happened to make you leave him?'

'I simply came to my senses one day and left. Just like that.' She clicked her fingers. 'He played a few nasty tricks on me afterwards then the trouble suddenly stopped. A friend told me he'd found another victim and it turns out it was you. But he still caught up with me one day, a month after he got together with you, and mocked me in front of a group of friends for not being able to hold his interest.'

'What? The cheek of it!'

'Yeah. I was still a bit fragile healthwise after I left him and it took months before I was in a fit state to come down here. I still don't really enjoy food, but if I stop eating he'll have won.'

'I don't fancy food much, either, but the thought of the baby needing me to eat more so that it can grow properly keeps me forcing it down.'

'You keep doing that. So anyway, that's the Revenge Club. We're going to get our own back on those who pushed us into anorexia.'

Peggy looked at her in alarm. 'What do you mean by that? I'm not doing anything illegal.'

'Neither am I. We're not going to break the law, but we are going to make them look stupid in public so that maybe they'll think twice about doing it to someone else.'

'Will that happen, do you think? I'd love to see it, mind.'

'We have to make it happen. Mike would hate to be made a fool of, don't you think?'

Peggy leant back in her seat, smiling at the thought. 'Yes, he would.'

'And if it doesn't make any difference to them, at least we'll have done our best and that'll feel more satisfying than just being a victim.'

'Well, I wouldn't mind *upsetting* him. He actually came after me in the hospital, sneaked in and tried to force me to leave with him. I don't see what we can actually do.'

Tessa smiled. 'I have an idea for how to get at Mike, and the others are going to help me. Lean closer. I hardly dare say it aloud at this stage.'

She began to whisper, gesticulating wildly with her hands. And Peggy had to chuckle at what she and her friends here had thought up.

Five minutes later a bell rang in the main building and two smiling young women wandered back across the lawn to the small sitting room for patients, where they drank their special shakes meekly.

After that, Peggy went to bed. She didn't expect to sleep but it had been a tiring day and she still wasn't as full of energy as she had been a year ago, thanks to Mike.

She chuckled again as she grew drowsy at the thought of what Tessa was planning. Oh yes, she definitely wanted to join in that.

Janice had watched them when she popped into the residents' common room for a few minutes, as she did regularly, but didn't try to find out what they were plotting. She didn't think it likely that they'd carry anything through, or at least not in the near future, especially as no one seemed to have managed to catch out Mike Cruikshank before. But it was good to see smiles on their faces.

And if they did serve up some mischief eventually, well, he deserved it, didn't he?

She could always step in and put a stop to it if it went too far.

Laughter, she sometimes thought, was a very good cure-all. Or in this case, mockery.

Chapter Twenty-Four

Charles North managed to get on an early morning flight from Sydney and arrived in Western Australia mid-morning, adding an extra three hours to his day because of the time differences between the two coasts of Australia.

At the airport he quickly claimed his hire car and set the satnav to take him south to the small holiday flat in Mandurah, which he'd booked yesterday for a week. He carried in his luggage, grimacing at how utilitarian and cramped the flat was, but at least it was conveniently situated. He then strolled out to find the shop of the real estate agent who was annoying his friend Hal.

He and Hal had been good friends for a while. They'd just clicked somehow. Like Hal, Charles had had enough of the way he was earning his living. Running the sort of business which meant being on call night or day, ready to go anywhere in the world could pall. He'd sold his company a while ago, still doing the occasional contract jobs for the new owner, but only ones that sounded interesting.

He envied Hal meeting a woman to love. He'd never heard quite that tone in his friend's voice before, and good luck to him. The only woman Charles had ever contemplated spending his life with hadn't wanted to settle down and had gone off to work in America. She'd probably be the CEO of a big business by now. He could have found her if he'd wanted to but that fire had died down.

He envied Hal his inheritance of a house in a beautiful setting, which was why he'd thought to take up the invitation to visit him. He hadn't expected Hal to need his help. So he was staying in the nasty little flat and no one would connect the two of them.

Maybe he'd have a look round Mandurah on his own behalf while he was here, if it had made such a good impression on Hal. And maybe not. Charles couldn't seem to settle anywhere since his semi-retirement. Maybe he'd left it too late to try to settle down in a forever home.

Ah, there it was! He stopped in front of the shop window full of photos of houses for sale, ignoring the holidaymakers coming and going around him, then taking his time to pretend to study the houses advertised. He even took out a notebook and scribbled in it to make it look like a genuine interest.

In the process he watched through his special dark sunglasses, seeing what was going on inside the shop without the people there being able to see what his eyes were really focused on.

Almost immediately he saw a showily dressed woman who matched the description of the annoying estate agent. She was sitting in a glass-walled miniature office to one side but seemed to be spending more time staring into space than working on the papers scattered across her desk. The woman's name was listed on several of the canal properties in the window.

It was clear even to a stranger watching her from outside the shop that her work wasn't making her happy at the moment. Her office was one of those boxes with clear glass 'walls' and he could see her chewing the end of her pencil and frowning. At one point she picked up a telephone and stared down at it, then shook her head and put it back in its cradle again.

Here we go! he thought and pushed open the door of the agency.

The receptionist smiled at him brightly. 'Good morning, sir. How may we help you?'

He answered more loudly than was necessary. 'I'm looking to buy a house on the Waterfront Canals.'

He saw the woman in the office jerk to attention and get up from her desk.

'Ms Vincenzo will be happy to help you, sir.'

Aha! He'd guessed correctly who the woman was. He turned as she came up to him.

'I specialise in canal homes, Mr . . . ?'

He didn't give his real surname. 'Smith. Charles P Smith.' He stretched out his hand to shake hers and held on to it for too long, giving her what he hoped was an admiring glance, though he didn't really admire such fussily dressed females or wish to gaze at her abundant breasts.

Her smile faded a little and she pulled her hand away. 'I have several canal homes I can show you, Mr Smith.'

'Oh, good. I've seen and admired such homes over east and I'm about to move across to the west so I thought I'd see if I could find one here to buy.'

'What exactly are you looking for in a house?'

'Not a small place. Something a bit special. I'll know it when I see it. How about we drive past the outsides of your houses and I'll tell you whether any of them appeal to me. No use going inside if I don't like the looks of the place it's situated, is there?'

'And your price range would be . . . ?'

He shrugged. 'Whatever it takes if I find a house I like the looks of. It'll be a cash offer.'

'Would your wife not wish to see these houses with you?'

He tried to look sad and in need of comfort. 'Sadly, my Mary died two years ago.' He could see her start to relax a little. Then an older man came into the agency and Ms Vincenzo stiffened again.

The receptionist stood up. 'Good afternoon, Mr Moretti. Can I get you anything?'

'No, no. Just carry on with your work.'

However, she opened the door of another office at the rear for him before she sat down again. This one had proper, opaque walls. The man went inside it with an air of ownership, stopping for a moment in the doorway to look across at Ms Vincenzo as if impatient to talk to her.

'Who is he?' Charles asked.

'One of the owners of this agency.'

'He looks as if he wants to speak to you.'

She shrugged. 'Well, I'd never abandon a customer and I'm sure Mr Moretti's business won't be urgent. Shall we go, Mr Smith? We can use my car, if you like.'

'Good idea.'

Charles followed her out, showed interest in one or two of the houses she took him past and asked their prices. 'I'll go away and study the areas around each of the homes you've shown me, then get back to you if I'm still interested.'

'May I have a contact number in case something else crops up?'

He gave her the number of a phone which had no greetings message or answer service. 'How about we look inside a couple of the houses later this afternoon? I'll phone you and let you know which.'

She sighed as if unsure he'd get back to her but didn't press the point. A cloud of worry seemed to settle around her as soon as he started to turn away and she hesitated, then got back into her car and drove off instead of returning to her office.

Charles strolled back to the flat, took off his jacket, shirt and tie, then put on a tee shirt and a shabby sun hat. He strolled back past the agency, moving slowly and wearily like an older person, fairly sure he looked different enough that the smiling receptionist would not recognise him.

He was in luck. A car stopped outside the entrance as he drew near it and the old guy the receptionist had fussed over came outside.

As the chauffeur drove away, the passenger slumped down, looking out. In fact, his expression was rather angry. Charles strolled on thoughtfully, buying a sandwich on the way back.

He ate the sandwich quickly, then set out again to drive to the street where Hal thought the old guy might live. He chuckled as he saw the car parked on the drive outside a house, which would be roughly opposite where Hal lived, according to the street map.

He stopped further along for a few moments and watched a shabby car stop and a guy who looked like a tradesman go into the house. Charles was fairly certain he'd recognised the type of person, a strong man, one who hired out as a bodyguard or to bully people.

'"*Curiouser and curiouser,*" cried Alice,' he muttered. It was one of his favourite quotations.

He took careful note of what the houses on either side of this one looked like, chuckling when he realised one of them was for sale and that Diana was the agent. Why hadn't she brought him to this one?

He went back into town and phoned her. She said she hadn't shown him that particular house because it wasn't up to much but when he insisted, she agreed to show him round it.

Was she avoiding Moretti and if so, why?

* * *

Diana arrived a few minutes later, parking her car behind his in the drive of the house, as if trying to hide from the house next door.

She got out and hurried to the front door, beckoning him inside.

He decided to confront her as soon as they got inside. 'You're trying to hide from Mr Moretti, aren't you?'

She stared at him in shock. 'How could you tell?'

'I'm an observant sort of guy.'

She shrugged, not elaborating.

'Let's sit down on that sofa and you can tell me about it. If it makes you feel any better I'm a registered private investigator and highly respectable.' He showed her his ID and saw her sag as if giving up hope. 'Go on.'

'Enrico hasn't been the same since his wife died. She kept him on the straight and narrow, I think. At the moment he's fixated on buying one particular house, I can't understand why and I think—' She broke off.

'You think he's hiring thugs to frighten away the poet's son. Why don't you trust me with the full story?'

She scowled at him. 'Why should I?'

'Because I'll find out anyway. I'm good at finding things out.'

Still she hesitated, then a tear rolled down her cheek. 'He owns part of the agency where I work. I don't want to lose my job.'

'Some people search desperately for a new aim in life when they lose a partner. Does he have any family left, children, siblings?'

'Two sons. Only they've not been close since their

mother died. Anyway, they live in the eastern states.'

'It's their job to look after him.'

'I don't think they realised why he was growing so – well, pushy. I think he must have been like that when he was younger, till he met Gina.'

'Phone them. Get them to come across to Mandurah and talk to him. In the meantime I'll keep an eye on what he's doing.'

'Has Kendrell hired you?'

Charles laughed gently. 'No. He and I are friends from way back. I'm helping him out because he's sprained his ankle and is afraid of the woman he loves getting hurt. Now, show me round this place quickly because I really am thinking of buying a house on the canals, then go away and phone Moretti's sons. Let me know how you go on.'

The way he said it made her stare at him and realise he wasn't going to go away without some resolution.

When he went back to his stuffy little flat, he phoned Hal and told him what he'd done and what he suspected. 'I can't do anything about Moretti. His family will have to get involved. In the meantime, make sure you keep the place locked up tonight. I'm going to have an early night. My body isn't tuned into West Australian time yet. But don't hesitate to phone if you need help suddenly. I can be there in ten minutes max.'

Hal put the phone down and went to tell Mara what Charles had found out.

'Already?'

'Told you he was good.'

'It sounds to fit,' she said.

'Yes, it does. On another topic, has Emma been in touch? I was wondering how Peggy was getting on.'

'Not a word from her. I'm going to phone my dad soon which will catch him in the morning UK time. I want to find out how things are going.'

But her phone rang before she could do that and it was Phil. After he'd assured her he was all right now, he said quietly, 'I think you'd better come back if you want to say farewell to your mother. Though it's only the shell of her that's left and she won't react to you, but you'll feel better for seeing her, I think. Well, I did. I've just come back from the hospital. Her deterioration has speeded up, apparently.'

His voice broke on the last words.

'I'll take the first flight I can get a seat on.'

'What about that chap you were telling me about? Will this break things up between you?'

'I'm not sure. He says he'll follow me to the UK, so me coming back early will either make or break us as a couple.'

'Well, that's a bright spot in a sad time, I must say. You'll be making me a grandfather yet.'

She could see that Hal had been listening and felt embarrassed by that, so said hastily, 'I'll have to see when I can book a seat. Bye, Da.'

Hal said, 'Get Emma to book a seat for you. Companies can often do such things better than individuals.'

'But they've just sold the company.'

'Ask her if she can help anyway. She's still nominally working there. I'll follow you to the UK as soon as I can make arrangements to have this house looked after.'

'I'll go across to see Emma straight away. Oh no, she's picking Aaron up from the airport this morning. She won't be in.'

'They'll be back by midday. That won't make much difference, surely.'

But before Emma and Aaron returned from the airport, there was another phone call from her dad.

'It's bad news, love. Your mother died an hour ago.'

She'd guessed before he told her. 'I wish she'd waited.' Tears welled in Mara's eyes. Her mother might have been getting stranger and more distanced from the world but it hurt more than she'd expected to lose the last of her.

'You don't need to rush to get back now. Why don't you wait and bring that chap with you? It's hard to face a funeral on your own.'

'You'll be on your own in the meantime.'

'Ah. Well, I won't. Sally is going round with me to sort the formalities out. She's been a tower of strength. I don't know what I'd have done without her.'

She blinked. Did that mean what she thought it might? Were he and Sally getting closer? She hoped so. Her mother had not really been acting like a wife for years now and he was such a loving man. 'I shouldn't have come here and left you alone.'

'Yes, you should. You couldn't have changed a thing. I won't hold the funeral till you're back, I promise.'

But she was determined to rejoin him quickly. It felt

like the right thing to do, the last thing she could do for her mother. And if that was a stupid idea, she couldn't help it.

She put the phone down and took Hal's hand. 'I'll ask Aaron and Emma if they can help. I need to get back.'

He studied her and nodded. 'Then that's what you must do.'

Chapter Twenty-Five

That evening Peggy and Tessa had a very satisfactory brain-storming chat, going over the details of their plot with Loreen and Jordan. It was a no-brainer to target Mike first for revenge, because he'd be nearby. She and Tessa were quite sure of that, knowing how he operated.

They felt so good about their chances of success that when they joined the other residents, they kept snorting with laughter, but refusing to explain why.

Loreen went to her room 'to freshen up' and returned half an hour later, looking distinctly gleeful. 'Let's go for a final stroll round the garden, girls.'

When they were away from the house, she said, 'We're in luck. Liam is only thirty kilometres away working on another photoshoot and if we can arrange it for around teatime tomorrow, he'll come and join the fun.' She sighed. 'I think he was interested in me as a woman till I got so thin he didn't even like to use me as a model. He said he was delighted that I'm getting better.'

'Can we organise it by tomorrow, though?' Peggy wondered.

'We can if you'll contact Mike. I bet he's just waiting for a chance to get at you again. If he isn't nearby already, he'll be down here like a shot if you tell him you want to escape from here.'

'I don't really want to speak to him again.'

'You must, if you and I are going to get our revenge,' Tessa said fiercely. 'I know I shall feel better for the rest of my life if we succeed.'

No one suggested she was exaggerating. They all understood.

'I'll phone him then,' Peggy said. 'Wish me luck.'

Janice, who had been watching them surreptitiously, leant towards a colleague and said, 'They're up to something.'

'Should we stop them?'

'No. Look at how alive they are all of a sudden. But we'll keep an eye on things.'

Peggy phoned the number she'd never expected to use again. She'd not have been surprised if he'd changed his phone number, but no, it was the same one.

'Mike?'

'Who's that?'

'Don't you recognise me?'

'Peggy? Oh, darling, I've missed you.'

'Have you? Look, I have to be quick. I've pretended I need to use the bathroom. Mike, they've sent me to a unit near Margaret River. I absolutely hate it here. The food is so . . . gross. They're forcing me to eat. Could you – rescue me? Or did you mean it when you said you never wanted to see me again?'

'I thought I did, but I found out differently after you'd left. It'll make me so happy to have you back.'

Liar! she thought. *You just want to get rid of the baby.* She faked a sob. 'I don't have any more personal time till tomorrow afternoon. Can you come for me then?'

'Of course I can. I—'

'Have to go. I'll phone tomorrow morning to tell you where to find me.' She cut off the connection and muttered, 'How dare you call me darling after what you've done, you nasty, sly rat?'

Then she went to tell the others what she'd arranged.

When Peggy was alone in bed she shed a few tears. She didn't want Mike back, definitely not, didn't want to see him either, but speaking to him had reminded her of how stupidly gullible she'd been.

Well, she'd get him here and from the way he'd lied to her, he deserved anything they could do to him.

They'd be waiting for him. Oh, yes.

Mara was surprised at how good it felt to see Aaron again. She hugged him back, then congratulated him on selling his business.

'Never mind that. I can see that you're upset about

something. Can I do anything to help?'

She explained about her mother and the need to go back to the UK as quickly as she could.

He was silent and she was surprised to see tears well in his eyes.

'Kath didn't have a very good life, did she?' he said eventually.

'We had a few fairly happy years as a family back when I was in primary school, but things went steadily downhill after that, though I don't think we realised it fully at the time. She hasn't been at all well lately, and apparently she attacked Dad physically just before she collapsed. Turns out she had a brain tumour.'

'It must have been so hard on you and your father.'

'There's never a guarantee that life will be easy or fair, is there? Your only choice is what to do about it.'

He gave her another quick hug. 'Emma will get you a flight and I'd back her to be more successful than anyone else could be. But even she can't guarantee how soon one will become available.'

'That's all right. It's not going to make a difference now, is it? I just – you know, want to be with my dad.'

'I'd like to meet him one day. I'm so glad you've had him over the years. Now, I'll come back with you and say hello to Hal. Is he walking well enough to join us for dinner, do you think?'

'Maybe.'

Hal insisted he could limp across if he took it slowly and used a walking stick.

When she got back, Mara put her dirty clothes in

the washing machine, then began to pack her suitcase again. It seemed a long time since she'd packed to come to Australia, but it wasn't. So much had happened since then in such a short time that it amazed her to think of it, not least meeting Hal.

It was hard to settle to anything, even chatting, but Aaron seemed to understand. He was a nice man, but he wasn't her dad.

That evening she let Hal lead the way next door at his own pace and they found Aaron waiting for them on the patio with an office chair on wheels.

Hal rolled it to and fro, paddling with his sound foot. 'This is the Rolls-Royce of office chairs.'

'It used to be in my office at work. I shipped some favourite bits and pieces home when I put the business up for sale.'

The food was good, as always with Emma in charge of the kitchen. The talk flowed easily, though Mara doubted she'd remember what had been said. She felt suspended, not quite here any longer, but not having left yet. Who knew when she'd get a flight? Or what would happen with Hal afterwards.

It was as they were about to set off back home that Aaron suddenly put up one hand to bar their way. 'Is it my imagination or is there someone in a small boat at the house beyond yours, Hal?'

'Yes. I bet it's Moretti.'

'He doesn't give up easily, does he?'

Hal explained quickly that Charles was dealing with

it for him. 'I'm not in the best condition to chase after anyone.' He glanced ruefully down at his ankle and took out his phone to wake his friend.

'Let's stay out of sight and see what happens, then,' Aaron said.

Everything seemed to happen very slowly after that and the moonlight made it feel like an old black and white movie with a chase brewing that the incompetent intruders didn't see coming.

The intruders tied up the boat to the jetty and one of them had peered over the top of the wall a couple of times. They seemed to be arguing about something.

Then the white-haired guy stood up waving his arms as if angry, though he was still speaking quietly. The boat began to rock and he started to wobble about, then let out a muffled yell. The other one tried to grab him, failed and set the boat rocking even more wildly.

'The Keystone Cops have nothing on this,' Aaron muttered, grinning.

'Who's the wobbly old one?' Emma whispered.

'It's the guy who's renting the big house a few houses up on the other side,' Hal said. 'The one that woman said wanted to buy my house. Moretti, he's called. Do you think he really did send those thugs to try to break into my house when I wouldn't sell? And then sent them into your house?'

'Who else would be interested? Let's creep out while they're busy and get closer to the action. It's a brilliant comedy performance.'

The boat had stopped rocking about and the older man in it now made another attempt to get out, with the help of the younger man. At that moment a passing boat roared into the canal, as they sometimes did, speeding way beyond the limit. A man on board was waving a bottle around.

That made the would-be intruders duck down again. The other boat didn't linger in their quiet, poorly lit side canal, but zoomed off back to the brightly lit main area at top speed.

This time when the older man stood up, disaster could not be prevented. He misjudged his moment completely and as the departing boat's wake hit them, he let out a wild yell, flailed about and tumbled overboard with a big splash. His companion began shouting for help.

Hal limped forward to the jetty and yelled, 'You get him out of the water, you fool!'

The man swung round and with a screech of shock at the sight of the group of people, he too tumbled into the water.

By this time the watchers were helpless with laughter but both men were yelling for help and panicking. They seemed incapable of saving themselves.

'I knew I'd use my lifesaving skills one day,' Emma said. 'I wish I wasn't wearing this dress, though.' She took a graceful dive into the canal from the edge of Hal's block, followed by Aaron.

Mara, who had also learnt lifesaving at school, hesitated but decided only to join them if they were having trouble. Sometimes panicking people could drag their rescuers down. But they only needed to be pulled a short distance here, so the rescue shouldn't be difficult.

Aaron found he had only to help the younger man to the edge and the fellow managed to drag himself up the jetty's ladder on his own.

'Can you help me, Aaron?' Emma called out. 'This guy isn't fully conscious.'

'Oh, hell.'

No one was laughing now. The two rescuers got the older man to the ladder then, with help from Mara and Hal above, Aaron got him up to the jetty.

'Is he breathing?' Emma called anxiously as she got out of the water.

'Yes, but something's wrong. I think he's had a seizure of some sort.' Hal turned round. 'Where's the other fellow?'

'Damn! I think he's legged it.'

'We'd better call an ambulance.'

Charles arrived before the ambulance could get there, checking Enrico Moretti. 'He may have had a stroke. He's breathing on his own, though, so I don't think he's in too much danger. How about you two change into some dry clothes and I'll stay with him in case he gets into trouble breathing. Mara, can you wait at the front door to let the paramedics in?'

'I don't think I've ever felt so useless in my life,' Hal grumbled.

'You set me onto him, so you played your part, but if you can limp into the house and put the kettle on, a hot drink might help us all afterwards.'

Hal lingered to say, 'Aaron and Emma probably saved his life. It might have looked like a comedy show at first, but it could have had serious consequences.'

'Yes. I hope the police catch the other guy.' Charles looked down at the still figure, breathing stertorously now. 'What the hell was he coming here for?'

'Heaven knows. To threaten me in person, perhaps.'

The paramedics turned up shortly afterwards and agreed that Moretti had probably had a stroke. They seemed at first surprised then annoyed when everyone declined to accompany the old man to the hospital.

Charles produced the business card Diana had given him and passed it to the paramedic. 'This lady knows the family. I'll give her a ring and ask her to go to the hospital.' As the ambulance drove away, he took out his mobile phone.

Emma and Aaron came down, having changed into dry clothes in record time.

'Brandy, anyone?' Aaron asked.

'Good idea.' Hal switched the kettle off.

'Yes, please.' Mara joined the others at the table. 'I'm certainly packing a lot into my visit, even though it's being cut short.'

She looked at Hal, who was smiling at her in that fond way that made her toes curl.

'I'm very glad you came,' he said softly. 'I shall miss you when you leave. But not for long, I hope.'

Emma nudged Aaron and they too smiled at one another.

'A nice ending to a horrid episode. I don't think Hal will need to fear intruders any longer.'

Just then the house phone rang and as Emma was nearest, she picked it up. 'Oh, heavens!' She looked across. 'Mara, can you be ready to fly out in four hours' time?'

'What? Um, yes. Of course. If someone will call me a taxi.'

'I'll drive you,' Aaron said. 'You go back and finish packing. I'll meet you at the front door when you're ready.'

Hal limped back home with Mara. 'I'm sorry I can't drive you to the airport. Sorry you have to go.'

'Life happens.'

'I'll join you in the UK as soon as I can. I have your address.'

She looked at him, hoping desperately that he meant this. 'Yes. Please do.'

But it was such a rush to put the last things into her suitcase and get ready to leave that she couldn't seem to say all she wanted to tell him.

During the hour's drive to the airport she thought of all she should have said, of course she did, and worried about that. But it was too late now. She had to be with her dad.

'We'll arrange another visit here later,' Aaron said as he put her luggage on a trolley. 'I'm sorry you and I didn't spend more time together.'

'We got enough time to find out that we get on well, don't you think? And that I like your Emma.'

His face lit up. 'That's how I feel. She's been the joy of my life. I'm sure I'll like your dad when I meet him and if there's anything you or he need, please don't hesitate to ask. I'm not short of money, just short of one daughter.'

Then she had to sort out her ticket, go through the airport formalities and board the plane.

She felt disoriented, didn't sleep much on the way back, even though she was once again in business class.

All she wanted now was to see her dad and get the funeral over. It all felt so unreal at the moment.

Around noon, Peggy texted Mike to tell him to meet her in the summerhouse at four o'clock that afternoon. She held out the message to the other conspirators before she sent it. 'How's this?'

Tessa grimaced. 'You haven't said anything affectionate. You know he'll be feeling amorous if he's been without a partner for a while.'

'I don't want him to touch me. I might give myself away.'

Loreen grinned at them. 'I've been thinking about it. We need to make the scene more visual anyway and if he's as vain as he sounds, he'll fall for it. How about you do it this way . . . ?'

They were all chuckling by the time she'd finished.

'That is brilliant,' Peggy said. 'I can do that if I keep the big picture in my mind.'

Mike turned up on the dot, looking so thin Peggy was amazed. Had she really fallen madly in love with this scrawny scarecrow of a man?

'Darling!' He held out his arms.

'Shhh! We have to keep quiet. There are bound to be people nearby.' But she forced herself to go up to him and let him put his arms round her. Eww! He was sticking his tongue in her ear.

'I can hardly wait for us to be together,' she whispered. 'In fact, why should we wait? If we're very quiet we could have a little reunion before we leave.'

He beamed at her. 'I can be very quick and quiet.'

'I want to see you without those clothes,' she said. 'It'll turn me on like nothing else will.'

He smirked and started taking off his clothes.

'Do it slowly,' she said, praying that the professional photographer was in place.

She pretended to smile, but in reality she was horrified at how scrawny he was and when she looked down at herself, she vowed to put more flesh on her own body if it killed her to eat.

As he took off the last of his clothes, he held out one arm to her. 'Your turn.'

She took a step backwards, then another. Ugh. How could she have thought she loved him?

'Peggy? What's the matter? Come on, darling.'

She turned and fled, calling out, 'Help! Help! There's a flasher in here.'

The security guard turned up within seconds and was up the steps into the summerhouse. He was followed closely by a grinning photographer, and then a woman in a white outfit.

Tessa came to join her. 'She's the physiotherapist. Jordan had the idea of bringing her over as well. Apparently she hates men who flash themselves at women.'

'He was so conceited he didn't realise I wasn't joining in till he had all his clothes off.' Peggy shuddered.

Yells and shouts from the summerhouse had them turning round and shortly afterwards, the guard led Mike out, with a blanket wrapped round him.

Peggy couldn't resist giving him a tiny, mockingly happy wave.

He looked shocked rigid as he noticed Tessa, who did the same thing. Then he stumbled past the group.

The following day there were photos in all the newspapers and Mike did not show up well.

Peggy and Tessa cut them out. They would look at them every time they had trouble eating.

Charles turned up at Hal's house the evening that Mara flew out, carefully carrying a bottle of champagne. He waited patiently while his friend came to the door.

'Aaron said you weren't feeling like company tonight so naturally I came round to see you.'

'I wasn't. But now I come to think of it, maybe I could just about tolerate you.'

'If I'm to drink you under the table, I'll need a bed for the night.'

'You can take the one Mara used but you'll have to change the sheets yourself.'

'Fair enough.'

When they were seated and had raised brimming glasses to 'absent friends', Charles said abruptly, 'It must be serious with Mara.'

'It is. But I can't just leave the house to fend for itself till we're sure Moretti was the only one involved.'

'I think you'll find he was.'

'You're sure?'

'Yes. How's the ankle?'

'Not good but I'll live. I need to find a caretaker for this house. Hey! Do you want the job?'

'I thought you'd never ask. I got you a seat on a plane, by the way.'

'How soon?'

'Not for a couple of days, I'm afraid.'

Hal sighed. 'I'm beginning to understand what they mean by the tyranny of distance. This country is a long way from the rest of the world.'

'And Western Australia is a long way from the rest of Australia.' Charles raised his glass. 'It's a pretty unique place, though. Here's to true love. It's about time you found someone.'

'Why did you never marry, Charles?'

'I found someone once and lost her to ambition. I'm a bit fussy and never seemed to luck out again.'

They finished off the bottle, together with some cheese and biscuits, then Hal went to bed.

Charles stood gazing out at the moonlit water. He was going to enjoy living here. But whether he'd want to stay in Mandurah was anyone's guess.

Chapter Twenty-Six

Mara arrived at Heathrow feeling exhausted but the sight of her dad beaming at her from the other side of the passenger barrier lifted her spirits considerably.

He gave her a big hug that said it all, and then took her trolley and began to push it towards the exit. 'It's a long flight. You must be exhausted.'

'I was in business class again, so I was quite comfy.'

'Do you need to sleep? I don't mind if you go straight to bed.'

'Not yet. I'll fit into UK time for as long as I can today.'

When they were driving west along the M4, he said abruptly, 'Do you want to see your mother one final time?'

She'd thought about that. 'No. I prefer to remember her as she was when I was a child, if I can. She grew so strange, especially towards the end. But I really want to be there at the funeral with you so that we can say a proper goodbye to her.'

'I've taken that for granted and arranged for the funeral to take place quite soon. We were lucky that a slot came vacant. There won't be many of us there, a few distant relatives and some friends of mine. And Sally of course.'

'Of course. That sounds – right.'

When they got to the house she stopped as she got out of the car to stare at her old home. Everything looked smaller than ever here after the big canal houses and wide, high sky of Australia. And it felt distinctly chilly, with a lowering grey sky.

'Coming inside?' he asked.

'Yes. Just, you know, reorienting myself.'

When they got inside he avoided her gaze and asked abruptly, 'Did you like this Aaron chap?'

'Yes. And you will too. He didn't feel like a father, though. More like a sort of distant cousin or uncle. His wife is nice as well.' She could see the relief on her dad's face. 'As if anyone could ever replace you, Dad.'

So they had another long, loving hug.

'I met a guy while I was there, as I told you.'

'This Hal chap?'

'Yes. He's really nice. He may be coming over for a holiday soon.'

Phil wasn't fooled. 'You like him that much.'

'Yes.'

'But you're not sure he'll come?'

'He said he would. I hope he does. After Darren, I'm

not as trusting.'

'I hope so too, then. And I'm sure Sally will give him a bed, if he does come.'

'I'm so glad you had her to help you.'

'She's a good friend, has been for years.' He took a deep breath and said hesitantly, 'Perhaps she'll be more than that one day. Would you mind?'

'Not at all. I hope she will. You've been lonely, in spite of Mum being there and your golfing friends.'

'Yes. I have. Very lonely when you weren't around.'

'No one could have done more for her.'

He shrugged but she could see the compliment pleased him. Well, he'd more than earned it.

With the help of a stroll out for some fresh if damp air, Mara lasted till shortly after teatime then fell asleep sitting in front of the TV. She woke as her dad shook her shoulder gently.

'Get yourself off to bed, sleeping beauty.'

She nodded and went upstairs.

Five days later the funeral took place, by which time Mara had pieced together a black outfit to wear. She had intended to buy new smarter clothes, but had seemed to hear her mother's voice in her head, saying how stupid that would be to spend all that money when she'd only wear the things once.

Her outfit was reasonably smart, making a statement that she was in mourning, which was what you felt mattered, after all.

Her father offered her his arm as they got out of the

black funeral limousine and went into the crematorium.

'There are more people than I'd expected.'

'Kath wouldn't have wanted a fuss made, but people like to do "the right thing" after someone dies.'

She didn't recognise most of those present and her father introduced her. He whispered as they took their places that they weren't having a funeral feast because Kath thought they were stupid. 'I'm trying to do what she'd have wanted. And anyway, I don't really know her relatives, so why should I spend a lot of my money on them? Though it's nice of them to come.'

The ceremony was brief and the only surprise was her father getting up to say, 'My daughter and I wish to thank you for coming to say goodbye to Kath. My wife wasn't perfect but she always did the best she could. No one can manage more than that, however hard they try. And she gave me the best daughter a man could ever want, which I shall always be grateful to her for.'

It wasn't till they were walking out that Mara saw the tall figure at the back of the chapel. He'd come. She stopped walking, mouthing his name and clutching her father's arm. 'It's Hal.' Suddenly she felt shy.

'Nice-looking chap.'

'How did he know to come here today?' she whispered.

'He phoned and I happened to answer it. I said to meet us here, then he could take you home again. Time now for you to go to him, lass. He came a long way to find you, so I think we can both trust him. Thank you for coming back for me first, though.'

'I don't want to leave you alone.'

'I shan't be alone, love. I shall have Sally. You don't mind, do you?'

'Mind? I'm delighted for you, both of you.'

He gave Mara a little push, then turned and held out his hand to their neighbour.

Mara walked along the aisle to join Hal and his face lit up as she came towards him, one hand outstretched.

'I'm sorry I couldn't get here any sooner,' he said.

'It worked out just right. I needed time with my father. And we needed to say goodbye to Mum.' She gathered her courage together, 'Now I need time with you.'

'I hired a car. Perhaps we can go somewhere for a meal and decide how to do this.'

'Do what?'

'Get together. If I had my way, I'd marry you tomorrow, I'm that sure of how right our love feels. But I'll give you as much time as you need to see your way clear.'

'I don't need any more time. If you hadn't come, I'd have coped. I always cope. But now you're here, I know that would have been a pale shadow of what life with you may bring me. And I'm ready for it.'

Heedless of the people standing nearby in quiet little groups, he picked her up and swung her round several times.

When he put her down, he saw that everyone was staring, so called out, 'She loves me and we're going to get married. I've never been so happy in all my life.'

Someone clapped and the rest of the crowd joined in, smiling, as people do when they see lovers happy together.

'You fool,' she whispered.

'I'd be a fool if I didn't shout for joy,' he insisted. 'And I'm sure your teddy bear will be pleased too.'

'You're definitely a fool, but I'm glad you like Archibald.'

'I more than like him. I'm going to invest in him and his tribe.'

She gaped at him.

He put one finger on her lips. 'But we'll discuss that another time. For now, we're going to focus on ourselves and our love.'

Outside the chapel, Phil and Sally had been watching them get together as the other mourners filed away. You didn't need to hear what they were saying. Their love for one another was shining brightly on their faces.

'I like the looks of him,' she said. 'Any man who can show his love so openly has a good chance of making his wife happy, I reckon.'

'Maybe I ought to shout out to the world that I love you, then.' Phil tried to summon up the courage to do that, but couldn't.

She chuckled. 'You're different, a very quiet sort of chap, and that will suit me just fine.'

So he summoned up all his courage and gave her a long, lingering kiss in public, blushing furiously as he did so.

'I know what that cost you,' she whispered.

'No more than I was prepared to pay.'

They walked along the path to the car park hand in hand but there was no sign of Mara and Hal waiting for them. A big luxury car was pulling out of it, however. The driver stopped at the exit and leant across to give the passenger another quick kiss on the cheek, then pulled out onto the road.

'That's the way to go,' he said. 'My lass will be all right with him. She's made the right choice.'

They got into Sally's small car, ten years old and a bit shabby, but it suited them.

'Let's go home now,' she said.

'Yours or mine?'

'Mine but it's going to be ours from now on, Phil love. Your Kath wouldn't want me living in her house and I'm sure it has too many bad memories for you as well. We'll rent that one out, eh?'

'Good idea. We'll need a bit of extra money to visit Mara in Australia.' And he kissed her again once he'd stopped the car outside her home, this time not blushing, just smiling tenderly into her eyes.

Author bio

ANNA JACOBS is the author of over ninety novels and is addicted to storytelling. She grew up in Lancashire, emigrated to Australia in the 1970s and writes stories set in both countries. She loves to return to England regularly to visit her family and soak up the history. She has two grown-up daughters and a grandson, and lives with her husband in a spacious home near the Swan Valley, the earliest wine-growing area in Western Australia. Her house is crammed with thousands of books.

annajacobs.com